My Mamma Mia Summer

Annie Robertson

ORION

An Orion paperback

First published in Great Britain in 2018
by Orion Books
an imprint of The Orion Publishing Group Ltd
Carmelite House, 50 Victoria Embankment
London EC4Y 0DZ

An Hachette UK Company

3 5 7 9 10 8 6 4 2

A CIP catalogue record for this book is
available from the British Library.

ISBN 978 1 4091 8311 2

Typeset by Input Data Services Ltd, Somerset

Printed and bound by CPI Group (UK) Ltd, Croydon, CR0 4YY

MIX
Paper from
responsible sources
FSC FSC® C104740
www.fsc.org

www.orionbooks.co.uk

For the original Annie Robertson

Prologue

2008

'Wasn't it brilliant?' said Laurel, brimming with excitement after leaving the cinema.

Marnie put her arm round her granddaughter as they walked in the cool night air, the summer sky only just beginning to darken, and pulled her close with joy. 'It was the greatest film I've ever seen!'

'I almost choked on my popcorn when they slid down the banister!'

'And those dance sequences – I haven't laughed until I've cried in years.'

'What about Pierce's singing?'

They paused to look at each other, both wincing in delight and bursting into fits of giggles.

'I still wouldn't kick him out of bed!'

'Marnie!'

'I'm serious. Would you?'

Laurel thought for a moment. 'Maybe Pierce but not Colin Firth!'

'Of course – it's always the shy, awkward one for you.'

Marnie linked Laurel's arm and they ambled home, singing ABBA hits and trying out Meryl's dance movements on the pavement.

I

At home Marnie put her keys on the sideboard and checked her reflection in the mirror. Her face looked younger to Laurel, glowing with happiness. 'Your mother would have loved it.'

'Do you think so?'

'I know it,' she said, turning to Laurel with a look of deep love in her eyes. 'It captured something of her spirit in a way I'm not sure anything else has since she died.'

Laurel wished, as she always did, that she had a memory of her parents, a memory of their spirit, the thing that made Laurel, Laurel. Marnie had tried to share as many memories of Laurel and her parents as she could – her mother dancing round the kitchen to ABBA with Laurel in her arms, her father sitting in their parked car with Laurel pretending to steer – but still Laurel hankered after a memory of her own, not one that she'd been told, but it was something she knew she could never have.

'Did I ever tell you your parents fell in love on holiday?' said Marnie, in the kitchen, putting on the kettle.

'You did.'

Laurel suspected Marnie had shared every scrap of information she had about her parents, and them falling in love was definitely one of Marnie's favourite moments.

Marnie made the tea, whistling 'Slipping Through My Fingers', and handed Laurel her mug. 'Do you know, I think it's time I gave something to you.' She left the kitchen and quickly returned with a shallow box not much bigger than a laptop.

'What is that?'

'Let's call it an early eighteenth birthday present.'

Full of excitement, Laurel opened the lid and unfolded the white tissue paper that concealed what lay inside. Peeling back the paper, she discovered an item in denim fabric. She pulled it up to unfold a pair of dungarees – she knew instinctively that they held a story.

'They were your mother's.'

'Really?' said Laurel in wonder. She held them against her body.

'They should be the perfect fit, you're exactly the same size as she was.'

Laurel immediately took off her skirt and popped them on.

'They feel amazing,' she said, going out to the hall mirror.

Marnie joined her. 'She used to wear them all the time. If you breathe deeply you can still smell the faintest trace of her scent.'

Laurel gazed in the mirror, imagining her mother was reflected there, feeling as close to her as she ever had, the scent of the dungarees bringing her to life.

'I love them,' she said, her voice catching.

'I thought you would. Your mother did too. When I saw Meryl wearing a pair, I knew it was time you had them.'

Laurel turned to hug her grandmother. 'Thank you, Marnie. I couldn't have wished for a better present.'

'You're welcome,' she said, brushing the hair from Laurel's face with her hand, and looking into her eyes as if they were her daughter's. 'I'll miss you when you head off to university.'

3

'I'll miss you too.'

But just then an idea came to Marnie and her face lit up, her violet eyes twinkling. 'Do you know what we should do?'

'What?'

'We should make a promise to visit the island in the film next summer, when you're back from uni – have a little adventure of our own.'

'Deal!' said Laurel, loving the idea, excited about the trip already.

I

2018

Laurel reread the email, removed an earphone and clicked open her calendar.

'Huh.'

'What?' asked Matt, the team-assistant, who sat next to Laurel in the open-plan office where they worked.

'I've still got ten days' holiday to take.'

'That doesn't surprise me,' he chuckled. 'You're *always* here.'

Laurel didn't like to admit it but Matt had a point. Since her grandmother died ten weeks ago, Laurel had thrown herself into work. It had been easier for her to focus on organising corporate events and weddings for the hotel she worked at than to dwell on the heartbreak of losing the woman she loved most in the world.

'So, are you going to take it?'

Laurel shrugged. 'I'm not sure.'

Matt didn't seem to hear her. 'Where will you go? God, just think of the choice! If I could go anywhere I'd go to Yosemite National Park and climb El Capitan.'

'Right,' replied Laurel, looking at the events planned for the next couple of months. She realised that if she were going to take leave it would have to be soon – next week soon – the big events booked in for July and August would require her to be there. Doubting that her boss Jacqui would agree to her taking time off, Laurel almost put the thought out of her mind. It was only when 'Dancing Queen' began playing through her headphones that she was reminded immediately of her favourite montage in her favourite movie, *Mamma Mia!,* and a flash of inspiration came to her.

'Matt?'

'Yup?' he answered, not looking away from his screen.

'Let me know when Jacqui's finished in her meeting, will you?'

'Sure.'

Happy that the coast was clear, Laurel did a sneaky Google search of Skopelos, the Greek island where *Mamma Mia!* was set. There was something irresistible to Laurel about the inimitable joy of the movie, the lavish dance routines and OTT performances. Regardless of whatever cloud darkened her day, there was always *Mamma Mia!* to make her smile.

Within seconds of her search thousands of images of crystal blue bays, rugged cliffs and white-washed homes with orange pan-tiled roofs flashed up in front of her.

Laurel was instantly transported to the night when she and Marnie had seen *Mamma Mia!* at the cinema, and the promise they'd made that the following summer they'd visit the island together. But one summer followed another, and before Laurel knew it she was laying her grandmother to rest. Laurel didn't have many regrets in life but not taking that trip was one of them.

With that thought in mind she pulled up TripAdvisor. Dozens of Skopelos hotels and guest houses appeared, all with perfect swimming pools, blue skies and large parasols. But for all their immaculate facades and crisp white bed linen it was something less perfect that caught Laurel's eye. Villa Athena, perched high on a cliff, overlooking a turquoise sea, looked a little tired – the bed linen had a definite whiff of the eighties and the décor was decidedly un-chic – but Laurel was drawn to its faded charm and its higgledy-piggledy feel. There was something about it that reminded her of Donna's guest house in the film.

Laurel skim-read the reviews.

'Quirky house but stunning location.'

'A bit like an episode of Fawlty Towers.*'*

'Owner is as mad as a box of frogs!'

And when she searched for Villa Athena on Google, the only result she found was via TripAdvisor – no

7

website, Facebook or Twitter. It was as if the place didn't exist, and yet Laurel was charmed and intrigued. She was about to check availability, when she felt a presence over her shoulder and heard the noisy clearing of someone's throat.

'How's the Dental Award Ceremony coming along?' asked Jacqui, who had appeared at Laurel's side like a ninja.

'Fine,' said Laurel, quickly closing the window and removing her headphones, hoping Jacqui hadn't spotted what she was looking at.

'Good, because I need the full itinerary on my desk by end of day. Understood?'

'Absolutely!' Laurel shot Matt a look that said, 'I thought you were meant to be my lookout, you git', and returned to her work, even though all she could think of was a trip to Skopelos.

'Only me,' called Laurel, entering her apartment.

Tom, her grandmother's ageing grey cat, slunk round the doorframe, his tail in the air, and meowed.

'Have you had a good day?' she asked, hanging her jacket on the back of the door.

He turned his back on Laurel and moseyed into the kitchen.

'Mine was pretty average too,' she said, removing her shoes and following him. 'In case you wanted to know.'

Tom stood next to his food bowl, his green eyes staring at Laurel.

'Hungry? What do you fancy?' Laurel asked from the

fridge, weighing up the cat-food options. 'Two-day-old tuna or something pertaining to rabbit liver?'

Tom meowed.

'Right,' said Laurel, scraping the last of the tuna into his bowl. 'I don't fancy my options much either.'

With a 'healthy eating' prawn curry heating in the microwave, Laurel went to her bedroom which, if she opened the Velux windows and stood on tiptoes, afforded her a view of Clapham Common. She took off her work clothes and pulled on her mother's dungarees, which always made her feel closer to her mum, and a bit like Donna, the character that Meryl played in the film, too.

The ping of the microwave took her back to the kitchen where she ate at her small table, *Mamma Mia!* on in the background, while browsing through a selection of brochures for the flats she planned to view at the weekend.

'I don't really like any of these flats,' she said to Tom, when he'd finished eating and had sat down on the floor beside her, no doubt hoping for a prawn to come his way. 'Plus they're all ludicrously expensive. How could I fritter away all of Marnie's money on just two hundred and fifty square feet?'

Although Laurel liked her job and loved her friends in London, she'd never quite felt she belonged there, and the more she looked at buying a flat in the city, the more she had a desire to go somewhere else. When her grandmother was alive, Harrogate had felt like home, but, having been through all the options of what to do with Marnie's home: live in it; sell it; rent it out; Laurel had even toyed with turning it into her own little boutique hotel, she decided to put it on the market. There were too many memories and without Marnie, it didn't feel like the home she'd loved.

Thinking of the trip to Skopelos, she pushed her supper aside and went to the framed picture of Marnie in her men's jeans and a pink and purple Liberty shirt, which she kept on the shelving unit beside the one of her parents in their high-waisted jeans and polo necks.

'Fancy a glass of wine?' she asked her grandmother, taking down the picture and pouring herself a glass. She sat down on the sofa, Tom jumping up beside her, and stared at Marnie's photo. She studied her violet eyes and every wrinkle around them, which her grandmother had spent hours trying to keep at bay with her beloved bottle of Olay, a scent Laurel would forever associate with her. If Marnie were here right now, Laurel knew she'd ask her three questions: Would buying a flat bring you happiness? Is that your dream? And, most importantly, what would Meryl do?

Stroking Tom from top to tail, it didn't take long for Laurel to come up with the answers: the flat wouldn't bring her happiness; her dream was to have her own boutique hotel, just like Donna's; and Donna would be impulsive, spontaneous, and throw caution to the wind.

Taking a deep breath and feeling a thrill of nervous excitement, Laurel chucked the brochures in the bin and placed the photo of Marnie back on the shelf, before reaching for her phone and typing in 'Villa Athena,

Skopelos'. The image of the higgledy-piggledy guest house came up and Laurel found herself smiling. Without thinking, she clicked on TripAdvisor and navigated her way to the availability checker. When she discovered they had rooms free for the following two weeks, she booked it then and there. The rush of happiness she felt almost matched Meryl's elation in the scene where she cavorted to 'Dancing Queen' with a feather boa round her neck. Laurel jumped up and, in her excitement, danced along to 'Gimme! Gimme! Gimme!', which was playing on the telly, shimmying her hips with her hands in the air.

Desperate to share her news with someone other than Tom, Laurel dialled her best friend.

'Hi, hon,' said Janey, her Yorkshire accent as strong as ever despite her years in London. 'What's going on?'

'How do you feel about looking after Tom for a couple of weeks?' Laurel asked, grinning from ear to ear and making silly faces at Tom.

'I'd love to. Why?'

'Because I'm off to Skopelos!' said Laurel with a squeal, which made Tom bolt for the cat flap.

'You're kidding?!'

'Nope. For once in my life I'm being spontaneous. Marnie and I always planned to go, so I'm going for her.'

'I'm proud of you,' said Janey, always supportive, but sounding excited too. 'Not only would it have pleased Marnie, it's exactly what Donna would have done!'

'And whatever Donna does—' said Laurel.

'Laurel does too!' They laughed in unison.

'It's exactly what you need – you might even meet your own Colin Firth!'

'That I doubt, but I can forget about work, visit all the locations, find an ABBA-themed bar, and swim in the sea. It's going to be great!'

Later, after she hung up the phone, Laurel poured herself another glass of wine, and hugged herself in anticipation. Whatever the next couple of weeks would bring, she was more than ready for an adventure.

2

'Jacqui?' Laurel knocked gently on her boss's open door the next morning.

'What is it, Laurel?' Jacqui looked up from a hefty document on her desk.

Laurel wished she'd been a little less spontaneous last night, seeing Jacqui face to face she wondered why she'd booked a holiday without clearing it first. 'HR told me I have to take my annual leave by the end of June or I'll lose it.'

'Uh-huh,' she said, removing her glasses and pinching the bridge of her nose. 'They copied me in. I assume you've come to tell me you're not taking it?'

Laurel laughed lightly at what she hoped was her boss's *very* dry sense of humour. 'Actually I've booked two weeks in Skopelos. I leave on Saturday,' she said, nervously.

'Lucky for some.' Jacqui gestured for Laurel to sit.

Laurel sat with her hands neatly placed on her lap. 'I've looked at the diary and I can have everything in order by the end of the week. I'll make sure Matt has copies of everything.'

'I'm sure you will. If anyone deserves a break it's you.'

'Thank you,' said Laurel, touched by her boss's kind comment. Jacqui was a bit of a peculiar character. She was exacting in her standards, had a quick temper, and her humour was as dry as the Sahara. But it hadn't taken Laurel too long to figure her out and she rubbed along with her better than most in the department. Jacqui had always been fair to Laurel, and when Marnie had fallen ill she'd given Laurel her full support.

'I had a holiday on a Greek island myself when I was about your age. I'm not so old as to have forgotten the fun one has in the sun,' she said, with a twinkle.

'I'm sure . . .' Laurel wondered where Jacqui was going with this.

'If you're as lucky as me you might even find someone to enjoy it with! I once met this gorgeous guy, muscles like you wouldn't believe—'

'Well,' said Laurel, her cheeks reddening, her boss lost in her memories. 'Thanks, Jacqui, I should get on!'

Laurel beat a hasty retreat and, back at her desk, started tying up every loose end she could think of before she left.

'It's as if you're planning on never coming back,' observed Matt.

'In my dreams!' For all Laurel dreamed of owning her own hotel, she couldn't quite imagine working anywhere other than The Higham, the place she'd worked since leaving university. Despite her flaws, Jacqui had been good to Laurel, promoting her regularly over the last six years.

'You never know – all that sun, sea and sex might just go to your head.'

'Hardly.' Laurel couldn't remember the last time she'd got laid, though the thought of a holiday romance with someone, after so many nights alone, was quite a nice one. She hadn't had a relationship since she broke up with Phil three years ago, after he decided he'd prefer to spend his life photographing spiders in South America than sharing a one-bed with Laurel in London. There had been an uncharacteristic one-night stand sometime last year, which Laurel had tried desperately to erase from her memory without success.

With things at work in order, Laurel hit late-night shopping. The only swimming costume she owned was the black Speedo she'd had at school for swimming lengths of the punishingly cold pool. It was now thread-bare and the Lycra had given up any sense of support years ago. More in need of support than ever, Laurel decided a new costume was in order.

'Do you want a one piece or two?' the department store assistant asked after Laurel had stared at costumes for the best part of ten minutes and come to no decision.

'One,' she said.

'Oh,' said the assistant, in a way that suggested that was the wrong answer.

'Why?'

'You've got a great bod,' she said, in a drawling sort of voice.

'You think?'

'Sure. You should definitely go with a two piece.'

'Oh, right, okay,' said Laurel, wondering why she was agreeing given that she'd never worn a bikini in her entire life.

'Something like this would be good.' The assistant held up a bright pink bandeau bra and tiny briefs.

'No. I need straps and bigger pants.'

The assistant rifled through the rail. 'This would complement your skin tone,' she said, holding up a padded bra in olive green with high-waisted ruched bottoms.

Deciding it was the best of a bad lot, Laurel went to the changing room where she stripped down to her underwear, trying the bikini over the top.

'How's it looking?' the assistant called.

'Fine. Good!' Laurel called back, checking the lock on the door to ensure she couldn't burst in and find Laurel with her M&S essentials poking out.

'Great! Throw it over and I'll wrap it for you,' said the assistant, before Laurel had really made up her mind. She wasn't sure how you were meant to tell if a bikini suited you from standing underneath a downlight in front of a three-way mirror with your undies and socks still on. Still, she reasoned, it was better than what she had already and at least it was something ticked off her list.

Somehow, in between buying new swimwear, dusting off her suitcase, searching every cupboard, drawer and file in the flat for her passport, and making sure everything was in order at work, the week flew by, and before Laurel knew it, it was Saturday morning and Janey was arriving to collect Tom.

'How did Jacqui take the news of your holiday?' she asked. Janey being very much up to speed on the peculiarities of Laurel's boss.

'With a little too much detail,' said Laurel, admiring Janey's batik headband, which held her thick, brown curls in place. 'I had to high-tail it out of her office before she told me all about her holiday fling.'

'Really? I don't know how you manage her so well.' She picked up Tom, scratching him beneath his chin in the way that he liked.

'What can I tell you, it's my USP: Laurel Dempsey, Crank Handler Extraordinaire!'

'You do attract oddballs.'

Laurel laughed, acknowledging that it was true; it was a quality she'd inherited from Marnie, who'd attracted lame ducks wherever she went.

'Help yourself to juice,' said Laurel, going into the bedroom to put her phone charger in with all her other packing on the bed. 'I need to empty the fridge before I go, so take whatever's in there.'

Janey came through and leaned against the bedroom doorframe, munching on an apple.

'You sure you've got enough stuff?' she asked facetiously, looking at the piles of folded laundry, books and toiletries.

'You think I haven't?'

'Laurel, are you mad? You've enough clothes there to dress the entire island.'

Laurel stood back to look at her belongings, fourteen of everything, neatly stacked. 'I haven't been anywhere before for longer than three or four nights.'

'Laurel, my little homebird, you look as if you've packed never to come back. They will have a washing machine, you know, and if not, you can always wash your pants in the sink.'

'What would you take?'

Janey, a seasoned traveller since her gap year in India, put down her apple on the bedside table and discarded four-fifths of Laurel's possessions. She undid in a minute what it had taken Laurel most of the week to put together.

'There,' she said, putting the suitcase onto the bed and throwing in the items. 'That should do it.'

'But that's barely anything,' said Laurel, surveying the contents, wondering how she was to get by with only one bra and two pairs of pants.

'Trust me. A pair of flip-flops, swimsuit and sarong, a dress and cardi for the evening, pair of shorts, skirt, trousers and three tops is all you need. Plus your dungarees.'

'Of course,' said Laurel, who went nowhere without her mother's dungarees. 'But I do need my shampoo and conditioner.' Laurel took the bottle from the pile Janey had created on the floor.

'They'll have toiletries at the hotel.'

'But not anti-frizz.'

Janey cast Laurel a withering look and held out her hand for Laurel to pass the bottle back. 'You are aware holidays are about relaxing, letting your hair down, right? You're supposed to forget about whether you have frizzy hair or not.'

Laurel hugged the bottle. 'There are some things I can never forget, and frizzy hair is one of them.'

'Well,' said Janey, realising she wasn't going to win this battle easily. 'I, Janey Andrews, your best friend since we were four years old, is on this day, declaring that Laurel Dempsey *will* survive two weeks with frizzy hair. Now hand the bottle over!'

'Fine!' said Laurel, grudgingly relinquishing it. 'But if I have a frizz emergency I will be cursing your name.'

'That's a risk I'm willing to take! And are you really planning on reading a book a day?' she asked, looking at the stack of fourteen books.

'You never know.'

'You can take three. No more. And I concede that your *Mamma Mia!* DVD is one of your life's essentials.' Laurel was about to open her mouth to object about the books when Janey raised a finger to tell her, no. 'Pick three, no more. Have you got your passport and currency?'

'Check.'

'Phone and charger?'

'Check.'

'Travel itinerary and directions?'

'Check.'

Janey threw in Laurel's choice of three books and the DVD, zipped up the suitcase and gave it a satisfied thump. 'Then that's it. You're ready!'

'Right,' said Laurel, the reality of setting off alone suddenly hitting home.

'Are you nervous?'

'A little,' she confessed, feeling in need of a cup of tea.

Janey followed her through to the kitchen. 'You're going to have the best time.'

'I know,' said Laurel, uncertainly.

'And more importantly, you're going to be doing something that you and Marnie always planned to do together.'

Laurel paused, swallowing a wave of emotion.

'I just wish she was here to do it with me.'

'I know,' said Janey, opening her arms to give Laurel a huge hug. 'She'd be so proud of you.'

Laurel nodded, and wiped away a tear, Janey still holding her by the arms.

'And you know, if she was going, she'd be here right now dancing round this room in excitement.'

'It's true,' Laurel laughed lightly, galvanised by Janey's pep-talk and the thought of Marnie. 'She'd probably have left by now, trying to sweet-talk the airport staff into letting her onto an earlier flight.'

'She was a great old girl.'

'One of a kind,' said Laurel.

'So, let's go?'

Laurel took a deep breath. 'Yes, let's go!'

Janey manhandled Tom into his cat box and Laurel gathered up her suitcase and bag and together they locked up the flat.

'When's your flight?' asked Janey, outside on the pavement.

'Eleven-thirty.'

Janey's eyes popped wide. 'You're kidding? It's already past nine.'

'Oh shit!' said Laurel, digging around for her phone to check Janey was right.

'You'd better run!'

Just as Laurel was about to pelt down the road to the Tube station the postman arrived at the gate.

'Morning,' he said, cheerfully, not reading the look of panic on Laurel's face. 'I've a letter for you to sign for.'

He handed Laurel an envelope and presented the gadget for her to squiggle something that bore absolutely no resemblance to her signature.

'Got to run,' she said, handing the postie back his pen-thing, stashing the letter in her handbag and kissing Janey goodbye.

Laurel made it on time to check-in by the skin of her teeth.

'Where are we travelling today?' asked the check-in assistant, brightly. She was jauntily clad in sky blue and white, with a neckerchief and eye-shadow to match.

'*I'm* travelling to Skiathos,' said Laurel, presenting her passport, marginally out of breath.

'You're almost late,' said the woman, bristling, her nails clicking on the keyboard of her computer.

Laurel resisted the urge to say, 'Almost late is the same as being on time'.

After checking in her suitcase, politely queue-jumping security – circumnavigating the barriers like a Jack

Russell on an agility course – she arrived at her gate just as final call was being announced.

'Made it,' she said, as she collapsed into her seat.

'You sound as if you need a drink, pet,' said a distinctly Geordie accent from above her.

Laurel looked up to see a voluptuous forty-something, peroxide curls springing from her scalp, boobs bursting out of a white cotton top, and a bottom concealed in white jeans, which Laurel wasn't at all certain would fit in the seat beside her.

'It won't be long until they bring round the trolley,' the woman said, stretching on tippy-toes to cram her bag into the overhead locker. 'We can have a couple then,' she continued, wiggling into her seat.

Laurel opened her book, hoping to make it clear that she'd like to sit quietly. Her ploy did not work. Within seconds the woman said, 'I'm Angie. What's your name?'

'Laurel.'

'Nice to meet you, Laurel. Are you going to Skiathos or somewhere else?'

'Skopelos.'

'Great,' she smiled. 'Me too!'

The announcement of the safety demonstration enabled Laurel to sit quietly again. She took out the safety card, craning her neck for a better view of the cabin crew. Angie, on the other hand, paid no attention. She was far more concerned with the in-flight magazine and checking out the latest duty-free bargains.

'If the plane goes down that safety stuff won't make a blind bit of difference,' said Angie, once the flight attendants had finished and were patrolling the aisles checking everyone's seatbelts. 'There'd be a brawl. Like Newcastle on a Saturday night, just at thirty thousand feet!'

Laurel couldn't help but laugh.

'Have you been to Skopelos before?'

'No,' replied Laurel, the force of take-off pushing them back in their seats. 'It's my first time.'

'Ooh, pet, it's been a long time since I said that!'

'How many times have you been?'

'More than I can remember, some I can't remember at all, if you know what I mean.' Angie winked. 'I've been coming since before it was famous, before Meryl and Pierce and his awful singing.'

Laurel knew it was ridiculous but she found herself feeling slightly hurt that Angie should be so rude about Pierce. It was as if she was at school again and an older kid had come up and told her Santa wasn't real, even though she'd figured it out for herself ages ago.

As soon as the seatbelt sign flicked off, Laurel tucked her book away and reached for the headphones, neatly coiled in their little plastic wrapper. She was thrilled to find *Mamma Mia!* was one of the film choices. If I'm lucky, she thought, I might even manage to watch it twice. But a nudge on her side suggested otherwise.

'You gotta love that movie,' said Angie, placing a tissue between her boobs.

'Yes,' said Laurel, who'd never seen anyone use cleavage as storage.

'Is that the reason you've come?'

'It's my favourite film. My grandmother and I always said we'd visit the island together but she passed away and now I'm visiting for both of us.'

'Ah pet, that's tough. But I tell you, you're going to love the island, you'll have the time of your life. I guarantee it.'

Just as Laurel thought she'd found an opportunity to duck out of the conversation and into the film, the drinks trolley arrived.

'What would your granny have had?' Angie asked, after the flight attendant had requested their orders.

Memories of Marnie drinking Smirnoff and orange on an evening by the fire, in the garden on a summer's afternoon, or at the funeral of a friend, came flooding back to Laurel. She remembered the smell of it, so toxic and sweet, and the sound of the ice cubes chinking against the edge of her grandmother's favourite cut-glass tumbler. Even now it made Laurel think of her.

'I'll have a vodka and orange.'

Angie looked impressed. 'Good for you, pet. Let's make it a double.'

'No—' Laurel began to protest but before she could finish Angie was poo-pooing her, saying, 'You're on holiday! Live a little.'

Aware that the advice was exactly what she would have received from both Janey and Marnie, had they been there, Laurel didn't put up a fight and received her drink gladly.

'Now, let's get that movie on,' said Angie. 'I'm dying to see that Pierce Brosnan – if I find someone half as tasty this holiday, I'll be a lucky, lucky girl!'

3

By the time the flight landed in Skiathos over three hours later, it felt to Laurel as if she and Angie had known each other all their lives. They'd drunk too many drinks, laughed, ooh-ed and aah-ed at all the same bits in the movie, and sung along together to the end credits. She was glad of her company and her knowledge. If it wasn't for Angie, Laurel would have stood at the airport dithering about whether to take a bus or a cab, and learning precisely (or as precisely as Google Translate would allow) how to say, 'Please can you take me to the port to catch the ferry to Skopelos.'

Instead, with Angie's help, Laurel picked her luggage off the carousel, left the airport and went straight to a taxi rank, where Angie, without a thought to the language, said, 'Ferry port, please' before opening the boot of the cab and throwing in both their suitcases.

At the port the same thing happened. Where Laurel would have procrastinated long and hard over which ticket office she should use, Angie just barrelled into the first, shouted what she needed and walked directly to the ferry.

It felt peculiar to Laurel, sitting on the ferry deck

waiting for it to depart, that only four or five hours earlier she'd been in London, racing through the busy streets to get to the airport, and now, here she was, on the sea, with a brilliant blue sky above her, just an hour away from the place she'd dreamt of for almost a decade.

'You thinking of your granny?' Angie asked as the boat began to move away.

Laurel stared straight ahead, torn between imagining Marnie beside her and embracing the moment as it was, with the force of life that was Angie.

'She'd have loved this,' she said, as they made their way out of the busy port. 'She'd have loved the expectation of how Skopelos would feel, if it would feel like being in the film.'

'Sounds like she really loved that movie.'

'I don't think anyone has loved it more.'

'What made it so special to her?'

Laurel paused before answering. 'My mum—' her voice broke. She cleared her throat, gathering herself. 'My mum loved ABBA more than anything. Apparently, she used to sing their songs to me when I was a little girl.'

'Apparently?' asked Angie, her voice softer than usual.

'She and my dad died when I was two. Granny Marnie raised me after that.'

Angie sat quietly. 'Sounds like you've been through the wringer.'

'No.' Laurel was quick to reply. 'Not at all. I was too young to remember and Marnie was the greatest granny-slash-mother I could ever have had – I got to grow up in her pottery studio, every day was messy and creative and full of fun. I can't imagine being raised by anyone else. If anyone had it tough, it was my grandmother.'

'But ABBA saw her through?'

'I believe so. And *Mamma Mia!* seemed to capture something of my mother in a way that nothing else had for Marnie, and I suppose for me too – I always wished I could have a stronger feeling of my mum's spirit and when I watch *Mamma Mia!* I get that, a bit. Whenever Marnie watched it she'd say, "It feels like coming home".'

'Sounds like this holiday is going to be a journey for you,' said Angie, the setting sun casting the most spectacular light on the water.

'A great one, I hope,' said Laurel, thankful for Angie's company even if it was unexpected.

They sat comfortably together, passing the time by watching fellow passengers on the boat and inventing stories about their lives. It wasn't long before the island appeared in the distance with its craggy cliffs plummeting into the sea.

'There it is,' said Angie, casting her arms wide. 'She's a real beauty!'

Laurel stared in wonder at the mountainous island, covered in dense trees and the cluster of buildings nestled in its bay. It was as beautiful a place as she'd ever seen.

'We're coming to you, baby,' called Angie, squeezing Laurel's hand in excitement, which Laurel felt too. 'You'd better be ready!'

★

When they arrived, the sun had almost set and the lights of the town were shimmering enticingly among the white buildings, which clung to the steep slopes. Laurel drank in the scent of the sea, of the local vendors cooking and the clean, fresh air that smelt so differently from London. All at once she felt nervous and excited and bursting to explore everything immediately.

'Meryl was here. And Julie, Pierce, Colin, and Stellan,' she whispered to herself as her fellow ferry passengers rushed by her on the quayside. She clutched the handle of her suitcase tightly; it was all she could do to stop pinching herself. 'And now it's my turn.' She smiled, feeling instinctively that she belonged here.

'You coming?' called Angie, already up ahead, trundling her suitcase behind her.

'Sure!' Laurel ran to catch her up.

In the car park next to the port there was a melee of passengers all looking for taxis and buses, and local men touting for fares. Laurel tried to make sense of the system, if there was one, but Angie barrelled straight into the heart of it, like a ball scattering skittles. Laurel lost sight of her for a brief second, until she saw a hand in the air and curls leaping and falling as Angie jumped to get Laurel's attention.

'Over here,' she yelled. 'Come see who I've found.'

Laurel edged her way through the crowd, trying not to bump into anyone.

'Sorry,' she said, when her suitcase became caught with someone else's. She turned to find a guy, about her

29

age, trying to steer his case out of the way.

'No trouble,' he said, doffing his straw trilby – he had a rather nice smile, she noticed – and heading off.

By the taxis, Angie was clutching the arms of a large, Greek man. For someone who Laurel guessed must be in his late fifties, he wasn't bad-looking at all, and had a roughish charm about him. His face lit up as he gazed at Angie.

'Alexandros,' she said, beaming from ear to ear. 'How are you?'

'Angie,' he said, in a thick local accent. 'How long it been?'

'Too long!' she replied, looking at him fondly. 'Look at you; you never age!'

'Eh,' he smiled, exposing a gold tooth. 'Women like you keep me young.'

'Alex!' she said flirtatiously, clearly enjoying the attention.

'And you have friend?' he asked, looking to Laurel.

Angie pulled Laurel closer.

'Alex, this is Laurel. Laurel, Alex.'

'Hi,' said Laurel, reaching out her hand.

'I met Alex the first time I came to Skopelos and he's been looking after me ever since.'

Alex moved his cigarette from his right hand to his left. 'Pleasure. Where you ladies stay?'

'I'm down the front this year so I don't need a cab but you could take Laurel to . . .' Angie paused, uncertain where Laurel was staying.

'Villa Athena.'

Alex dragged on his cigarette and laughed, smoke rushing all around him.

'You stay with Mama Athena?'

'That's right.' She pulled out her itinerary to check she had the correct details 'Villa Athena,' she read, and handed the paperwork to him.

'Sure, sure,' he said, shooing away the papers. 'Everyone knows Athena!'

Laurel frowned, uncertain if everyone knowing Athena was a good thing.

'I'm sure it's fine, pet,' said Angie.

'I hope so,' said Laurel, feeling a sudden knot of anxiety in her stomach.

'Alex, can you take her?'

'For you, anything,' he said, stubbing out his cigarette under his trainer.

'If there's a problem, bring her to me at Hotel Skopelos,' she instructed Alex, taking Laurel's number and hugging her tightly. 'And if there isn't a problem, bring yourself!'

The interior of Alex's taxi was immaculate, with no trace of the scent of sick, which Laurel had smelled so often in the mini-cabs that she took in London, usually badly masked by some cheap, novelty air-freshener.

'Why you no stay with Angie?' asked Alex, glancing in the rear-view mirror.

'We only met on the plane.' Laurel wasn't quite sure whether to speak to the mirror or the side of Alex's clean-shaven, leathery face.

'You no friends?'

Laurel looked out of the window as they drove past the bars and restaurants of the town centre. 'I think we'll become friends.'

'That's good. Angie is good woman.'

'Yes,' said Laurel, thinking how kind she'd been to her. 'I believe so.'

They continued on their way out of town, through tightly packed streets with cars parked bumper to bumper. In the fading light Laurel caught glimpses down alleys and up steep stairs of courtyards, and flowers, and chapels, and a myriad of places to explore.

Before long they were leaving the town's higgledy-piggledy charm behind and were onto roads surrounded by dense trees through which Laurel spied the darkening sea.

'This is far as I go,' said Alex, after five minutes or so, as they pulled up outside a large guest house.

'Is this Villa Athena?' Laurel was surprised by its smart exterior, it wasn't quite what she'd been expecting.

'No!' laughed Alex. He pointed to a track in the trees and, in the distance, high above them, where a dim light shone, a building that Laurel could only just make out. 'That's Villa Athena!'

Laurel watched Alex's tail-lights disappear back to town. She resisted the temptation to go into the guest house beside her to ask if they had a room for the night and instead, dug out her phone, put on its torch, and began walking.

'I'll bet Meryl didn't have to do this,' she said, walking deeper into the woods, following a track that crunched beneath her and proved almost impossible to pull a suitcase on.

It felt like an eternity to navigate the track, which wound its way up the hill in a series of bends. Laurel stopped every few minutes to un-jam her suitcase from a rock or to heave her handbag back onto her shoulder after it had slipped. By the time the large gates of the villa came fully into view she was tired and sore and ready for a lie down.

'How do I get in?' she asked, having tried the handle and found the gates to be locked. She stared at the two large, arched wooden gates in front of her and shone her torch to the right, which highlighted a wooden sign with Villa Athena etched in it, then to the left and above, which showed nothing that resembled a bell. She tried the black, cast-iron handle again but it twisted and turned without success.

'Crap,' she said, searching for her paperwork. She hoped there might be a telephone number, or an email address but when there wasn't she found herself asking: What Would Meryl Do? There were three options: 1) Walk back down to town. 2) Camp out for the night under the stars. 3) Yell!

She quickly eliminated option 1, given there was no guarantee she'd find another room. Option 2 might have been okay if it wasn't for the fact Janey had deposited all her warm clothes on the bedroom floor, which left option 3.

33

'Hello!' she called, timidly at first and then, when that bore no result, a little louder. 'Hello! Is anybody there?'

The villa was so remote that her voice, whipped by the wind, seemed to carry into nothingness.

On her third attempt, Laurel roared from the bottom of her lungs, long and loud, 'Hell-o'. Suddenly, like music to her ears, came the sound of a door being opened and keys jangling.

'Who is it?' a voice asked from behind the gate.

'Laurel Dempsey,' said Laurel, relieved to have made contact with someone, anyone.

'Who?' the voice asked, abruptly.

'Laurel Dempsey. I have a reservation.'

Laurel heard a harrumph, a key in a lock, and saw the handle turn before one of the gates squeaked open.

'I didn't think you were coming,' said the voice, which belonged to an elderly woman wrapped in a dressing gown, with thick, dark-grey hair that flowed around her shoulders. She held a torch under her chin that lit up her oval face like a ghoul.

'I'm so sorry,' said Laurel. 'It's a long trip from London.'

'This way,' said the woman, directing her torch across the courtyard towards the front door.

The house was dimly lit and musty, as if in need of an airing. The old woman led Laurel up a steep, winding flight of stairs, down a narrow corridor and into a small room.

'This is you. Bathroom's through there,' she stabbed a finger at a door. 'Breakfast's at eight.'

'Thank you,' said Laurel, as the woman departed.

Laurel sat down on the bed, and tested its springs.

'Right, not the best start,' she said, looking around. For all it was small, the room was clean and tidy with an eclectic range of charming, vintage furniture that wouldn't have felt out of place in Marnie's house. But the hours of travelling had caught up with Laurel and all the vintage charm in the world couldn't stop her from wanting to close her eyes and wake up at home. She suddenly wished she'd paid more attention to the TripAdvisor reviews, that way at least the start of her holiday might have lived up to her dreams.

4

'Guess I'll be looking for somewhere else to stay,' Laurel muttered to herself the next morning, stretching and groaning awake. The previous day came to her in flashback: the rush to the airport; Angie; the ferry ride; the taxi drive; the final schlep on foot up to the villa. Not to forget the old woman. But, still intrigued by what lay behind the shutter doors, shafts of sunlight creeping through, Laurel got up and pulled them open.

'Wowsers!' she said, as the bright morning light struck her eyes and the view from her bedroom became clear.

The doors led onto a large balcony with table and chairs, where Laurel gazed in amazement at what the darkness of the night before had concealed. Reaching out in front of her, far into the distance, was the sea, sparkling and radiant in the morning sun. To her right, a way off, she could make out the town and its harbour wall, and, to her left, golden beaches. Below the balcony lay terraced gardens of the brightest green. It was paradise.

'Unbelievable,' she said, taking a moment to absorb it all, then, brimming with excitement, she sent Janey a picture of the view with a big thumbs-up emoji. Janey replied immediately with a huge smiley face. Laurel wanted to sit a while but, recalling what the old woman had said about breakfast at eight, she showered in the pretty, tiled bathroom, dressed, and ventured downstairs.

'Ah, there you are!' called a voice as Laurel arrived at the bottom of the steps into the wide entrance hall, which housed a large sideboard, hall stand and bench. It was bright with antique mirrors and coloured, patterned rugs.

Following the voice, strong and Greek with a slight American twang, Laurel found herself in the guest sitting room – a room with shuttered windows, and the soft rustle of leaves from the garden. Laurel, stroking the worn leather of the art-deco armchairs, glanced through to the dining room beyond.

'It's Laurel, yes?'

Standing in the doorway was the woman from last night, this morning fully dressed in a long, loose linen dress with large amber beads around her neck. Behind her was the kitchen, which led off the sitting room.

'Yes,' said Laurel. 'I'm sorry, I didn't catch your name last night.'

'Athena!' she said, as if stating the obvious. 'Come!'

Athena showed Laurel to the dining room, a garden room full of large plants and a life's collection of art-work. She pulled out a cafe-style chair at a small antique table. 'Sorry about last night. I get real cranky when I'm tired!'

'That's okay,' said Laurel, taken aback at Athena's transformation. The woman in front of her was clearly older but her eyes shone, her skin was soft, and her lips were plumper than Laurel's had ever been. 'I didn't mean to arrive late. I must have lost track of time.'

'That happens,' said Athena, sprucing up a jug of pink flowers on the buffet table. 'You're from London, yes? Two hours. That's the time difference. And I can tell you, two hours to me is the difference between charm and hostility!'

'I'll remember that,' laughed Laurel, and Athena laughed too, presenting her with a basket of warm bread. Laurel admired her rings with huge turquoise stones.

'So, what would you like for breakfast? We have pastries, cheese, yoghurt, meat, honey, olives, juice, cereal, eggs – whatever you like.'

'Gosh,' said Laurel, struggling to take it all in. 'Perhaps I might try a little of everything?'

'Good girl!' said Athena, with a smile, and a wave of her hands, which made her wooden bangles clatter together. 'I like a girl who's not afraid to eat.'

With Athena in the kitchen, Laurel helped herself at the buffet and took in the view beyond the patio, over the gardens to the sea. She only snapped out of her daze when a young woman, tall and slender with dark hair in a tight ponytail, entered with a pot of tea.

'Good morning,' said Laurel.

The woman didn't reply, rather, she bowed her head, poured Laurel's tea and scurried away. Laurel shook off the incident, drizzling honey on bread.

Moments later, Athena swooshed back in, her robes flowing, with a selection of eggs.

'Enjoy!' she sang, leaving Laurel to enjoy her breakfast in peace.

When Laurel felt she couldn't eat anything else, possibly for the rest of the day, she returned to her room to unpack. She hadn't wanted to unpack the night before, it had felt like too much trouble if she was just going to find another place in the morning. However, now with the beautiful scenery spread out before her, seeing the charming, if slightly dilapidated guest house in the daylight, and having met Athena properly, she felt like she may never want to leave.

She placed her clothes in the painted wardrobe and her passport, travel documents and cash in the vintage bedside cabinet. At the bottom of her handbag she discovered the letter that she'd signed for the previous morning.

'What is this?' she asked, examining the envelope with its Yorkshire postmark and handwritten address. She ran her finger under the fold.

Inside Laurel discovered a letter from the lawyers who'd settled her grandmother's estate.

Dear Ms Dempsey,
Please find enclosed two documents, one pertaining to our fees and the other . . .

There was a knock on her bedroom door. 'Laurel?'

'Yes?' she called, putting the letter back into the envelope and tucking it away to read later, alongside her trusty copy of *Mamma Mia!*, at the back of the drawer.

'It's Athena. Would you like a tour of the house?'

'Yes, please,' said Laurel, opening the door to find Athena in a wide-brimmed straw hat ready to play tour guide.

'Let's start outside,' she said, dismissing the upper quarters with a shoo of her hand, and heading downstairs.

The front door opened onto a large, bright courtyard, surrounded by high white-washed walls. Laurel couldn't help but chuckle at the very Greek, gigantic crazy-paving that covered the area, which she remembered so fondly from *Mamma Mia!*. She noted the gate, which didn't look as foreboding as it had when she'd arrived, the beautiful terracotta pots planted with figs and geraniums, and the bright pink bougainvillea that crept over the roofs of the outbuildings, which stood between the gate and the house, with their orange tiled roofs.

'Tsk,' said Athena, grabbing a stool and clambering up to tighten one of the bulbs that criss-crossed the area on wires.

'Can I help you with that?' asked Laurel, hovering beneath Athena to ensure she didn't fall.

'I'm fine!' she said, screwing the bulb and putting a hand on Laurel's shoulder to climb back down. She wiped her hands of dirt. 'You think I'm so old I can't fix a light bulb?'

'No,' stammered Laurel, not meaning to have offended Athena.

'I'm messing with you!' Athena's dark eyes lit up. 'I know I look as old as the crows but I'm still pretty able.'

'Of course.'

'Of course I look as old as the crows, or of course I'm still pretty able?' she laughed.

'Now I know you're messing with me,' Laurel laughed back, knowing she and Athena were going to have fun.

'I am! I am! I love to mess!'

As Athena put the stool back in the outhouse – a store piled high with furniture stacked this way and that, which looked as if it might topple at any moment – Laurel cast her eye around the courtyard. 'It's so peaceful here.'

'It won't be when high season comes. You might be the only guest at the moment but come the middle of summer there'll be a lot of life again.'

'I can imagine,' said Laurel as she walked to the far side of the house to another paved area where the woman who'd served Laurel her tea was hanging out laundry.

'Hello, again,' said Laurel when they passed. The woman nodded shyly.

'Don't mind her, she's quiet as a mouse. You're more likely to get conversation out of one of those olive trees.'

'Oh,' said Laurel, fascinated by the woman whom Athena didn't introduce.

Beyond the washing lines was the start of the garden, terraced lawns descending towards the edge of the cliff. The grass needed cutting and the windows of the house required a fresh lick of paint but, in the most part, Villa Athena, like her owner, looked good for her years.

'How long have you been here?' Laurel asked, as they reached an archway, just like the one in the movie, which led to stone steps and the beach below.

'Over fifty years.'

'And do you look after it alone?'

'I have Helena.' Athena motioned her head towards the drying area. 'And when it's busy Nikos stops by to help out. Other than that I'm on my own.'

'It must be a lot of work.'

'I manage.' Athena sat down at a table near the arch. 'Why don't you go down the steps, check out the beach? I never did see the appeal of sand!'

At the bottom of the craggy steps Laurel discovered a small private beach, where a tree leaned out over the water with a little wooden boat tied to it. It was idyllic.

Bounding back up, surprised at just how steep the stairs were, Laurel found Athena, still in her chair, holding a Polaroid camera.

'Smile!'

Laurel put her arms high in the air and grinned. Athena clicked the camera and within moments it spewed out the photo.

'Let's put it on my wall of fame!'

In the house, just off the hall was an office, the walls of which were covered from floor to ceiling with photos of decades' worth of guests. All were happy, smiley shots with a backdrop of brilliant blue sea and sky.

'Did you grow up on the island?'

'I moved here, when I was about your age,' said Athena, distantly, rifling around in a drawer. 'But that's a whole other story. For now, we need to think about you.' Athena looked Laurel up and down. 'I'll bet that you like *Mamma Mia!*.'

'I can't deny it.'

42

'Then you must go on the tour.'

'There's a tour!'

'There is. And it's got your name written all over it.'

As Athena pinned Laurel's photo to the wall Laurel felt a surge of happiness and a sense of belonging she hadn't felt since Marnie died.

5

Alex leant against the bonnet of his car, drawing on a cigarette. 'Good morning.'

'Isn't it,' said Laurel, a wide smile on her face. The day was bright and warm and everything seemed to shimmer and sparkle around her, even the path that had felt spooky and intimidating in the dark was now full of birds chattering. It was glorious.

'Where you going today?'

'I'm going on the *Mamma Mia!* Tour.'

'Ah, you like the film?'

'I love it!'

Alex laughed. 'So, I take you to harbour.'

At the harbour, where boats knocked together gently and tourists milled peacefully eating ice creams, Laurel struggled to find the tour operator. She'd walked from one end of the quay to the other and still hadn't found it. Worried that she would miss her opportunity, she approached a pregnant woman wearing flares and carrying an ABBA tote bag.

'Excuse me,' said Laurel, tentatively. 'Do you speak English?'

'Yes, we're English,' said the woman, her tall partner holding her hand.

'Do you know where I can buy tickets for the *Mamma Mia!* Bus Tour?'

'Are you going on it too? I'm so excited!' The woman's small porcelain face lit up. The guy, large with mid-length floppy hair, rolled his dark eyes affectionately. They reminded Laurel of a chihuahua and a Great Dane.

'Me too,' said Laurel, thrilled to have found a fellow fan.

'Do you love the movie?'

'More than you can know!'

'Oh, I'm glad. It will be so good to have someone on board who shares my passion, unlike some around here.' She gave her partner a poke in the stomach.

Laurel laughed. 'Hi, I'm Laurel.'

'Chris,' said the tall man.

'And I'm Emily.'

Laurel shook both their hands. 'It's really nice to meet you.'

'The ticket office is just over there,' said Chris, pointing to a small shack underneath a tree.

'And the bus leaves from here. We'll make sure it waits for you.'

'Thank you!' Laurel rushed to the ticket office, feeling even more in love with the day than ever, and returned just as the bus was pulling up.

'I heard it's best to sit on the right side,' said Emily, on the bus. 'That way you get the best view of the coast.'

'You've really done your research.' Laurel took a seat behind them, and made herself comfortable.

'Research is Emily's middle name,' said Chris, in a tone that suggested, as much as he loved her, her attention to detail sometimes wore a bit thin.

Emily screwed up her face. 'There's nothing wrong with being prepared.'

'And there's nothing wrong with going with the flow.' Chris stretched his legs far into the aisle, his arms folded in a way that suggested he might have a sleep.

The doors of the bus swooshed closed and the engine rumbled to life when Laurel heard a holler. She looked out of the window to see Angie, clad from top to toe in a pink maxi-dress, running alongside.

'Wait,' she yelled, waving her ticket in the air. 'Stop the bus!'

The driver stopped and opened the door.

'Thank you,' she said, fanning herself with her ticket. 'You're a darlin'.'

'Angie!' Laurel called, when she saw that she was about to take a seat at the front on her own.

'Hi!' She climbed over Chris's legs and plonked herself and her enormous bag beside Laurel. She patted her brow with a hanky, 'Woo-ee, I'm hot!'

'Me too,' said Emily.

'And I'm not seven months pregnant!'

'How do you know how far on she is?' asked Laurel.

'I'm a midwife – it's a busman's holiday wherever I go!'

'This is our last trip before the little one arrives.' Emily rubbed her bump as she spoke.

'Make the most of it,' said Angie. 'Babies change your life for ever, whether you want them to or not.'

'I'm sure we'll manage; we're pretty well organised.'

Chris, eyes closed but listening, raised an eyebrow, which Laurel suspected meant that Emily had the entire nursery kitted out already.

'Just give a shout if you've any worries.'

The girls chatted amiably as the bus wound its way along winding narrow roads. At its first stop the driver announced,

'Glysteri Beach, where you see famous arch.'

'Oh my gosh,' said Emily, jumping up and shoving Chris to get out of her way. 'How exciting is this?'

Laurel squeezed past Angie and allowed Emily to take her by the hand. The two of them hared down the path like small children towards the little cove with its crystal clear water.

'Can you believe it?' Emily cooed, as they arrived on the pebble beach, staring out to sea and the tree-covered land that curved round to create the cove. 'They filmed all around here, all of this is in the movie.'

They stood in awe, taking it all in.

'Do you think Meryl stood here?' Laurel asked, her body tingling with excitement.

'I believe she did!' said Emily, wrapping an arm around Laurel. 'I can feel it in my bones.'

It wasn't long before the girls' reverie was broken

by Chris and Angie, who'd walked rather more slowly down the path.

'Think I'll have a drink,' said Chris.

'Don't you want to take it all in for a while?' asked Emily, gesturing for him to join her.

'I can do that sitting with a beer.'

'Make that two,' said Angie, both of them going to find a table at one of the beachside tavernas, leaving Emily and Laurel alone.

'It's perfect,' said Emily, unable to peel her eyes away from the scene.

'Completely perfect.'

'And look what's over here,' called Chris, from where he was sitting.

Emily and Laurel turned to see what he was referring to.

'Oh my god!' Emily dragged Laurel once more by the hand.

'The arch! The arched entrance to Villa Donna!'

'We *have* to do photos,' said Emily, after both of them had rubbed their hands over it several times knowing that all of the cast must have touched it at some point.

Emily stood under the arch and did a series of baby bump poses. 'This is insane!'

'Completely,' said Laurel, who was quite giddy with it all and delighted beyond measure to have found Emily to share it with. Marnie would have been thrilled.

'I can't believe how happy you both are,' laughed Chris, when Laurel and Emily had at last feasted enough on the scenery and had sat down for a drink.

'What's not to be happy about?' said Emily, her feet up, cradling her bump.

It was then that Laurel noticed the guy she'd seen at the quay in the straw trilby, sitting alone at a table, reading. Laurel noted his clean-shaven face, short-sleeved shirt and semi-tailored shorts and she couldn't help but wonder about him. He looked a little out of place among the couples in their casual shorts and T-shirts, and parties of scantily clad young women.

'Laurel!' called Angie.

'Hmm?' she replied, dreamily, her eyes still on the guy.

'We were just asking, do you fancy a bite to eat? Turns out Chris and Emily here are foodies; they want to sample as much local cuisine as they can.'

'Sure.'

After a light lunch of chilli octopus and fries, the foursome set off round the island to the next location. Laurel noticed that the guy in the hat was on the bus too, sitting on his own near the front.

'Angie,' said Laurel, a little later, when Chris and Emily were having a quiet moment together, chatting to their unborn baby. 'Have you noticed that guy on his own over there?'

'Where?'

'There,' said Laurel, trying not to point.

'Well,' she said, getting up. 'We can't have that.'

Angie had drunk several beers at lunch, and Laurel – in dismay – only realised now what that meant. Angie got up, despite Laurel telling her not to, and introduced herself.

'Hiya,' Laurel overheard her say. 'My friend over there saw that you're on your own,' Angie pointed straight at Laurel, who waved feebly, 'and thought that you might like to join us.'

'Ah, thank you, but I'm fine on my own,' he replied, in a lilting Irish accent.

'Nonsense,' said Angie, too tipsy to take no for an answer. 'There's plenty of room. Come on!'

Accepting his fate the guy moved to a seat across the aisle.

'This is Laurel.'

'Hi,' said Laurel, with a shy, embarrassed smile. He acknowledged her with a small nod and faint smile of his own, his eyes soft and kind.

'And Chris and Emily.'

'I'm Mark.'

Emily waved.

'Nice to have some male company,' said Chris. 'Tell me you're not a *Mamma Mia* fan.'

'Ah, no!' he laughed. 'I was just looking for a way to see the island.'

'I don't believe him,' Angie whispered. 'He's just embarrassed to admit his love of Meryl!'

Laurel laughed, still looking at Mark. He had a quiet intensity about him that captured her attention.

'Agios Ioannis sto Kastri,' the driver announced, pulling over. 'Track is small so you walk.'

'Do you know where we are?' Emily asked, her head popping up above the seat.

'Where?' asked Laurel.

'It's the chapel, you know, where the wedding scenes were shot!'

'You're kidding!' said Laurel, jumping up and heading down the aisle once more.

'You need shoes,' said the driver when Laurel passed wearing only her flip-flops.

'I'll be fine,' she cried, springing off the bus and following the narrow road, which led to the chapel.

'Oh my word,' said Emily, when they'd descended the winding road and turned the final corner, which gave them the most spectacular view of the huge chunk of rock that jutted out into the sea, on which, at its very top, was the tiny chapel.

'This is unbelievable,' said Laurel. 'I genuinely can't believe I'm here.'

The two women began to climb the very same steps that Donna and Sophie, and all the rest of the characters, had climbed for Sophie's wedding. Laurel drank in every moment.

'I read there are one hundred and ninety-eight steps carved into the rock,' said Emily.

'I can believe it,' said Laurel, already slightly out of breath and not even a quarter of the way up. 'Are you sure you should be doing this?'

'I have to,' said Emily, stopping and clutching her side. 'There's no way I'm coming all the way to Skopelos and not seeing inside the chapel where Sam proposed to Donna.'

'Good point!'

'If it takes all day, I will make it.'

They were about to set off after their rest when Chris and Mark arrived.

'If what takes all day?'

'Getting to the top of these steps,' said Emily.

'It sure is a hike,' said Mark, looking up to see how much further they had to go.

'Where's Angie?' asked Laurel.

'She decided to sit this one out,' laughed Chris. 'I think she's made friends with the ice-cream vendor.'

On the small beach below, Laurel could make out a flash of pink waving at them. She waved back.

'Why don't you guys go on ahead?' said Chris. 'I'll take it slow with preggers here.'

'Only if you're sure,' Laurel said to Emily.

'Of course!' she said. 'Just promise not to go in until I get there.'

'Deal,' said Laurel, who set off alone with Mark, trying to ignore the slight flutter of nerves in her tummy.

'I'm not sure I've ever seen anywhere so beautiful,' she said, a little further up, with the chapel in view.

'It's certainly unique.' Mark stopped to admire the view.

Laurel loved an Irish accent, and Mark's was beautiful. She could fall asleep listening to a voice like that, soft and soothing . . . She gave herself a mental kick. What was she like? Thinking this man into bed already.

'You haven't been to the island before?' she asked, as they set off again. Laurel was trying to keep up without getting too pink or sweaty.

'Not to Skopelos, but I've been to a few of the other

islands.' He walked steadily in front of her, his sinewy calf muscles flexing with each step. She liked his calf muscles, she decided. He wasn't a big man, but he had strong shoulders. She'd always liked a good pair of shoulders.

'It takes your breath away,' said Laurel when they finally reached the top. She held on to one of the railings. 'Literally!'

'It really does,' said Mark, who wasn't out of puff at all.

They stood at the top of the rock and looked out in awe at the sea and island stretching in front of them. Laurel found herself humming 'The Winner Takes It All'. Despite her aching feet from where her flip-flops had rubbed a blister, she was still blown away by its beauty. She thought of the end of the movie and of Marnie, and was surprised to find her eyes misting over.

'Are you okay?' Mark asked

'Yes,' she laughed, a little embarrassed. 'I was thinking about my grandma; she'd have loved it here.'

'Has she passed?' he asked, gently.

'A couple of months ago.'

Mark gave Laurel a moment to compose herself before saying, 'I'm sure she's looking down from heaven, wishing she was with you.'

'Thank you,' said Laurel, touched by Mark's kind words.

They stood together quietly, the small chapel behind them, both lost in thought. Laurel couldn't help wonder what Mark was thinking – for all he seemed comfortable in his own skin, he also seemed to be carrying the weight of the world on his broad shoulders.

'Mother Nature is a glorious thing,' he said.

'Yes,' said Laurel, searching for the words that summed up the beauty in front of them. But her thoughts were broken with the arrival of Chris.

'Look who's made it!' he called to them.

They turned to find Chris carrying Emily by piggyback.

'Chris,' laughed Laurel. 'That's so romantic.'

'Isn't it?' said Emily, sliding off his back as easily as a seven-month pregnant woman is able to do. 'Have you been in?'

'Without you? Never!'

They went into the chapel together, marvelling at how tiny it was, and sat on the little wooden benches. Here was where Sophie and Sky decided not to marry and to travel instead, and where Sam proposed to Donna, having loved her all his life. Marnie loved that scene; she was all about people following their dreams.

'I could stay here for ever,' whispered Laurel, staring up at the simple wooden cross, realising she wasn't talking to Emily but to Marnie.

6

'Man, that squid was good,' said Chris, leaning back in his chair, contented and full after supper.

'Doesn't get much better,' agreed Emily.

Laurel sipped her red wine, thinking how much Marnie would have enjoyed this evening at the tiny outdoor restaurant, set among orchard trees with tables on the grass. 'It was a great choice for dinner, Angie. Thanks for bringing us.'

'A real treat,' said Mark, raising his bottle of beer. 'Thank you.'

'You're welcome – I've enjoyed having the company.'

'If it wasn't for the fact I'm trying to figure out the recipe for that dipping sauce, I might even feel a bit romantic,' said Chris, dabbing his finger into the small white dish for the umpteenth time and licking it.

Emily sidled up to him and, in a corny American sweetheart accent, teased, 'Gee, honey, you say the sweetest things.'

Chris wrapped his arm round his wife. 'What was that final flavour?'

'I don't know; we can always ask one of the staff.' Emily yawned, exhausted by the day's excitement.

Laurel felt pretty zonked too. If she had it her way she'd happily sleep in the orchard under the trees and stars instead of hoofing it up the hill to Athena's.

'You guys really know how to do romantic,' she laughed, looking at them cosied up together; it was evident how much they doted on each other, for all their different ways.

'We've done the romance,' said Emily, pointing to her belly. 'And food is our passion. Wherever we go we're always on the lookout for new things to add to our menus.'

'You have a restaurant?' asked Laurel.

'A catering company,' said Chris. 'It started out as a small cafe back in Warwick, where we met at uni, and developed rapidly. Now we've over twenty staff.'

'How's parenthood going to fit around that?' asked Angie, who was keeping a close eye on the men at the bar.

'We've plenty of employees who can help out at the start,' said Emily. 'But ideally we'd like to find something like this – a home and a business – that would allow us to have the family around us.'

'Overseas?' asked Angie.

'Possibly,' said Emily.

'Wow!' said Laurel, in awe of their adventurous spirit. She wished she had more of that herself. Maybe, she thought, it's easier to be adventurous and make big decisions when there are two of you. Perhaps making decisions alone is harder. She felt she knew something of that since losing Marnie and the decision about the house and her own future. 'Are you excited about being parents?'

'Terrified!' said Chris.

Mark laughed.

Emily gave Chris a slap. 'I can't wait to meet whoever's in here. It will be the biggest adventure of our lives.'

Laurel couldn't help but feel a little envious of their adventure, of having something of their own to look forward to.

She looked fondly at Emily and her bump until Angie piped up with, 'And Mark, I haven't had a chance to ask – what brings you to Skopelos?'

Emily and Laurel, even Chris, looked towards Mark, all interested to learn something about him. Laurel could sense it made him feel a little uncomfortable to be put on the spot but, as curious as the rest, she didn't intervene. While he'd bantered with Chris throughout the day he hadn't revealed anything about himself.

'I'm here doing some work,' he faltered, his thumb rubbing his bottle of beer.

'What d'ya do, pet?'

Mark cleared his throat. 'I'm a writer.'

'What sort of writer?' asked Emily.

'A novelist.'

Emily nodded approvingly.

'Like a proper novelist?' asked Angie.

'Thankfully, yes,' he said, modestly.

'Get away!' said Angie. 'I've never met a real-life novelist before. What's your name? Are you famous?'

'Angie!' said Laurel, sensing Mark wasn't interested in

divulging too many details, even though she was keen to find out more.

'What?! We could be sitting in the presence of genius.'

'Sadly not,' he replied, taking a swig of his beer. 'I'm just a bit of a hack, really.'

'Well, if that's all you're telling, I'm gan the bar.'

Angie departed, going straight to the bar, where she took a seat between two young Greek men, who were probably half her age. It made Laurel think of Tanya in *Mamma Mia!* and the sexy barman.

'Anyone for pudding?' Laurel asked.

'Sure,' said Emily. Chris held the menu open so Emily needn't move.

'Mark?'

'Yeah, that'd be great,' he said, his Irish accent like music to Laurel's ears.

After Laurel had decided what to have she looked up to find Mark watching her intently. They fleetingly held eye contact, his sensitive dark eyes pulling her in.

'On second thoughts,' said Emily, noticing the look. 'Maybe there's no room left at the inn.'

Chris looked at her incredulously. 'You always have room for pudding.'

'Baby must be pushing upwards,' she said, giving him a discreet dig in the ribs, which didn't go unnoticed by Laurel. 'Plus I'm wiped out.'

'Right,' said Chris, eventually catching her drift. 'Maybe I'll get something at the hotel.'

Emily and Chris said goodnight, and Laurel felt suddenly exposed, as if Mark could read her thoughts.

'Actually, I might call it a night myself,' he said.

Laurel felt relieved not to have to think of dazzling conversation but she also felt the dull ache of disappointment, not to have the opportunity to spend some one-on-one time with him.

She put on the pretty cardigan Janey had packed for her. 'It is getting a little colder.'

'Can I walk you back to your hotel?'

'That would be lovely,' she said, the prospect of strolling side by side and chatting being so much nicer than having the intensity of sitting at a table face to face. Then it dawned on her that she wasn't a walk but a cab ride away from Villa Athena. 'But I'm out of town.'

'So I'll walk you to the harbour, find a cab for you there.'

They left the little restaurant behind and wound their way down a narrow, cobbled alley with houses that leant inwards and lines of laundry criss-crossing the way.

'Angie's a character,' Mark said, breaking the silence between them.

'That's an understatement,' said Laurel. 'I've known full orchestras with less brass than her.'

Mark laughed. 'I hope you won't take this the wrong way, but she seems like an unlikely companion for you.'

It was hard to know what Mark meant by that – she hoped that he wasn't being unkind about Angie, but when she looked into his face for a clue, there wasn't unkindness there, not at all. He smiled at her, and Laurel turned her gaze to the ground, unaccountably embarrassed. She couldn't say that he was the most gorgeous man she had ever seen, but the combination of his dark eyes, his shy smile and his amazing accent certainly made him one of the most intriguing.

Laurel cleared her throat. 'We met on the plane – she took me under her wing. And I'm glad she did. I may still have been looking for the ferry if she hadn't!'

Mark smiled at Laurel's self-deprecation, who was suddenly aware that she was being followed by a neighbourhood cat.

'I think that cat likes you,' he laughed, watching it trotting along at Laurel's heel, only falling back when Mark turned around.

Laurel bent down to coax it to her and give it a fuss, admiring its patch of black around its eye. 'He reminds me of Tom.'

'Who's Tom?'

'My grandmother's cat. He lives with me now.'

'Has he settled into his new life?'

'He has!' laughed Laurel. 'He likes being around people more than hunting so he's fine in my flat and just pootling round the garden. Mostly he likes a tickle, and a prawn.'

Laurel gave the cat one last stroke before they continued towards the harbour, the cat following at a distance.

'It must have been a difficult couple of months?'

'Yes,' said Laurel, recalling not only the last two months of grieving and all the paperwork that came with bereavement but also of the year before with all the travelling back and forth at weekends to care for Marnie. 'It's good to get away.'

'And you chose to come alone?'

'My grandmother and I were always meant to do this trip together but we ran out of time. It didn't feel right to bring someone else.'

'I understand,' he said, as they arrived at the quay. 'I know how it feels to travel alone when things change.'

'Were you meant to be here with someone?' she asked. If I was Marnie, Laurel thought, I'd come right out and ask if he has a girlfriend. How could someone with those eyes and that smile not have one . . .

Mark didn't answer. 'I think the best place to pick up a cab is over there.'

'Yes,' said Laurel, wondering why Mark had deflected the question. Did he not want to talk about something, or was she reading more into the situation than was there?

Just then she heard a voice call her name. She saw Alex beside his car waving at her. 'You need ride?'

'Angie's taxi driver,' Laurel explained.

'You trust him?'

'Of course,' said Laurel. She thought it was sweet that Mark was concerned about her safety.

'Well, I guess we say goodnight then,' he said, a touch awkwardly, faltering for a moment. Laurel thought he was going to suggest going on somewhere else but instead he said 'goodnight' and turned to leave.

Laurel felt a pang of disappointment; she'd been enjoying their slightly delicate conversation, tip-toeing around Mark's shyness. Before Laurel knew what she was doing she found herself calling, 'Wait!'

She walked towards him, not quite knowing what she was going to say. They stood for a fraction of a second in uncomfortable silence. 'Uh,' said Laurel, hoping not to make a fool of herself, wishing she was more like her Marnie, who was never self-conscious. 'It would be nice to see you again. I mean, if we're both travelling alone, maybe we could do something together during our time here?'

'Sure,' said Mark with just enough of a smile for Laurel to feel he was pleased by the idea and not just being polite.

'We should exchange numbers,' she said.

'Right,' he laughed nervously, taking his phone from his back pocket. 'Good plan.'

'You like that boy?' Alex asked as the taxi drove past Mark and Laurel gave him a wave, thankful that she'd plucked up the courage to ask for his number.

'Maybe,' said Laurel. 'He's quite shy.'

'It's a curse,' said Alex. 'I know.'

'But you're not shy,' said Laurel as they sped out of town.

'As young man I no speak to girls.'

'But you don't seem shy now.'

'Because I grow old. But I never marry. Never many girlfriends.'

'There was never anyone special?'

'Maybe one,' he confided, as they arrived at the path to Villa Athena. 'But it was not to be.'

'I'm sure someone was broken-hearted because of it,'

said Laurel, handing Alex his payment.

'Perhaps,' he said, shaking off a memory. 'Goodnight, Miss Laurel. I see you soon.'

Laurel wound her way leisurely up the path to the villa, tired but contented. As she was closing the gates behind her she heard a sudden scream from the house and she ran to the front door.

'Who left the stove on?!' she heard Athena yell from the kitchen.

Bursting in, Laurel found Athena clutching her hand, plumes of smoke in the air, and the acrid smell of a burnt-out pan, which was now tossed in the sink.

'Athena!' she said, rushing towards her. 'Are you okay? What happened?'

'Just an accident,' she said, slightly unconvincingly. 'Helena must have left the stove on.'

'Right,' said Laurel, opening the back door and taking a cloth to help fan out the fumes. 'Is your hand okay?'

Athena clutched it tightly. 'It'll be fine.'

'Let me see.' She opened the hand to expose a searing burn. 'That's going to need treatment.'

'It'll have to wait until morning. There isn't a hospital and the medical centre only opens out of hours for emergencies. And this,' said Athena, clearly noting Laurel's look of concern, 'is not an emergency.'

'Then we need to cool it down,' said Laurel, emptying the sink and running the cold tap.

'Put it in the cold water,' she said. Athena did as Laurel said. 'How does that feel?'

'Better, thank you,' replied Athena, looking pale.

'You need to keep it there for at least twenty minutes.'

Laurel placed a stool beside Athena and went to get ice from the freezer.

'How was your day?' asked Athena, as Laurel poured ice into the water.

Laurel told Athena all about the *Mamma Mia* Tour, meeting new friends – and about Mark. She neglected to mention the glorious, bustling restaurant, uncertain if Athena would want to know about other businesses being so busy.

'You think you might have a little romance while you're here?'

'If I do,' said Laurel, reaching for the cling film to wrap Athena's hand, 'it'll be the first in a very long time!'

7

The following morning, Laurel opened her bedroom door to hear Athena ranting animatedly at someone downstairs. It crossed her mind to remain in her room a while longer until the situation had cooled off, but, curious by nature, she continued down to breakfast.

In the sitting room, where part of the kitchen was visible from behind the little bar, Laurel caught sight of Athena throwing the contents of a frying pan into the bin. Then followed the sound of the pan being slammed back onto the stove and Athena continuing her rant. It was only when Laurel heard a small voice say, 'Naí, Athena' that Laurel realised Athena was shouting at Helena.

Not wanting to intrude, Laurel went to the empty dining room where she sat and read her book, hoping to give the impression she hadn't overheard the dispute. It was several minutes before Athena arrived, her hair unkempt and eyes raging.

'Huh!' she said, on seeing Laurel. 'I didn't know you were here.'

'I haven't been waiting long,' said Laurel, trying to look as if she hadn't heard anything.

Athena carelessly poured Laurel a glass of water,

spilling it over the tablecloth in the process. 'What do you want for breakfast?'

Laurel remembered what Athena had told her about being cranky when she was tired, and wondered if she hadn't slept well because of her hand.

'I can make you an omelette.' Athena said 'an omelette' loud and slow then, turning towards the kitchen she said, even more loudly, 'It's the house speciality.'

'Then I'll try that,' said Laurel, not daring to request anything else.

Athena returned to the kitchen where Laurel overheard her barking further instructions at Helena. She came back shortly afterwards shaking her head and muttering heavenwards.

'How's your hand this morning?' asked Laurel, searching for neutral conversation.

'It's fine,' dismissed Athena. 'Nothing to worry about.'

'You should have someone look at it; you wouldn't want it to become infected.'

Athena rolled her eyes. 'You young people run to the doctor if you sneeze. There's nothing the matter. It's a burn. It will heal itself.'

'If you're sure,' said Laurel, who had been used to similar conversations with Marnie, who categorically refused to waste doctors' time unless something was hanging off or an orifice was bleeding that shouldn't be!

Laurel was thankful when Helena appeared with the omelette.

'Oh, that looks spectacular. Thank you!' she said, glancing up to see Helena's eyes smiling.

As Laurel took the first mouthful Athena started questioning Helena in Greek. Helena answered quietly. Laurel wondered what they were saying and why Athena was so hard on the timid young woman.

'It's delicious,' said Laurel, encouragingly. The zingy tomato, salty feta and fleshy olives all combined with the egg into a glorious taste sensation.

Helena nodded courteously, looking pleased that Laurel was satisfied, and then hurried back to the kitchen.

'Has Helena worked here long?' asked Laurel, who wondered if Athena was 'breaking her in'.

'She's been helping me since she was a teenager.'

'She isn't a full-time employee?'

'She's meant to come each morning.'

'Meant to?'

Athena took a deep breath and shook her head.

'There can't be much work on the island.'

'Most young people leave to find work but Helena . . . Helena can't.'

'Why?'

'She hasn't the skills or the confidence,' said Athena, brushing the matter away. 'All her life she's been the way she is; she won't change.'

Laurel wanted to challenge Athena, to suggest there might be something that could be done to help Helena gain more confidence but sensing she wasn't much in the mood, she left the subject alone.

After breakfast, Laurel returned to her room where she sent messages to find out if anyone fancied spending the afternoon on the beach below the villa, maybe taking the boat out for a ride, having a picnic, that sort of thing. Within seconds Angie replied saying she'd be there with bells on and Emily replied a few minutes later to say she and Chris would love to come and they'd bring a picnic. It was only Mark who was slow to reply, which Laurel tried hard not to over-examine as she tidied her room and organised herself for the day ahead.

Later, in the sitting room, Laurel found Athena up a ladder, cursing and muttering as she attempted to take down curtains from the shuttered window.

'That looks like a job for a person with two working hands, not one.'

'You may have a point,' conceded Athena, battling with the curtain pole.

Laurel put down her book. 'Let me go up.'

'I hate this job,' Athena grumbled, descending the ladder, her bracelets clattering against the metal frame. 'But I have to do it while it's quiet, there isn't time when we're full.'

Laurel climbed the ladder. 'When does it start to get busy?'

'Usually around May.'

'Oh,' she said, surprised, given that it was already late May and she was the only guest.

'Or June,' Athena was quick to reply. 'Sometimes June.'

At the top of the ladder Laurel released the knob of the curtain pole and allowed the curtains to fall to the ground. 'There, done!'

Athena immediately began the process of gathering up the fabric but on doing so she stumbled and let out a moan, and the curtains dropped to the floor.

'Athena?'

'It's nothing,' she said, attempting to lift the curtains.

Laurel, not wanting to draw attention to her loss of balance said, 'I was going out to the terrace to read for a while, will you join me?'

'I suppose a quick sit down wouldn't hurt.'

'Good,' said Laurel, reaching out an arm to offer support, which was stubbornly brushed aside.

'You said you moved here when you were my age,' said Laurel, when they were both seated on the terrace, sun hats on and cold drinks in hand.

Athena nodded. 'When I married.'

'You married an islander?'

'Stephanos,' she said, in a way that suggested there were many stories to be told about the man, and not all good. 'We met one summer when I holidayed here with my family.'

It wasn't easy for Laurel to imagine Athena as a young woman, but she put her mind to it. She imagined her in caftans and smoking cigarettes from elegant holders, and sporting fabulously daring swimsuits on the beach. 'Where did you grow up?'

'In Athens,' said Athena, closing her eyes and allowing the morning sunlight to warm her face. 'But my father was American so we travelled a lot.'

'And you didn't mind the change in lifestyle?'

'No,' laughed Athena, looking at Laurel. 'I loved it here from the moment I saw it come into view from the boat. I had a feeling that, one way or another, Skopelos would end up being my home.'

Laurel wanted to say she'd had a similar sensation herself but she knew she couldn't compare two days of holiday to a lifetime of living here.

'And how did you come to be in Villa Athena?'

Athena took a sip of iced water before answering. 'It wasn't always Villa Athena. When we married it was Stephanos's mother's house. When she died it was left to him and we made it into our family home.'

'You have children?' asked Laurel. She didn't think of Athena as the most maternal of women.

'Three sons.'

Laurel whistled. 'My grandmother had three children too, so I know from her stories that it's a lot of work.'

'It certainly is – particularly when your husband ups and leaves.'

'Oh, you're kidding?'

Athena brushed it off. 'Don't feel too sorry for me. I was better off without him. And he did do one good thing for me: he left me this house.'

Laurel looked at the house behind them, which had a faded, feminine charm. 'How old were the boys when he left?'

'Five, ten and thirteen.'

'Ouch! Did you name it Villa Athena after he left?'

'You bet I did! I wasn't having him have anything more to do with the place, we were rid of him.'

'So you turned it into the guest house?'

'I had no choice; he left me no money.'

Laurel imagined the old house with fresh paint and three young boys haring about the place with Athena, no doubt shouting at them, up a ladder hanging new curtains.

'And it did well?'

Athena nodded proudly. 'In the eighties and nineties we were the island's destination of choice, to stay and to dine. Everybody came. Our food was legendary.'

It occurred to Laurel that the nineties were almost thirty years ago, when Athena must have been in her fifties. She wondered if, since that time, the guests were no longer coming in the numbers they used to.

'But times change,' said Athena, drifting in and out of sleep. 'Times change.'

Laurel crept away, not wanting to wake Athena. In the sitting room she found Helena, standing on the sofa, in the midst of her own battle with the curtains.

'Can I help fold?' asked Laurel.

Helena offered her a corner of fabric.

'Athena's sleeping,' said Laurel, mimicking sleep, uncertain of how good Helena's English might be.

'Good.'

Together Helena and Laurel billowed and folded the curtains.

'Thanks again for the omelette,' said Laurel, as the two women moved together for the penultimate fold. 'You like to cook?'

Helena's face lit up. 'Very much.'

71

'That's great,' said Laurel, handing the curtain to Helena. 'Do you do most of the cooking here?'

Helena shook her head, her smile dwindling. 'Athena doesn't like it, only when she's sick – and Athena is never sick.'

'No, I can imagine,' said Laurel, who'd sensed the tension between the two women. She wondered if there was any way in which she could help them rub along a bit better.

From the window Laurel saw Athena awaken in the garden. She rubbed her temples and reached for a tub of tablets before swallowing a handful down. Laurel couldn't help but wonder if Athena's health wasn't all that she made it out to be, in the same way that Marnie had tried to hide the truth of her own ill health for so long.

8

2012

'Surprise!' cried Marnie, as Laurel stepped through the patio doors into the garden to find her friends, young and old, all blowing noise-makers and pulling party-poppers. She immediately spotted Janey.

'I wondered why you weren't at the flat this morning!'

'Did we surprise you?'

'Yes, big time!'

'Congratulations!' said Marnie, coming up to hug her. 'We're so proud of you.'

Laurel laughed at them both. 'I only graduated – I didn't win the Nobel Prize!'

Marnie squeezed her closer. 'We couldn't be any prouder if you had.'

'Thank you,' said Laurel, touched by their generosity.

Laurel mingled with friends from school whom she hadn't seen in months as she'd prepared for her finals. She laughed with friends from uni about how they'd managed to keep the surprise a secret, given that not one of them had been known for their discretion. And she chatted with Marnie's friends, women she'd known since she was tiny and who were like aunties to her. She felt a little as she thought she might feel on her wedding

73

day, with everyone that mattered in life all in one place.

'Adrian's being very manly with the barbecue,' Laurel said to Janey, taking a breather from all the catching up. Janey's boyfriend was effortlessly flipping burgers while making sure the chicken and sausages didn't burn.

'I know – I'm quite impressed!'

'Janey,' Adrian called. 'Could you grab the salad from inside?'

'I'll get it,' said Laurel, glad to grab a quiet moment in the kitchen with Marnie.

She found her grandmother chopping stems off salad leaves at the breakfast bar. 'I'm so happy you're home.'

'Me too.' Laurel took a seat and pinched a piece of spinach.

'It's not the same round here without you, even after four years.'

'I know,' said Laurel, who missed Marnie too. For all it was fun living in London with Janey it wasn't home. It never would be. 'But you know I can't feel too sorry for you – you've more friends than I have.'

'I've been alive longer,' laughed Marnie. She slapped Laurel's fingers away from the salad. 'How's the job hunting going?'

Laurel watched her grandmother washing the salad leaves at the sink. She wondered if she looked a little tired, lacking her usual vim.

'I found one.'

'When?'

Marnie abandoned the salad in the sink and was about to sit down next to Laurel when the phone rang, taking her out to the hallway.

'Marnie Ferguson speaking.'

Laurel loved the way her grandmother answered the phone.

'Oh yes, hello.' There was a silence as the person on the other end of the phone spoke. 'Very good. Dr Aitken. Four-thirty. Thursday.' Another pause. 'Thank you. I'll see you then.'

'What was that about?' asked Laurel when Marnie returned to the kitchen.

'Oh nothing. Nothing at all,' she said, sitting down beside Laurel. 'Now, tell me all about this job of yours.'

Laurel brushed off the incident, trusting that Marnie would tell her if there was anything to worry about.

'Don't get too excited,' she laughed. 'It's only an admin job, but it is for an events management team at a swanky hotel.'

'That's wonderful! Events management is exactly what you wanted.'

'I'm just the admin assistant.'

'Not for long – soon you'll be running the department, just you wait and see.'

It made Laurel happy that Marnie was so enthusiastic about the position but for all her enthusiasm Laurel thought she saw the tiniest hint of disappointment in her eyes. Laurel knew that more than anything, even above having her own daughter back, Marnie wished Laurel would come home.

Laurel placed her hand over Marnie's. 'It's not for ever.'

Marnie placed hers on Laurel's with a squeeze and a shake and looked deep into her eyes. 'You must live your life, Laurel, not mine, not someone else's, only yours.'

For all Laurel knew it to be true, she loved her grandmother far more than she could ever love a job. To her their lives were not separate, they were inextricably intertwined.

'And how's Anthony?'

'Anthony?'

'That fella of yours.'

Laurel wondered if Marnie was kidding around, giving the guy she'd been seeing for over a year a different name, but when her grandmother's eyes didn't sparkle mischievously she realised she wasn't. Laurel worried something was wrong.

'You mean Phil?'

'Right,' said Marnie, after a beat, getting up to finish the salad. 'How is Phil?'

Laurel shrugged, watching Marnie more closely. 'He's all right.'

'Why didn't he come with you today?'

'He had some exhibition he wanted to go to – it was the only chance to meet the photographer or something, I don't know,' she said, trying to pass it off as if it was nothing.

Marnie picked up the salad bowl with a flourish and put her arm supportively round Laurel. 'Sounds entirely stuffy and not half as much fun as hanging out with my granddaughter. Come, let's go feed our guests!'

9

2018

'Coo-ee,' called Angie, picking her way down the precarious stone steps from the villa to the beach.

'Morning,' waved Laurel, who'd already set out the sun loungers, she and Athena having dug them out of the store and dusted them down.

'How was last night?' Laurel was keen to know just what Angie had been up to.

'Oh you know,' she said, coyly. 'Just making new friends.'

Laurel pulled her shades down past the bridge of her nose. 'Friends or friends with benefits?'

Angie giggled.

'Honestly, Angie, I don't know how you do it. I can barely attract mosquitoes,' she said, her mind flitting to a thought of Mark and his charming, slightly awkward, way.

'Rubbish!' said Angie, flicking out her towel. 'Look at you. You're gorgeous.'

Laurel bent her pale white legs to one side and examined her arms to see if anything of a tan had formed since she'd arrived. It hadn't.

'I'd give anything to have big lips like yours again

– mine seem to get thinner every year.'

'I'm sure that's not true.'

'Plus you've got those big green eyes, and that hair!'

'Yes,' groaned Laurel. 'That hair. Some days I wonder if I'm related to Chelsea Clinton!'

'Nonsense!' Angie removed her tunic top to expose a strapless, exotic-flower swimsuit – it made Laurel's choice seem positively demure. 'I'll bet there are dozens of men back home all clamouring for you.'

Angie was lathering on her sun lotion and filling Laurel in on the joys of virile Greek men when Emily and Chris arrived with a gigantic hamper.

'We've been food shopping,' called Emily, who was smiling broadly, her bump wrapped in a sarong.

'We bought most of the island,' said Chris, putting down the hamper and adjusting his cargo shorts.

Laurel looked in the basket to discover a plethora of local produce – fresh fish, salad, breads, large round olives, cheeses, pies, honey and plums.

'Where did you get all this?' she asked, salivating at the prospect of it all.

'We just walked around the town,' explained Emily. 'We stumbled down alleys and into squares. It's the sweetest place. I can't get enough of how close the buildings are to each other with their balconies and pots and bright pink flowers, and how easy it is to get lost and discover something completely unexpected in doing so.'

'Sounds like you've fallen for the town in the same way that I fell for its men,' said Angie, who was now happily reclining with her sunhat over her face.

'I think you might be right,' said Emily, positioning her towel on the lounger and digging out her book.

The four friends were quiet for a time, Laurel drinking in the beautiful scenery and feeling a sense of relaxation that she couldn't achieve at home. Emily was reading, gently stroking her bump as she did so, Chris was busy laying out the picnic, while Angie . . .

'Has she fallen asleep already?' asked Chris.

'Looks like it,' laughed Emily, as Angie snored lightly.

'I think she had an eventful night,' Laurel whispered to Emily, when Chris had gone to collect firewood.

'Lucky for some!'

'Tell me about it.' Laurel had never had the confidence to simply pursue a man she fancied, she envied Angie's brass.

'Did you and Mark chat for a while after we left?'

'We strolled down to the harbour.'

'And?'

'And,' said Laurel, enjoying Emily's interest. 'I guess I have a little crush.'

'I knew it!'

'But that's all it is. I doubt very much that it's reciprocated.'

Emily cast her a look of 'get over yourself'. 'Is he coming today?'

Laurel scrunched up her nose. 'I don't know.'

'I'm sure he'll come if he's able, and we'll see what we can find out.'

'Please don't be obvious,' said Laurel, hoping she hadn't spoken too hastily. 'He doesn't strike me as the sort of guy who responds well to that.'

'Stop worrying, it'll be fine.'

Emily had turned back to her book, and Laurel had just fished hers out of her bag when Chris returned with wood for the fire.

'Let's get this beauty burning,' he said, dumping the wood and rubbing his hands gleefully at the prospect.

'Men and fire,' mused Emily as she watched Chris position the wood in a pyramid formation. 'It's such an elemental thing.'

Chris beat his chest. 'Me Tarzan, you Jane.'

Emily rolled her eyes. 'It does make you think though, for all we strive to progress, some things never change. The woman carries the baby, the man carries the wood.'

'He'll make a lovely father,' said Angie, drowsily. 'You found a good one there.'

'Thanks, Angie. It means a lot to hear you say so. You must have seen all sorts in your time.'

Angie stretched awake. 'I have, so I know a good one when I see one.'

'Chris, let me help you,' said Laurel, leaving Angie and Emily to chat about her birth plan.

'You fancy making a quick salad?' Chris asked.

Laurel cut tomatoes, cucumber and onion as Chris prepared the fish on the fire. It reminded her of the times she and Marnie cooked together for Sunday lunches or celebrations. It was never anything fancy but it always tasted so much better for being prepared together and shared with friends.

When everything was ready they all sat on the rug together and tucked in.

'These olives are divine,' said Laurel. 'I've never tasted any as juicy and flavoursome.'

'They're the Pelion variety, apparently,' said Emily. 'They're grown here on the island.'

'And what is this?' asked Angie, pointing to something that looked a little like a cross between a quiche and a Cornish pasty.

'Tiropita,' said Chris. 'It's a cheese, egg and filo pie.'

'It's sensational,' said Laurel, her mouth full. 'I could live here for ever and never tire of these flavours.'

'Agreed,' said Emily. 'There's nothing quite like eating sun-drenched local produce.'

'That's the truth,' said Laurel, selecting a piece of Chris's expertly baked fish, which flaked as soon as her fork touched it.

They chatted some more about the island's produce, gorging themselves as they did, and finished with fresh plums, which Chris had roasted on the fire and served with a dollop of thick yoghurt.

'Who fancies a swim to burn some of this off?' asked Angie, when everyone was satisfied.

'I won't, if you don't mind,' said Emily. 'Nobody wants to see a beached whale!'

'I will – race you!' called Laurel, and the two of them dashed in to the crystal-clear, turquoise water.

'It's as warm as a bath,' said Laurel, far enough out to start swimming.

'An enormous one!' said Angie, bobbing under the

water and reappearing with her hair soaking wet and her curls straightened out. She shook herself off. 'It's beautiful under there, you should try it.'

Laurel dived down and swam below the surface for as long as her lungs would allow, feeling as if London and all her grief had been momentarily washed away.

When she resurfaced, her eyes stinging, nose running and her hair plastered against her head she saw, on the cliff, a figure coming down the steps.

'Here comes trouble,' said Angie, with a wink.

Laurel knew at once whom Angie was referring to. As she rubbed the water away from her eyes she could make out the trilby hat and the strong shoulders of Mark.

'Great,' she said, instantly regretting her choice of swimwear and dunking her head under the water. 'Flabby midriff and frizzy hair. Go Laurel.'

'Let's say hello,' said Angie, dragging herself out of the water, seemingly without a thought to her appearance.

Laurel, on the other hand, waited until the final moment to stand up, adjust her bikini, suck in her stomach and scrunch her hair. She walked up the beach, behind Angie, grabbed her towel and wrapped it around her before Mark had the opportunity to lay eyes on her body.

'You made it,' she said, shaking water from her ear, trying not to make it obvious that she was delighted he'd arrived.

'I only just got your message,' he said, watching Laurel rubbing her hair dry. She was inwardly cursing Janey for not allowing her to bring her anti-frizz. 'I was working all morning from the hotel. The signal isn't strong there.'

'It's good you're here now,' said Emily, joining Laurel supportively. 'Chris is in need of some company.'

Lucky Chris, thought Laurel, a light flutter of butterflies passing through her tummy.

'What's the craic with the villa?' asked Mark, sitting on the picnic blanket with a plate of food. 'It's kinda off the beaten track. I wasn't certain I'd come to the right place.'

'It used to be *the* place to stay on the island,' said Angie. 'A sort of precursor to the boutique hotel. Loads of famous artists and writers stayed here, it was a bit of an artisans' retreat.'

'Really? Did you ever stay?' Laurel asked, intrigued by all the summers gone by that Angie had spent on the island.

'I came for dinner once. Athena treated us like royalty. Her attention to detail was exceptional, and the dinner was divine.'

'Cool,' said Chris, nodding approvingly. 'I like a hidden gem.'

'That was in the late nineties, just before it began to decline, I think.'

'That sounds about right,' said Laurel. 'Athena mentioned the eighties and nineties but that's what, twenty, thirty years ago and currently I'm the only guest. I think it's becoming a bit much for her.'

'It certainly is a handsome home,' said Mark, looking towards the house. 'It seems a shame it's not being run at full capacity. Is there anything obvious that needs work?'

'It's a little tired but I think it's more that she doesn't promote it or make any changes. I suspect she relies on what worked in the past, rather than what might work in the present or the future.'

'What's the food like?' asked Chris.

'Good.'

'Has she a website?' asked Mark.

'No. No website, no Facebook page, Twitter, nothing.'

'No wonder she's not getting any punters,' said Chris. 'How did you find out about it?'

'TripAdvisor. But I only chose it because it reminded me of Donna's guest house in *Mamma Mia!*. Everywhere else on the island looked much fresher.'

'Poor thing,' said Emily. 'It must be really tough to keep up if you don't do tech.'

'We could offer to help,' said Mark. Laurel wondered if everyone else was thinking how nice it was of him to offer, or if it was just her.

'We could plan a party for her,' said Angie. 'Bring back the spirit of yesteryear, just a bit more, well, now.'

'Yes,' said Laurel, who was thrilled by Angie's suggestion. But would Athena be open to their plan? 'Perhaps with just a little help we could get her back on her feet. I'll ask her.'

'Who's up for another swim?' asked Angie, a little later.

'Me!' said Chris, jumping up and running to the sea.

'I'm happy reading,' said Emily, laughing at her husband bombing into the water.

'Me too,' said Mark.

'You should take a dip,' said Emily, which Laurel recognised instantly as gentle meddling. 'Wash off some of those writerly cobwebs.'

'I'm afraid I'm more of a watcher than a doer,' he said, sieving sand through his fingers. 'Us Irish don't really do swimming!'

'Or how about a boat ride,' she suggested. 'You'd like a boat ride, wouldn't you, Laurel?'

'Sure,' she said, blushing.

'Mark?' said Emily. 'You wouldn't disappoint a poor young maiden, would you?'

'How could I?' he said, gallantly getting up and offering Laurel his hand.

'Thank you,' she said, hoping not to show that the touch of his hand made her tingle.

'I should warn you,' he said, putting on his hat. 'I'm not much of an oarsman.'

Mark waded into the sea and untied the rope, which secured the boat to the small tree leaning over the water.

'M'lady,' he said, once the boat was released. He held out his hand and tried to keep the rocking boat steady for Laurel.

'Thank you,' she said, climbing in, but as she did so the boat tilted dramatically to one side and she lost her balance.

'Whoa!' said Mark, trying to hold the boat still but, as he did, Laurel's weight shifted and before Mark could grab her the boat tipped and Laurel fell, head over heels, into the water.

'Oh God!' shouted Mark, wading as fast as he could to her rescue. 'Are you okay?'

'I'm fine,' laughed Laurel, sitting up to her waist in the warm water, feeling like Julie Walters when she fell out of the boat.

'Let me get you your towel,' he said, running back to the loungers and returning immediately. 'I'm so sorry!'

Laurel looked at Mark and then at herself, both of them soaking wet, and burst into laughter. It wasn't long before Mark did the same and the two of them were in fits of giggles.

'Shall we try again?' asked Mark, after Laurel had dried herself down, and they'd both composed themselves.

'Yes,' she said, diverting her eyes form his clinging shorts. 'I'd like that.'

The boat wobbled dreadfully as she stepped in again and for a split second she thought she was going to fall once more but this time Mark managed to steady it and between them they got the thing moving, Laurel pushing off from the tree and Mark in charge of the oars.

'There's something wonderfully Victorian about row boats,' said Laurel, relaxing at the end of it as Mark tried to get the swing of steering.

'They always make me think of *Wind in the Willows*.'

'*There is nothing, absolutely nothing, half so much worth doing as simply messing about in boats,*' said Laurel, charmed that Mark should reference the book.

'I'm impressed.'

'It was one of my grandmother's favourites.' Laurel remembered how Marnie would always say she'd read her one chapter each night and go on to read two or three, sometimes four. 'She always said it reminded her of her husband.'

It was then that it came to Laurel whom Mark reminded her of, her grandfather. He had died fifteen years before Laurel was born so she never met him but Marnie had talked at length about his life and character and it felt to Laurel as if she'd known him.

Physically Mark and her grandfather were similar, not tall, of medium build, and with similar eyes, which Laurel knew through the photographs she used to pore over with her grandmother. Marnie would describe her husband's eyes as 'dancing with a faraway look'. Laurel thought the description suited Mark too, a look that suggested he was always in a world of his own.

'It's one of my favourites,' he smiled, holding Laurel's gaze for a fraction longer than could go unnoticed, giving Laurel the confidence to believe her feelings might be reciprocated after all.

10

Laurel spent the next morning exploring Skopelos town, winding her way through endless alleys of little white buildings, draped in the boldest pink bougainvillea, strong against bright blue skies. Every way she turned she stumbled upon colour and vibrancy and another architectural treasure, which she knew Marnie would have delighted over.

By late morning, she'd wound her way down to the port where she happened upon a beautiful white church, perched on a cliff, with a grey slate roof and domed tower, reached by white stone steps.

'Incredible,' she said, arriving at the top and gazing out over the Aegean Sea to an island in the distance and a tiny bay below. 'You would have loved this, Marnie.'

Feeling in need of a coffee, Laurel went in search of a place to sit for a while. She found a small waterfront cafe, where she took a seat and ordered a coffee and some loukoumades, a Greek treat, which Emily had told her about on the beach the previous day.

'They make you fat,' said a voice, as Laurel was biting into a second little ball, which was like a round doughnut

– crisp and sticky on the outside with a fluffy inside, but tasting of honey and cinnamon.

Alex was grinning at her.

'I can imagine!' said Laurel, undeterred. She had walked sufficiently far to warrant a treat.

'You alone?'

'Yes.'

Alex hesitated. 'I join you?'

'Of course,' said Laurel, surprised that he should want to.

He ordered a coffee and took a seat. 'It is beautiful day, no?'

'Aren't all days on Skopelos beautiful?'

'In summer, it is true. But winter, no.'

'Does it get cold?'

'Not cold like London but Skopelos cold.'

Laurel struggled to imagine the island with grey skies, flowerless plants and no boats bobbing in the water.

'Have you been to London?'

Alex shook his head. 'I always want to go.'

London suddenly felt very far away to Laurel. The prospect of leaving all this beauty and returning to the noise and bustle left her feeling quite cold. 'It couldn't be any more different from here.'

'Where Angie today?' asked Alex, after they'd sat quietly for a while, watching the world go by.

'Probably sleeping off a hangover,' laughed Laurel. As they said their goodbyes yesterday, Angie had said she planned to hit the bars after she left Villa Athena.

'She is fun, no?'

'She certainly is!'

Alex looked out over the boats lost in a thought.

'Wait,' said Laurel, suddenly recalling what he'd said about the woman who got away. 'Do you like Angie? Is she the one who got away?'

Laurel wasn't certain but she thought Alex blushed.

'I . . .' he faltered.

'Alex,' Laurel teased. 'Am I right?'

'It stupid,' he dismissed, waving the matter away.

'No!' insisted Laurel, never happier than when she had the opportunity to play matchmaker. 'It's brilliant. Why wouldn't you have a thing for Angie? She's fabulous.'

'I am old.'

Laurel looked at Alex with a 'come off it' expression. 'A little older than Angie maybe, but not old.'

'She has many men.'

'None of whom are suitable,' said Laurel, deciding to talk to Angie. 'You leave it to me, let me see what I can do.'

At that moment the cat from the alley brushed up against Laurel's leg.

'Hello again,' she said, recognising the patch on its eye.

'You have way with cats.'

'What makes you say that?'

'That cat has no home, it shy of people.'

'Poor thing,' said Laurel, stoking it from head to tail, the cat nuzzling for more attention until the arrival of the waitress frightened it away.

'Alex?' asked Laurel, after the waitress had served fresh coffee. 'What do you know about Athena?'

'Athena,' he said, smiling irreverently. 'She strong woman. She came here when I was boy, over fifty years ago.'

'She told me she came here when she married.'

'She married rich man of island but he leave when children small.'

'Do you know why?' asked Laurel, feeling a little guilty about asking Alex rather than Athena.

'Pretty young tourist.'

'Oh.' Laurel grimaced.

'Then she open house, she cook beautiful food, treat everyone well. She big success, all with three boys. She was talk of island.'

'And what happened?'

Alex shrugged. 'Then she disappear; nobody know why. She come to town hardly ever.'

'But it doesn't make sense,' said Laurel, wondering what had happened to Athena and the villa.

'People say she had no money, or she lost her mind when children left – I don't know.'

'No,' said Laurel, thinking that none of those things rang true. 'I wonder if anybody really knows for sure.'

'Athena, what are you doing?' asked Laurel, who had returned to the villa to find the courtyard scattered with old wooden chairs, and Athena, muttering, deep in an outhouse.

'I'm organising,' she replied, reaching for another

chair, which was perched precariously on top of a tower of stacked tables. It reminded Laurel of how Marnie used to have sorting sessions in her studio when she'd group pots of all shapes and sizes together like miniature Towers of Pisa.

Laurel edged her way into the old brick building, which was chock a block with old furniture and pots and crockery, and smelt oddly reminiscent of Marnie's studio. There were baskets hanging from the ceiling and kids' bicycles attached to the walls. Barely an inch of space remained.

'I'll get it,' she said, reaching for the chair far more easily that Athena could manage. Laurel surveyed the space. 'You have a lot of stuff.'

'I've lived a lot of years!'

'So, what can I do to help?'

'I need things categorised, tables with tables, chairs with chairs.'

'Fine.' Laurel was glad she'd worn her mother's dungarees. 'While I do that why don't you tell me a little about the villa?'

Athena unfolded an old deckchair, happy to take a short break.

'I didn't start the business with any great intentions, it was just a way to put food on the table for my sons.'

'How did they respond to you working?'

'It was tough. They'd lost their dad and in his place they found a bunch of strangers traipsing through their home, taking up all their mother's time and attention. It wasn't easy.

'Christos was thirteen so he was able to help around the place, and Stelios made friends with visiting children, but George found it difficult – he was only five – and he hated the fact he had neither his father nor his mother's full attention.'

Laurel dragged an old barbecue from the outhouse. 'It sounds hard.'

'It was but, one way or another, we stumbled through the first few years and emerged with a successful business. People came from all over, and we developed a reputation as a bit of a retreat. We had all sorts of artists and writers visit, sometimes staying for months on end. But most of all we became known for the restaurant.'

'How did you manage to run the restaurant with three young children?'

'I'm not sure! At first I cooked great batches of things when the boys were at school but as they grew, and didn't need me so much, I became passionate about the food I was preparing and serving. But it wasn't without its moments.' Athena laughed wryly, recalling something.

'Go on,' said Laurel.

'George went through a stage of practical jokes, you know the sort of thing – changing all the clocks in the house by an hour, cling-film on the toilet, soap in the toothpaste tube – but he soon became inspired to try something more elaborate.'

Laurel beat the dust off a sun-lounger and cringed in anticipation at the story Athena was about to tell.

'We'd been tipped off about a restaurant critic's visit – an important critic – I told the boys all about it and how it was extremely important that Mama was left to prepare something exceptional for him and off they went, seemingly obeying my instructions. Little did I know they set about an array of pranks to make the inspector's visit memorable for all the wrong reasons.'

'What did they do?' Laurel asked, perching on the sun-lounger.

'Christos greeted him, took his coat, and sprinkled itching powder round his collar! Stelios cut a centimetre of wood off the leg of the table I'd prepared especially for him so that it rocked and wobbled throughout his supper, and earlier in the day George had snuck into the kitchen and kneaded a spoonful of salt into the bread mix so that the first thing the inspector tasted was a disaster.'

'That's terrible!' said Laurel, shocked that Athena's boys would do such a thing.

Athena laughed heartily, clutching her stomach.

'I was so mad at the time. They were grounded for weeks. I thought if we'd got that star it would have changed our lives, that we would somehow have been living the dream, but of course I was wrong. My boys knew what they were doing that day.

'If we'd got the star the pressure to maintain the standard would have been enormous, and family life would have suffered. They did me the biggest favour. For the rest of our time together we were happy, comfortable running our home as a much loved and respected restaurant and guest house, but not trying to keep up with anyone other than ourselves.'

'It's good you were able to see that,' said Laurel,

thinking how similar Athena's lack of greed and wisdom was to Marnie's. 'It sounds as if people loved being here.'

'They did,' said Athena, fondly.

'Do you ever think about having a party?' said Laurel, surveying her handiwork, everything now accessible and in order. 'A revival of the glory days?'

Athena was quick to dismiss the suggestion. 'Those days are gone.'

'Right,' said Laurel, still curious as to exactly why they'd slipped away. 'I just mean something that shows off the house again and the food, a sort of re-launch party, if you like.'

'The house is too tired.' Laurel could sense Athena trying to close the conversation down.

'Not really,' said Laurel. Seeing Helena at the washing lines, she beckoned her over. 'It's nothing Helena and I couldn't sort out with a few cushions, curtains and throws.'

'What is, Miss Laurel?' Helena asked.

Laurel explained her idea.

'I could help.'

'You could cook!' said Laurel, clapping her hands, delighted with the idea.

'Helena hasn't the time!'

'Why not?' asked Laurel.

Athena began muttering in Greek and started to get up.

'Okay,' said Laurel, realising Helena in the kitchen was a sore point. She gestured for Athena to sit back down. 'Helena stays out of the kitchen but I will need her help sprucing up the house.'

'And when are you planning on this party?' asked Athena, grudgingly.

'In a week?' Laurel suggested tentatively, feeling she was on the brink of Athena agreeing to the plan. 'It's no trouble; I do this sort of thing for a living.'

'And who's paying for all this?'

Laurel was happy to cover the cost herself but knowing Athena was too proud for charity she suggested a small ticket price instead.

'Fine,' said Athena, wiping her hands of the matter. 'But don't forget who's boss around here.'

'Oh, thank you, Athena,' said Laurel, kissing the old woman on the cheek. 'I know you won't regret it. We'll make it a party to remember!'

11

'Do you want to hear my news?' asked Laurel, greeting Angie at the bar she'd chosen for the night – a terrace overlooking the yachts in the harbour, laid out with tables and chairs, and large almond trees in containers. The smell of lamb cooking on an open grill made Laurel's mouth water.

'What is it?' asked Angie, taking a seat at a table nearest the water.

'I know someone who fancies you,' Laurel sang, feeling like a teenager again.

'Who?'

'Alex!'

'Oh.'

Laurel couldn't help but feel a little deflated by her friend's lack of excitement. 'You don't sound very interested.'

'That's because I'm not.'

'I thought you liked him – you teased him that night when we first arrived about him coming to see you!'

'That was just friendly banter,' she said, shrugging off the incident.

'But didn't you once have a thing with him?'

'About twenty years ago, when we were both young enough to know it was nothing serious!'

'Don't you want something serious?' asked Laurel, who couldn't quite understand why someone like Angie should be on a one-woman conquest to sleep her way through the island.

'I don't know,' said Angie, shaking her head.

'Alex is so nice,' said Laurel. 'He's really respectful and considerate. You could do a lot worse than him.'

'I know . . .' said Angie, gazing out across the boats.

'But?'

'I want to enjoy myself while I still can. God knows I'm not getting any younger.'

'You're not exactly ready for the grave, Angie. Don't you think it would be nice to have someone to share your life with more fully?'

'Perhaps,' she said, a naughty grin forming as she tilted her head towards a guy at a table of four younger Greek men.

'Angie . . .' Laurel began, worrying that this was the second or third man Angie had her eye on in as many days, but as she did Chris and Emily arrived.

'Nice place,' said Emily, impressed, looking out over the port with all its boats and people milling about. The evening sun had gone and the lights of the harbour reflected and danced in the water.

'I chose it with Laurel in mind.'

'How so?' asked Laurel. Angie nodded to the back corner of the terrace where a man was setting up a small sound system. 'I don't understand.'

'Karaoke!'

Laurel looked aghast, which made Chris chuckle in amusement.

'What made you think *I* would be into karaoke?'

'You love ABBA. You love Meryl. Why wouldn't you love karaoke?'

Laurel was about to explain the difference between the enjoyment of watching and the dread of performing when Mark arrived.

Emily leaned over and whispered, 'You guys were having a good time on the beach yesterday, do you think he likes you?'

Laurel bit her lip, uncertain of her own feelings, let alone his. 'I don't know.'

Emily clutched Laurel's hand. 'Leave it to Auntie Emily!'

'Good evening,' said Mark, looking casual in a black polo shirt and khaki shorts, which showed off his tan. 'What can I get everyone?'

'Cocktails!' said Angie.

'Non-alcoholic for me,' said Emily, looking rather sorry at not being able to drink.

'Beer,' said Chris.

'I'll have a cocktail too,' said Laurel.

'Anything in particular?'

'You choose.'

With Mark at the bar Laurel probed everyone about their days.

'We hired a car and drove to a cheese producer on the other side of the island,' said Chris. 'The island has lots of goats so the cheese has a really distinctive zing.'

Laurel loved the fact that Emily and Chris did their own thing. When everyone else was lying poolside soaking up the sun they were beetling about looking for new flavours.

'What about you, Angie?'

'I hung out at the pool, topped up my tan, caught up on some reading. It was nice.'

Mark returned with a tray of drinks.

'For Angie,' he said, offering her a lurid orange and red cocktail, 'Sex on the Beach!'

Angie laughed, as did the others. 'Yes, please!'

'And for Laurel, the house speciality,' he said, presenting her with a rather more sophisticated-looking cocktail. 'The Meryl Streep.'

'Thank you,' smiled Laurel, touched that he'd remembered her passion.

'We couldn't possibly have cocktails and karaoke in Skopelos without Meryl somewhere.'

'Quite right,' said Angie, as Mark took the tray away. 'To Meryl!'

'To Meryl,' they said in unison, chinking glasses.

Mark returned and took a seat at the head of the table. Laurel felt a twinge of rejection that he hadn't chosen to sit next to her.

'So what did you do today, Laurel?' asked Emily.

'I did a little exploring and then I helped Athena clear out her outhouse.'

'I'm sorry,' said Chris. 'You helped the owner of the villa, where you're staying, clear out her outhouse?'

'Right, I know,' said Laurel, a little embarrassed. The trouble was she was enjoying helping Athena, even if that wasn't normal for a paying guest. 'It sounds like a bit of a weird thing to do on your holiday—'

'*A bit*,' interjected Chris, which received a quick 'behave yourself' stare from Emily.

'But there's something about her,' continued Laurel. 'I don't know, maybe she reminds me of my grandmother, but I want to help her. Plus I enjoy her company.'

'It's nice that you're helping her. She sounds like a real character,' said Mark. 'I'd like to meet her.'

'Well,' said Laurel, warmed by Mark's interest. 'It's funny you should say that . . .'

Laurel told them how Athena had agreed to Angie's suggestion of a party. 'And I was wondering if you guys might help in some way. Some food, party ideas, a little advertising. What do you think?'

'I think it sounds like a great idea,' said Mark. 'I'm happy to help out with promotion.'

'And we can definitely do the catering,' said Emily. Chris nodded, accepting that his wife's commitment was his too, whether he liked it or not. 'We've heard of lots of little producers on the island that we're desperate to visit so this will give us a real focus to our outings.'

'And I can help out with entertainment,' Angie said.

'Perfect,' said Laurel, thankful for her new found friends. 'So it's settled; I'll let Athena know.'

It wasn't long before the karaoke was up and running and Angie was in position ready to give it a go.

'Mark,' said Emily. 'Do you mind moving to Angie's seat, you're blocking my view?'

As Mark repositioned himself Laurel smiled covertly at Emily, whom she knew had moved Mark to be closer to her.

'There,' said Emily. 'That's better. Now I've got a great view of Angie.'

Laurel had a good view of her own – Mark.

'She's not,' said Chris, despairingly when he heard the opening few bars of 'I'm Every Woman'.

'I think she is,' laughed Laurel, all four of them fearful for what was to come.

As Angie began her assault on Whitney, Laurel searched for an opener with Mark.

'What did you do today?' she asked, sipping on her Meryl Streep for courage.

'More work, I'm afraid,' he said. 'And a couple of strolls to clear my head.'

'Did you discover anywhere interesting?' she asked, wishing she'd been able to join him.

'A nice little cove, past the headland, with a barbecue place.'

'Barbecue?' said Chris, his ears pricking up.

'Excuse my husband,' said Emily, shooting Chris daggers, which said, 'leave Laurel and Mark to talk alone'. 'Chris hearing "barbecue" is like a dog hearing walkies.'

'Maybe we should check it out,' suggested Laurel. 'What about supper tomorrow evening?'

'I'd like that,' said Mark, looking at Laurel with an

intensity that caught her off-guard; tiny goosebumps appeared on her arms.

'Great!' said Chris, rubbing his hands. 'Nothing beats a barbecue.'

'Chris, we have that *other thing* tomorrow night.' Emily's tone of 'it's meant to be a date' couldn't have been any clearer but – distracted by the prospect of man-sized portions of meat sizzling on a hot grill – it passed Chris by and he lost himself in a soliloquy of steaks.

Emily closed her eyes and shook her head listening to her husband blethering on and on about different sauces and meat-smoking techniques. 'Chris,' she said, when he'd eventually finished. 'Why don't you go get some more drinks from the bar?'

'I can help,' said Mark, the two of them heading off together.

'I'm so sorry, Laurel. I'll work on distracting him. We can go another night.'

'Don't be silly,' said Laurel, who couldn't help but look over Emily's shoulder to check out Mark's broad shoulders that tapered to a slim waist as he leaned against the bar. 'It might be more comfortable with the five of us. I'm sure they'll be another opportunity at some point to chat to him alone.'

By the time Angie returned to the table Laurel had drunk another two cocktails and was beginning to feel decidedly tipsy.

'Anyone up for singing?' she asked.

'Me!' said Laurel, more drunk than she'd realised.

'Brilliant!' clapped Angie, taking her by the hand. 'What do you want to sing?'

'ABBA of course!' said Laurel. 'We should do "Chiquitita".'

Angie handed her a microphone and another cocktail.

Laurel began to sing and as she did she thought of Marnie, who always sang as if no one was listening. She imagined herself as Rose, with Angie at her side as Tanya, and together they took it line by line, alternating between drinking and singing, until they were in relative harmony. When they reached the high of the first chorus Laurel suddenly lit up, dancing to the music as if no one was watching. She opened her eyes to find Angie, cocktail in hand, singing straight at her, having the time of her life. They sang the rest of the song, oblivious to everyone in the bar, at the top of their lungs.

'You were incredible!' said Angie, hugging Laurel, when the song was finished.

'You were too,' said Laurel, feeling invigorated and giddy. 'I want to do another!'

'Okay!' agreed Angie.

'But wait,' said Laurel, leaving Angie and walking towards Mark. Laurel saw Emily, at the table, shaking her head lightly but Laurel was too drunk to interpret its meaning. She offered her hand to Mark and said, 'Come on, sing with me!'

'No,' he laughed, nervously. 'You were amazing but, really, karaoke isn't my thing.'

'Go on!'

'No, thanks.'

'Really?' she said, incredulous in her drunkenness that anyone could turn down such a proposition.

'Laurel,' said Emily, placing her hand on Laurel's back. 'Why don't you just go sing with Angie; maybe Mark will join you later?'

'But I—'

When Laurel wouldn't take no for an answer Emily stood up and gently led Laurel aside. 'Mark isn't as drunk as you,' she whispered, hoping to make Laurel realise she was on the brink of embarrassing herself.

'Right,' said Laurel, half getting Emily's message, and suddenly feeling a bit swimmy and sick. 'Maybe I should just go back to the villa, forget about singing.'

'That's probably for the best,' said Emily kindly, gathering up Laurel's things and calling Alex to take her home.

'Did you talk to him?' Laurel asked, outside the bar, the fresh air going some way to sobering her up. 'Is that why you stopped me, because he's not interested?'

'No,' said Emily, softly, with a light laugh, amused by Laurel's drunkenness. 'He just didn't want to sing, he wasn't as drunk as you.'

'Are you sure?'

'Yes,' said Emily. 'I didn't want you to say something you'd regret. I promise, I haven't probed and he hasn't said anything. Now look, here's Alex – go have a relaxing sleep. You'll see things more clearly in the morning.'

'You had good night?' Alex asked, once Laurel was in the car and he was winding his way through the traffic congestion of the narrow streets.

'Until the end,' she said. 'When I made a fool of myself.'

'Never, Miss Laurel.'

'You might be surprised.'

'What you do?'

'I misread a situation and made someone feel uncomfortable.'

'Someone you like?'

'I think so,' said Laurel, unable to make sense of what she felt. All she knew was that she wished Marnie was with her and that she hadn't had so much to drink.

'I'm sure it okay.'

'I'm not,' said Laurel, feeling unusually maudlin. It had been such a long time since she'd felt even an inkling of attraction towards anyone and, now that she did, she'd blown her appeal by being hideously drunk.

'He like you, Miss Laurel. Everyone like you.'

Laurel raised an eyebrow.

'Angie like you.'

'Angie,' said Laurel, thinking about her friend who was probably still belting out eighties anthems at the top of her lungs.

'You speak to her?'

'Yes,' said Laurel, sober enough to know she should choose her words carefully.

'What she say?'

Laurel thought before answering. 'She said she's seeing someone else but she's flattered to know how you feel.'

'You mean, she say no.'

'No. That's not what she said at all.'

'Hmmm.' Alex didn't seem to believe her, and they drove the rest of the way in silence.

Later, as she climbed into bed, the room spinning, Laurel thought about what she could do to help Angie focus on Alex, and why other people's love lives always seemed so much easier to sort out than her own.

12

'Good grief!' said Athena, when Laurel arrived down-stairs in the morning. 'What happened to you?'

'Don't ask.' Laurel's mouth was as dry as sand and her head was pounding. 'May I have a glass of water?'

Athena went to the kitchen and returned with a glass of water and the Greek equivalent of Alka-Seltzer, which Laurel took dubiously. 'I wondered why you didn't come down for breakfast.'

The mere mention of breakfast made Laurel's stomach flip.

'Were you out sampling Skopelos's nightlife?'

Laurel swallowed some of the Greek Alka-Seltzer, which tasted of aniseed and made her gag.

'Where did you go?'

'I've no idea,' said Laurel, who could barely remem-ber arriving at the bar let alone getting its name. 'Some karaoke cocktail bar on the waterfront.'

Athena raised her hands in delight. 'Ha!' she laughed. 'Sounds like Dafni's. They're notorious for their deadly cocktails. Did you try them? Did you have more than one? I spent a night there years ago; I only had two drinks and still I ended up singing my way home without my shoes and handbag.'

'What happened?'

'Your guess is as good as mine,' laughed Athena at the memory. 'Mysterious things happen at Dafni's!'

'Tell me about it,' moaned Laurel, unable to recall why she'd thought it was a good idea to attempt to drag Mark up to sing. In the cold light of day she could see perfectly well that he hadn't wanted to do it. Why, she wondered, couldn't she have seen that the night before?

'Did you do something you regret?'

Mark had been the first thing Laurel had thought of on waking, followed by a sinking feeling in her stomach and a general sensation of dehydration and pain. It had taken her ages to pluck up the courage to open the curtains and let in the brilliant morning light, which 1) was like needles to her eyes, and 2) brought home the harsh reality of the night before.

'Maybe,' said Laurel. She thanked her lucky stars Emily was pregnant and off the booze and had had the wherewithal to stop her when she had. If it hadn't been for Emily, Laurel may well have dragged Mark up to the front and embarrassed both of them rather than just herself.

'Do you want to tell Athena about it?'

Laurel shook her head. 'Only that any chance of romance I might have hoped for on this holiday has been well and truly eradicated by me making an idiot out of myself.'

'It's probably not as bad as you remember it.'

The look on Mark's face as she pleaded with him to get up and sing was burnt on Laurel's memory.

'I suspect it is,' said Laurel. 'But, no matter, I guess I never have to see him again – that is, after today.'

'Why? What's happening today?'

Laurel took another drink of water and began to feel the effect of the Alka-Seltzer. Some of the self-inflicted pain in her body began to disperse.

'The friends I told you about have offered to help out with the party plans. Mark is one of them. You don't mind, do you?'

'I don't suppose so,' said Athena. 'The motto of the house is "the more the merrier" – it will be good to have some young life about the place again.'

'I'm so pleased you've arrived first,' said Laurel, greeting Emily and Chris at the gates to the villa. 'I was worried Mark might get here before you and I wouldn't know what to say.'

'Oh yeah,' snorted Chris, 'after you tried to drag him, like a sack of spuds, up to sing.'

'Chris!' said Emily, sharply. 'Not helpful.'

'It's fine,' said Laurel. 'I did make a giant tit of myself.'

'No, you didn't,' Emily soothed.

Laurel wasn't sure whether or not to believe her.

'Only because you stopped me before I had the chance to really embarrass myself, which I'm sure he realised.'

'I doubt it,' said Emily. 'He'd had enough beers not to know what was going on.'

'Really?' said Laurel, desperate for any glimmer of

hope that things might not be quite as bad as she thought. 'Did he say anything after I left?'

'I think he was too traumatised by Angie's singing,' chuckled Chris. 'I think we all were!'

Emily paid no attention to Chris. 'He didn't say anything specific per se, but he did ask me if you were okay.'

'*How* did he say it?'

Emily shrugged. 'I couldn't really say. He just asked.'

Laurel didn't have the chance to enquire further as Athena was beckoning her and her guests over to the front door.

'Chris and Emily run a catering company,' said Laurel. Marnie had taught her always to tell people something interesting or relevant about the person she was introducing. 'And Athena has run this beautiful villa for almost forty years.'

'Don't make me sound so ancient!' she said, inviting Laurel's guests into the house.

In the kitchen Athena showed Chris and Emily everything from her cast-iron, wood-burning stove to the refrigerator, 'almost as old as me', to the larder stuffed floor to ceiling with every ingredient imaginable.

'Have you thought about what sort of food you'd like to serve at your party?' asked Emily, the four of them standing round the large, wooden table.

'The house specialities always go down a storm,' said Athena.

'Great,' said Chris, rubbing his hands. 'What are they?'

'Moussaka, spanakopita and keftedes, with baklava for dessert.'

Chris's face fell. 'Can we add in a few dishes that we've discovered on our travels around the island?'

'Like what?' Athena asked, crumpling her brow.

'There's plenty of—' started Chris, but a quick shake of the head from Emily, who saw Athena's reluctance, told him to stop. 'There's plenty of time for me to learn your recipes,' he improvised, receiving an approving smile from his wife.

'But *I* can manage!' said Athena, irritated by the implication that she'd need Chris's help.

'But it might be nice to have someone else do the cooking for a change,' Laurel intervened, increasingly aware that Athena was territorial about the kitchen. 'There's so much to do.'

'True,' she agreed, the moment being defused by a call from out front.

'Hello,' the voice said. Laurel recognised the accent instantly and her heart-rate quickened.

'We're through here,' Laurel called, going to greet Mark at the front door. He seemed even more attractive today – more tanned, and sporting stubble rather than his usual clean-shaven look.

'How are you feeling?' he asked.

'Oh, you know,' she said, trying to play down how drunk she'd been. 'A little worse for wear but Athena's been plying me with remedies . . .'

'Good,' he said. 'I was worried about you.'

'You were?' said Laurel, far too keenly. 'I mean, that was kind of you, but I was fine. Alex brought me back.'

A momentary pause fell between them, their eyes meeting. It was Laurel who broke it. 'I'm sorry if—'

'Laurel,' Athena called, coming into the hall. 'Who is it?'

'It's Mark,' stammered Laurel, flustered by the interruption.

'Ah, Mark!' sang Athena, mischievously, linking arms with him. 'I've heard all about you.'

'And I've heard all about you,' said Mark, clearly taking an instant shine to her.

'Mark might be able to help with promoting the party,' said Laurel, ashamed that she felt a twinge of jealousy that Athena was touching Mark and bringing him out of himself in a way that she had not so far been able to do. 'He's a writer.'

'I've had many writers here,' said Athena, patting his arm. 'They always bring such mystery to the place.'

Yes, thought Laurel, watching the two of them head into the office, and this one is no exception.

Angie arrived a little after everyone else. By the time she got there Emily and Chris were engrossed in Athena's vast collection of cookbooks, and Athena and Mark were squirrelled away in the office, putting together a website and social media feeds, the pair of them intermittently pealing with laughter. Laurel was busy in the courtyard sanding down the sideboard from the hall.

'That looks like hard work,' said Angie, pushing her

sunglasses onto her head to look at what Laurel was doing.

'I don't mind.' Laurel stood back to see how she was getting on. 'I enjoy the transformation, and it'll really brighten up the hall.'

'I never met anyone who wanted to restore furniture on holiday,' laughed Angie, sitting on the small bench by the front door. 'Especially furniture that isn't their own!'

'It's fun,' said Laurel, working on a small section of varnish that she'd missed.

'Not fun as I know it!'

'Was it a late night?'

'You could say that,' she winked.

'Angie,' said Laurel. 'You didn't hook up with someone else, did you?'

'No!'

'The same guy?'

Angie giggled.

'Do we get to meet him?'

'I don't know,' she said. 'Maybe.'

'Honestly, Ang,' said Laurel, rubbing a stubborn spot more vigorously. 'Don't you ever have a hangover?'

'I've had more practice than you,' she laughed. 'I was downing beers when you were still on formula.'

Laurel laughed too. She hadn't thought about the age difference but now Angie mentioned it she realised it was the best part of twenty years.

'In fact,' said Angie. 'There's a chance that I was here having dinner when you were still in nappies.'

'That's just weird,' said Laurel, looking out over the courtyard and trying to imagine how it must have been with guests arriving and departing. 'What do you remember of the place? It might be nice to bring a flavour of how it was at the party.'

'I remember the courtyard was lit up with lanterns and strings of bunting, there were tables under large parasols, and live music. You could be inside or out, eat or just drink. It was all very mellow.'

'Sounds gorgeous,' said Laurel, hoping she could recreate such a relaxed vibe. 'But the emphasis was on the food?'

'The food was definitely the thing.'

'I love food!' sang Athena, coming out to join them, with a tray of fresh orange juice.

'The food here was sensational,' said Angie, taking a drink.

'Still is!' said Athena. Laurel introduced them.

'You've really spruced that up,' said Athena, admiring Laurel's work. 'It's always been such an ugly old thing; it was my mother-in-law's. Never much cared for it, or her, now I come to think about it.'

'With a lick of paint and some wax it should come up nicely,' said Laurel, happy that Athena was pleased. 'And I found some pretty drawer knobs in the outhouse, which I'll use. It'll feel like a completely different piece when I'm done.'

Athena nodded approvingly, sitting next to Angie on the bench. 'Have we met before?'

'I came to the villa, years ago, we chatted for a while.'

'You do look familiar.'

'You look just the same.'

'I doubt that!' laughed Athena. 'But I'll take it. Who did you visit with?'

'With Alex,' said Angie, with what Laurel detected as bashfulness. 'One of the local taxi drivers.'

'That's right,' said Athena, clapping her hands in delight. 'I remember you now. Alex was crazy about you. What happened?'

'I don't think he was crazy about me,' said Angie, obviously trying to defuse Athena's enthusiasm.

'Sure he was! For months after that all he could talk about was the woman he brought to dinner that night.'

'You see,' said Laurel, taking a well-earned glass of juice. 'Didn't I tell you he liked you – you're the one who got away!'

'Hardly,' laughed Angie, but there was a note of fondness in her voice that belied her dismissal.

'You should go out with him again,' said Laurel, 're-kindle old flames.'

'I think that spark died out a long time ago.'

'Not in his mind,' pointed out Laurel, who had begun hatching a plan to set them up on the night of the party if she hadn't made it happen before then.

'Anyway, this isn't about me, this is about Athena, and how *you* are going to make this a party to remember.'

'Yes,' cried Athena. 'Maybe we could make it themed!'

'A theme might take the focus away from what we're trying to achieve,' said Laurel.

'Which is?' asked Angie.

'To show off Athena's beautiful home and fine food. Anything else detracts from that.'

'So speaks the professional,' laughed Athena.

'I suspect she knows what she's talking about,' said Angie. 'It is what she does for a living. And she does seem pretty good at this interiors thing.'

'Well, far be it for me to meddle,' said Athena, taking the tray. 'Help yourself to whatever you need, Helena can show you where everything is but, if you'll excuse me, I need to go for a lie down. You bright young things have worn me out.'

'Of course,' said Laurel. 'Do you need anything?'

'Just a little peace and quiet,' said Athena, gingerly getting up to leave, reminding Laurel of how Marnie had moved in her later years. 'That should do it for now.'

13

The pop-up barbecue shack in the tiny cove, which Mark had discovered, was a hidden treasure. It was just far enough from the main town to be quieter than the bigger venues, and its position, nestled between two headlands, made it sheltered and warm, even in the cooling evening air. It was the perfect location after a busy day at Athena's and the debauchery of the previous evening.

'This is heaven,' said Laurel, lying on a rug on the small beach listening to the lapping waves, and breathing in the scent of charcoal that filled the air.

'I couldn't agree more,' said Emily, who was sitting comfortably on a canvas chair with her feet on a cool box.

'The boys are in their element,' said Angie. She watched them loitering round the barbecue, beers in hand, with a few other guys, chatting to the owner about different cuts of meat and the best types of wood.

'Chris hasn't been able to talk about anything else since Mark mentioned it.'

'Fire and meat, it's all they need,' laughed Angie.

'There's something quite nice about that,' said Laurel,

who was enjoying keeping an eye on Mark, looking all manly by the huge metal drum, positioned under a makeshift shelter at the edge of the beach.

'How's the hangover?' asked Emily.

'Better,' said Laurel, 'but not sufficiently so that I plan to drink tonight.'

'Not even for a little Dutch courage?'

'Dutch courage for what?' asked Angie. It was then Laurel realised Angie hadn't witnessed the exhibition she'd made of herself last night.

Laurel was spared having to explain by the arrival of Chris and Mark carrying a tray each. One was laid out with every cut of meat imaginable, the other laden with breads and salad and condiments.

'It's a man feast!' said Angie.

'You'd better believe it,' said Chris, who was beaming like the Cheshire Cat.

'Such a great find, Mark,' said Emily. 'You've made Chris happier in this last half hour than I've made him in five years.'

'I doubt that,' laughed Mark.

Chris guffawed, 'I'm not sure I would!'

'Why don't you guys do a barbecue for Athena's party?' suggested Laurel, who was determined not to allow her awkwardness to show around Mark.

'It's a good thought,' said Chris, gnawing on a rib covered in a sticky, dark sauce. 'Athena's ideas are stuck in the past.'

Laurel bristled at Chris speaking unkindly about Athena, but when Emily agreed she realised they were only speaking the truth to try and help her. 'She needs to move her cooking out of the eighties if she's going to attract new punters.'

'We've got so many great recipes that we could use,' said Chris, sauce smeared all over his mouth. 'At the walnut grove we tried this incredible olive and garlic spread with crushed walnuts, it's so simple to serve on fresh bread as an entrée.'

'Right,' said Emily, putting aside her steak and rubbing away heartburn. 'And we could easily serve it alongside one of Athena's classics, to elevate the experience.'

It made Laurel happy listening to Emily and Chris tossing ideas about, even if it was slightly at Athena's expense.

'What about that grilled lettuce dish with feta, spring onion and dill?' continued Emily. 'All those ingredients are grown on the island. People love to eat local and to know the provenance. It's a no-brainer.'

'Again, so simple, but—'

'Let me guess,' said Laurel before Chris could finish. 'Athena was having none of it?'

'She was pretty hostile towards us trying anything new,' said Chris.

'It doesn't surprise me,' said Laurel. 'She doesn't seem to like other people in her kitchen, which is understandable after running it on her own for so long. Helena would like to help and, from what I can gather, she's pretty good, but Athena won't hear of it.'

'Can you talk to her?' asked Emily. 'Try and win her round to the idea of something different?'

'I can try,' replied Laurel, wondering how and when she might broach the subject. 'But I can't promise anything.'

'She was pretty receptive to the website,' said Mark, gripping the enormous burger he'd made, stuffed full of salad and pickles and sauce. Laurel couldn't help smiling at his 'man-sized' portions.

'Probably because she knows nothing about it,' said Chris. 'She's not prepared to relinquish her grasp on what she knows.'

'You may be right but I like to think she'll come round. She's a spry old girl with more life in her than a lot of people our age.'

'You're right,' said Laurel, who loved that Mark saw the same thing in Athena that she did, her vitality, rather than her just being stuck in her ways. 'She won't let that place go without a fight, she's still got fire in her belly.'

'I wonder how much,' said Angie.

'How do you mean?'

'Only that I wasn't quite telling the truth today when I told her that she looked the same. Actually, I saw a big difference in her. She was hardly recognisable as the woman she once was. But that's not to say we shouldn't put all our effort into the best party we can make. We can make the place really magical again, I'm certain.'

'Absolutely,' said Mark. 'The website's set up, I've asked all my Twitter contacts to follow her, and there's a Facebook page set up specifically for the party. We could probably do with some fliers and posters about the island though, if we want to generate interest among the locals.'

'I can do that,' said Laurel, happy to be something more than just the coordinator.

The evening passed easily, the boys going back and forth to the barbecue, the girls relaxing quietly after such a hectic day. It was just after nine when Emily suggested she and Chris head back to their hotel.

'My heartburn is bad and I feel a bit sore,' she said. 'Sorry to be a kill-joy.'

'Not at all,' said Laurel, concerned for her friend. 'Will you be okay?'

'A good sleep should sort you out,' said Angie, reassuringly.

'Yup,' agreed Emily. 'Just too much steak and standing.'

'I'll share a cab with you,' said Angie. 'I'm double-booked for the evening.'

'You be careful,' said Laurel.

'Don't worry about me.' Angie winked. 'I'm fine!'

'Guess that just leaves us,' said Mark, when the others had gone.

'Guess so,' said Laurel, feeling even more exposed than she had at the restaurant in the orchard. At least at that point she hadn't made a fool of herself.

'Shall we take a stroll along the beach?'

'That would be lovely.'

They walked for a while, their feet crunching on the gravelly sand, the waves lapping over their flip-flops.

'It was good of you to stand up for Athena earlier,' said Laurel, watching out for pretty shells.

'It was nothing.' Mark picked up a smooth stone and skimmed it. It bounced three times. 'I like her very much. I'd have done the same for anyone.'

'All the same, it was kind.'

'You're the kind one. You're the one giving up your holiday to help her. I respect that.'

'Thanks,' said Laurel, wondering if, after last night, that was the only thing he respected about her.

'Not many people would offer to do what you're doing.'

'I just like her. She reminds me of Marnie.'

'Your grandmother?'

Laurel was impressed that Mark should remember her name. 'She was a bit outspoken and eccentric too.'

'She sounds important to you.'

Laurel stopped herself from telling Mark that she'd been a mother to her. It felt a bit much for a relaxed, summer night to be talking about your dead parents and being brought up alone by your grandmother.

'She was. Until I met Athena I'd never known anyone else like her. She was very free. Free of inhibition, free from others' opinions; she exuded love and knew no conflict. And that's not to say she hadn't known it in her life, she had, she just learnt how to rid herself of negativity and worry.' Laurel considered all the worrying she'd done over the last twenty-four hours and how Marnie would have dismissed it out of hand. 'I wish I had a fraction of her freedom.'

'Wow,' said Mark, watching Laurel. 'I've never heard anyone speak so passionately about their grandmother before.'

Laurel smiled faintly, pleased to have honoured Marnie. 'It's only been a couple of months. My emotions are still a bit raw.'

'I understand how you feel,' said Mark, placing his hand briefly on the small of her back. Her whole body shivered in unexpected delight. 'My grandfather passed away this time last year. I still can't quite get my head around him being gone.'

'Were you close?'

'Sometimes I think he was the only person in the world who truly understood me.' Mark glanced at Laurel who was listening carefully. 'We were very similar.'

'How so?'

'He was a bit introspective, like me. An observer, like me! And he was a creative thinker. It was my grandfather who introduced me to writing.'

'So not only were you similar but he was instrumental in your life.'

'He was,' said Mark, skimming another stone, which sunk straight to the bottom.

Laurel laughed. 'Did he teach you to skim stones?'

'Not at all!'

They walked a little further, Laurel trying not to focus on the couples who passed by hand in hand.

'Did he live to see you become a writer?'

'He did.'

'He must have been proud.'

'First in the queue at the local bookshop, even though I sent him several copies!'

'That's sweet,' laughed Laurel, imagining the scene. 'He sounds very dear.'

'A more gentle spirit I'll never know.'

Touched by Mark's words, Laurel felt a tear for Marnie escape her eye, and had a sudden, strong desire to live more like her. Thinking about what Marnie would have told her to do she seized the moment and turned to him.

'I'm sorry I was so insensitive last night. I didn't mean to make you uncomfortable. It's really not like me. Those drinks got the better of me and—'

Mark's eyes smiled affectionately and Laurel knew in that look that he held no ill will, that, in fact, he was sorry she should feel any discomfort about what happened.

'Don't be silly,' he said, stopping her from saying anything more. 'The truth is I was glad you wanted me to join in, I'm sorry I didn't feel able.'

He took her hand in his and for a split second Laurel thought he was going to kiss her. But then something in his gaze changed and she felt a 'but' coming on.

'But?'

'But I'm not sure I'm looking right now.'

'Oh,' said Laurel, gulping back the disappointment.

'It's nothing to do with you,' he said, quickly, reassuringly. 'It's just . . .'

'What?'

He shook his head. 'I'm not ready to talk about it, not yet.'

'I understand,' said Laurel. Although she didn't, not

really. But she knew that she couldn't push him further.

As they turned to head back along the beach Laurel felt any optimism she might have had about Mark fancying her fizzle away, and was left with the dull reality of accepting that he didn't.

14

Laurel climbed into Athena's battered old, soft-top jeep. 'Are you sure you can drive with your hand like that?'

'I've driven while breast-feeding my sons and eating breakfast,' Athena replied, incredulous at Laurel's remark. 'I'm quite certain a burnt hand isn't going to stop me.'

'Right,' said Laurel, not entirely sure if Athena was exaggerating or not.

'Off we go!'

Laurel clung tightly to the grip bar as Athena drove perilously fast down the steep woodland track, which was barely wide enough for two people to walk down let alone drive.

'There's no need to hold on,' she laughed, as the vehicle bumped through potholes deep enough for Laurel to be thrown around in her seat. 'I've never had an accident, yet!'

The sight of the road at the bottom of the path didn't come a moment too soon for Laurel and, even though it was really just a track, it felt comparatively smooth and secure.

'Where do you want to start?' Laurel asked, steadying herself.

Athena turned onto the tarmac road at the end of the track. 'Down at the waterfront in town.'

At the harbour Laurel jumped out of the jeep with a handful of posters and fliers, which Mark had designed. With Athena waiting in the car, she ran along the front sticking a poster to every other lamp post and handing out fliers to whomever she passed.

'Come to Villa Athena on Tuesday evening,' she said, repeatedly, feeling a buzz of excitement at being the party girl talking to strangers and spreading good cheer. A thrill raced through her body when she recognised the difference between 'London Laurel' and 'Skopelos Laurel'. London Laurel would never be so uninhibited; London Laurel didn't look anyone in the eye on the Tube, let alone hand out fliers and talk to strangers. She felt more like the version of Laurel that Marnie would want her to be, and that made Laurel very happy indeed. 'We're having a party; it's going to be great!'

With the harbour complete she ran back to Athena.

'Done,' she said, jumping back into the jeep. 'Where next?'

Athena put her foot down and sped up the winding roads, as fast as the traffic would allow her, and out of town.

'What's that?' asked Laurel when she spotted an ancient building up on the hillside surrounded by dense trees.

'A monastery,' said Athena, taking her eyes off the road for an uncomfortably long time. 'I think it was built in the eighteenth century. There's quite a few on the island, maybe ten or twenty.'

'And so many churches,' said Laurel, catching sight of a steeple among the trees. They seemed to be everywhere.

'People say there are enough churches or chapels on the island for there to be one for every ten people. And they say, if a south wind blows the church bells can be heard on the mainland.'

'How romantic,' sighed Laurel, as they wound their way through the mountains.

'Romantic, yes, but odd that someone like me should live on such a religious island.'

'You seem very spiritual to me.'

'Spiritual isn't the same as religious,' said Athena, tearing round a blind corner in the middle of the road. It occurred to Laurel that perhaps the islanders needed to pray so much because of Athena's driving.

'But you believe in something beyond life on earth?'

'At my age you have no choice but to believe!' said Athena, rounding a bend to reveal a stunning sea view, with a tiny little village clinging to the cliffs, a curved bay and views towards a neighbouring island.

'What is this place?' gasped Laurel.

Athena took a left turn onto another dirt track. 'Stafylos,' she said. 'I need to drop in on Helena.'

A little way down the track they pulled up outside a small dwelling perched on the edge of the village. There were brown-and-white horned goats bleating contentedly, and scruffy-looking hens pecking and scratching in the dust. Athena sounded her horn.

'Helena!' she yelled.

'I can go and find her,' said Laurel, feeling uncomfortable about Athena demanding Helena's attention with the horn.

'No, let her come!' she said, sounding the horn again.

'Athena!' shouted Laurel. 'Let me go.'

'Fine, fine,' she said, digging around for an envelope in her bag. 'Give her her wages.'

The goats and hens scattered as Laurel walked to the front door of the little house.

'Hello,' she called, knocking on the door.

'One moment,' came the reply.

When Helena opened the door Laurel found her in her apron, which was smeared with tomato sauce.

'Hi,' said Laurel, hoping it wasn't a bad time.

'Miss Laurel,' she said, tucking her hair behind her ears, resulting in streaks of tomato sauce running through it. 'Why are you here?'

Laurel handed her the envelope. 'Athena wanted me to give you this.'

'Thank you,' she said, taking the packet. As she did, a door on the far side of the kitchen opened and a small child, around four years old, came and hid behind her.

'Hi,' said Laurel, smiling.

The boy retreated further behind Helena, who stroked the child's hair.

'He's shy, like me.'

'He's yours?' asked Laurel, surprised. Athena never said anything about Helena having a child.

'Yes. His name is Yanni.'

'Hi, Yanni.' The boy peered out. 'He's very handsome.'

'Thank you,' smiled Helena. 'Will you come in?'

'No, no,' said Laurel, not wanting to inconvenience her at home. 'Athena is waiting.'

'Just for one minute?' she asked, her eyes suggesting it was something she really wanted. 'Will you try something for me?'

Laurel entered Helena's home into a general purpose room with a tiled floor and a large range, which Yanni's clothes hung on. A thin dog with big ears lay in the corner, unperturbed by Laurel's arrival. There were toys scattered about the floor and laundry hanging everywhere but the thing that struck Laurel most was the smell – the tiny house was filled with the aromas of cooking, the stove was crammed full of pans and the large table was heaving with ingredients.

'I made a new recipe,' she said, untangling Yanni from her leg and bringing a pan of sauce over for Laurel to try. 'How does it taste?'

Laurel sampled the tomato sauce, which was rich in herby flavours. 'Heavenly!'

'Really?' Helena's face lit up.

'Really!' said Laurel, smiling back at her, wondering how she could possibly get Athena to agree to let Helena help with the party food.

'Thank you,' she said, ruffling Yanni's hair. 'Thank you very much!'

Laurel, fully aware that Athena would be growing impatient, said her goodbyes and left Helena and Yanni.

'What took you so long?' Athena asked, back at the jeep. She took off immediately, throwing up dust in her wake.

'She was in the middle of something.'

'Daydreaming, no doubt.'

'Actually, cooking,' said Laurel, determined to take the bull by the horns. 'It's her passion and, for what it's worth, she's good at it!'

Athena turned and stared at Laurel.

Laurel folded her arms defensively. 'You don't have the monopoly on good cooking on this island.'

'I never said I did.'

'So then why won't you let Chris and Emily introduce some new recipes for the party?'

'Because people want what they know!'

'No, Athena,' said Laurel, aware that she was being confrontational and uncertain if Athena would be receptive to it. '*You* want what you know. *Other* people like change.'

Athena drove silently for a while, and a little faster.

'I'm not saying this to offend you,' said Laurel, after it became obvious that Athena was sulking. 'I'm saying it to help.'

'What do you know about running a restaurant?' she snapped.

Laurel sensed that she was wounded rather than angry.

'I don't know anything about running a restaurant, that's what you're good at,' said Laurel, more softly. 'But I do know what I like to eat, and I know Chris and Emily know what other people like to eat. I'm simply suggesting that it might be worth being open to new ideas.'

Athena shrugged, staring at the road straight ahead. 'It's my business.'

'I know, but you've said yourself, things change. If you don't move with the times you might find things don't change for the better.'

Laurel watched Athena twist her lips, thinking.

'You could let them try a recipe or two for you to taste,' tip-toed Laurel, sensing Athena might be on the brink of submission.

'Oh fine!' said Athena, throwing a hand up in the air. 'I can see you won't give me a moment's peace until I do.'

Laurel grinned. 'Oh thank you, Athena, I promise you, you won't regret it!'

'Humph,' said Athena, who couldn't hide the glint in her eye. 'While we're on the subject of meddling in other people's lives,' she said, as they whizzed past another track end. 'There's a beach down there you should visit. It's one of my favourites. Maybe you could take Mark.'

'Maybe,' said Laurel, hesitantly.

Athena glanced over. 'Did you sort things out with him?'

'In as much as I know where I stand.'

'So no romance, yet?'

'After last night I don't think there will *ever* be a romance.'

'I doubt that!'

'I'm serious. I don't think he's into me in that way.'

'Well, if I were you I'd persevere,' said Athena. 'And I reckon some time on that beach might help you find your answer.'

'How do you mean?'

Athena didn't respond to Laurel's question. Instead she said, 'You know he's quite successful. It was good of him to give up his time to help at the villa.'

'He likes you; he was happy to help.'

'Even so, it's not often you receive help from a prize-winning author.'

'Prize-winning?' asked Laurel.

Athena turned to Laurel. 'Mark is Mark Embry.'

'Oh,' said Laurel, who didn't like to admit that she didn't know who Mark Embry was.

'My boys used to love coming here when they were little,' said Athena as they wandered through a small food market. 'We'd come on a Saturday morning and they were each allowed to choose one thing each. Christos always chose cake, Stelios nuts, and George chocolate.'

'It must have been a tough choice,' said Laurel, admiring the beautiful displays of gourds and tomatoes sitting in colourful crates at the first stall.

'It used to take us most of the morning.' Athena smiled at the memory.

At the next stall, Laurel breathed in the scent of fresh peaches and apricots, her mouth watering.

'Athena?' cried the owner, opening her arms wide. 'How long's it been?'

'Odele!' Athena cried in delight. 'Look at you!'

The woman, in her sixties, held out the corners of her apron and did a silly curtsey. 'Don't we both look grand!'

'We certainly do!' laughed Athena, who introduced Laurel.

'How are you enjoying the island?' Odele asked, her eyes dark and gentle.

'Very well – what's not to enjoy?'

'That's what I say!' said Odele, handing Laurel a peach. 'And Athena, how are the boys?'

'They're fine, Odele – but still too far away.'

Odele nodded knowingly. 'My two don't look like they're coming back either.'

'Ah, Odele. So sorry.'

'What can you do?' she said. 'There's not enough work. They have no choice.'

The two women chatted a while longer, catching up on the island gossip.

'Come to the party on Tuesday,' said Laurel as they left Odele, handing her a flier.

'Yes, come!' said Athena. 'It'll be like old times.'

'Then I'll be there,' she sang. 'I wouldn't miss a Villa Athena party for the world!'

Laurel and Athena meandered some more, admiring the beautiful olives in purples, greens and black, and the cheese-rounds piled high.

'Where are your children now?' Laurel asked, picking up on what Athena had said about being too far away.

'In America.'

Laurel brushed her fingers over the feathery leaves of a large bunch of dill. 'What took them there?'

'My parents moved back to my father's home town when the boys were young. Christos, my eldest, went to college there, as did my youngest, George. Stelios studied in Athens but moved there for work.'

'And you were never tempted to move there yourself, to be near them and your parents?'

'I thought about it about twenty years ago when my parents were sick and George had just graduated but . . .' Athena paused, thinking for a while. 'Well, they were spread out all over the country and I had the business. It wasn't so simple.'

'Do they visit?' asked Laurel at the bread stall. She admired the different shapes – plaits with almonds, flat breads, and rings with sesame seeds – and the beautiful, colourful lanterns that adorned the front of the stall.

'They have free holidays to a Greek island, of course they visit!'

'Mama Athena!' someone called out. Laurel turned around. Athena had been greeted by the attendant at the bread stall.

It seemed to take Athena a moment to recognise the man who was greeting her but when she did she exclaimed joyously. 'Theo!'

The man, slight of build and around Laurel's age, hugged Athena warmly.

'You look good, no? Where you been?'

'Keeping busy,' said Athena.

'And who's your friend?' he asked, noticing Laurel, his eyes smiling.

'This is Laurel, she's staying at the villa.'

'Laurel,' he said, cheerfully. 'Good to meet you!'

'And you,' she said, liking Theo instantly.

'How's Nikos?' he enquired.

'He's fine, Theo,' said Athena. 'Here, there and everywhere.'

'Still doing his vlogging?'

'I believe so.'

'You tell him to come see me next time he's here. I miss that guy!'

'I'll do that, Theo,' sang Athena as he kissed her goodbye.

They walked back towards the jeep. 'Everybody knows you!' said Laurel, remembering Alex had told her exactly that on the evening she arrived on the island.

'Theo is a friend of Nikos, one of my grandsons.' Laurel recalled Athena mentioning him in the garden.

'What does he vlog about?'

'Food and travel. I don't understand how he makes a living out of it but one way or another he does. And from time to time he stops by to help out in the kitchen when it's busy, just for a few weeks – long enough to get his laundry done!'

'Sounds mutually convenient,' laughed Laurel, arriving back at the jeep. 'I can't believe how friendly everyone is here,' she said, thinking how stark a contrast it was to London. 'It's like one huge family.'

'You're right,' said Athena, setting off again. 'And

what of your family? I hear you mention work, and maybe buying a flat in London, but you rarely talk about family.'

Laurel thought of the little family she had. 'I have an uncle and aunt and some cousins, who I never see, but other than that I'm on my own, I have no siblings.'

'You seem too young for that.'

'Hmm,' said Laurel, wishing it were true. 'My grandmother, Marnie, passed away recently, she was the last of my immediate family.'

'What about your parents?'

'They died when I was little, which leaves me rather rootless and without much sense of belonging.'

'Hence the holiday?'

'I thought it would do me good to get away for a bit, try and get a sense of perspective.'

'And have you?'

As she asked they came round a corner and saw a beautiful village in white, orange and blue, clinging to the green hillside, which sloped down to the water's edge. 'Oh Athena! What is this place?'

'Glossa.' Athena pulled over for Laurel to admire the view, who sat awestruck by its beauty.

'We have to get out and take a picture!'

Together they set up a photo of Laurel with the village in the background.

'Smile!' called Athena, holding up Laurel's phone.

Laurel beamed.

'It's a good one of you,' said Athena, showing Laurel the picture. 'Definitely one for the office wall.'

At first Laurel didn't understand what Athena meant, she didn't recognise the girl in the photo, who looked so at ease and full of joy, she didn't look like London Laurel at all. Instead, captured for a moment in time, was Skopelos Laurel.

'It's perfect,' said Laurel, now knowing the answer to Athena's question – she had found perspective, suddenly everything was becoming clear. 'I only wish I could stay for ever!'

15

The island was peppered with posters by the time Laurel and Athena returned to the villa just before supper. They took a seat in the sitting room, the early evening sun filling the room with a soft light.

'I doubt we missed a single noticeboard or village shop,' said Athena, rubbing her forehead.

'I believe you,' said Laurel. She placed a traditional, woven blanket over Athena's legs.

'All we can do now is wait.'

'And plan some more,' said Laurel. 'I'm certain a lot of people will come.'

'Let's hope so,' said Athena, sounding tired. 'I'd hate for you to go to all this work for nothing.'

Laurel thought of Marnie and how she had always said the same thing: 'I hate you going to all this trouble to look after me when you should be out having fun with your friends.' Little did she realise that Laurel loved to look after her – that given the choice, she'd choose Marnie over a night out with friends any day of the week.

'Let me get you something to eat,' said Laurel.

'I should do that,' said Athena, but she was too tired to attempt to move.

In the kitchen, Laurel found a loaf of olive bread and goat's curd, a tomato and red onion salad, and some traditional meatballs, which she heated in the microwave, even though she suspected Athena wouldn't approve.

'Here we are,' she said, returning with a tray for Athena's lap.

'Where did you find all this?'

'It was all prepared in the fridge,' said Laurel, surprised that Athena should ask.

Athena shook her head, dismissing her comment. 'Of course it was.'

'Wow!' said Laurel, as she dug into her meatballs. 'These are sensational.'

'Are they?' said Athena, sounding less than interested and edging on tetchy.

'Don't you think? And this bread is so rich in flavour. It's heaven.'

'I can't say I'm that hungry,' said Athena, putting down her knife and fork and leaning back in her chair.

Having looked after Marnie in her old age, Laurel recognised that Athena needed her bed. She took her tray and held out her hand.

'Come on, let's get you to bed, before you turn cranky!'

'All right then,' said Athena, taking Laurel's hand to be helped up.

'Can I help you with anything?' Laurel asked at the door to Athena's private quarters.

'I'll be fine,' she said. 'Thank you for today – it was quite the treat to be out and about.'

'You're welcome,' said Laurel, picking up that it sounded as if Athena didn't get out the way she used to, as Alex had alluded to. 'Sleep well.'

In her room Laurel caught up with messages from the day. Emily had sent one to say that she and Chris were going to have a quiet night, the events of the last few days having caught up with her, and Angie texted to say she was out on the town. Laurel had been hopeful there might have been something from Mark but, when there wasn't, she decided on a relaxing evening in her room in front of *Mamma Mia!*.

Raking around in the bedside drawer for the DVD she discovered the letter she'd put aside on her first morning at the villa. She removed the contents from the envelope and was astonished to discover that it wasn't just a letter from the lawyers about fees but that there was also a personal document enclosed – a letter from Marnie. With trembling hands Laurel sat in the armchair and read the words aloud.

My Dearest Laurel,
I know when you receive the inheritance that you'll want to invest it carefully, probably in a place of your own. If I may be allowed one last request, I ask that you remember that a home is more than bricks and mortar, it is built on hopes and dreams and, most important of all, the love of those who fill it.
If your mother and father had been alive they'd have told you the same – their dream was to live on the Greek

143

island where they fell in love. They often spoke of their days there in a villa way off the beaten track, perched high on a cliff.

Follow your dreams, Laurel, and you will find where you belong.

Your loving grandmother,
Marnie x

P.S. Never forget the words of Christina Rossetti – 'Better by far you should forget and smile than that you should remember and be sad'.

As Laurel read the letter tears blurred her eyes; when she blinked they plopped onto the paper, smudging some of the words.

'Oh God,' she said, mopping the rest of her tears with a tissue, not wanting to destroy the last words she would ever receive from Marnie.

She read the letter several times, delighting most in learning that her parents had fallen in love in Greece – she'd only ever known it was on holiday – in a place that sounded similar to the one that Laurel was staying in now. Reading that made her feel closer to them, as well as to Marnie.

Laurel was about to read it again when her phone rang.

'Janey!' she said, wiping her nose and shifting about to get comfy on the bed, preparing herself for a marathon catch up. 'How are you?'

'I'm hunky-dory!' said Janey. It felt good to hear her best friend's voice, the most familiar voice she knew, now that she hadn't Marnie to talk to. 'How are you? How's it going out there? Surviving without your anti-frizz?'

'It's great,' said Laurel, tucking the letter back into the drawer so that she could focus fully on Janey. 'I'm having the best time. I don't know how I'll ever return to smelly old London after this!'

'The photos do look amazing. Especially the house.'

'Janey, it's beautiful, you'd love it. And the woman who runs it reminds me so much of Marnie. She's strong and spirited and not afraid to say what she thinks.'

'Marnie certainly never had that problem,' laughed Janey, who'd been in the firing line of Marnie's tongue more than once in her life. 'Do you remember the time she dressed me down for putting Chris Skelton ahead of preparing for a GCSE?'

'She was furious.' Laurel smiled fondly at the memory of how embarrassed she'd been that her grandmother should reprimand her best friend. 'I guess if you're passionate about women's rights, it must sting to see some gobby teenager prioritise a spotty oik over their own future.'

'I didn't get it at the time but I'm glad she spoke up. Mum wouldn't have fought so hard.'

'No,' said Laurel. Janey's mum had had three younger kids to look after. 'I think you're right.'

'And are you coping okay on your own? You're not feeling too blue?'

'I have my moments of missing Marnie, I do, and

wish more than anything that she was here with me, but I've made some new friends and they're keeping my spirits up.'

'No one I should be jealous of?'

'No!' laughed Laurel, who loved that Janey was a little possessive of her. They'd been friends since they were four years old.

Laurel could remember very clearly the first day of nursery when they'd met at the coat pegs, Laurel's with a rainbow sticker, Janey's with an ice cream. They'd sat beside each other, while their mother and grandmother changed their shoes, and Janey had asked, 'Will you be my friend?' They'd been joined at the hip ever since, like sisters.

'There's Angie, a midwife in her forties, who's big and jolly and kind, but hell-bent on sleeping her way through the island. And Emily and Chris, who're expecting a baby in two months' time.'

'Anyone else?' asked Janey, who knew Laurel so well she could tell when she was withholding any scrap of information, even when they were a thousand miles apart.

'Just some guy called Mark.'

'Just some guy?'

'Hmm – just some guy I might have a little crush on.' Laurel enjoyed telling Janey about Mark, even if she did think it was a dead-end scenario.

'Oh really?' sang Janey, who'd always had more interest from men than Laurel, but who was always thrilled when one guy or another had his eye on her friend. 'Do tell.'

'There's not much to tell. He's Irish, a writer, kind of shy but kind, sensitive . . .'

'And let me guess,' said Janey, knowing Laurel's type. 'He has a slightly mysterious air?'

Laurel laughed at her own predictability.

'He's a guy travelling to a Greek island alone; he hinted at his plans having changed last minute, and then he told me he wasn't ready to talk about something – so, yes, I guess he is a bit mysterious.'

'You think he has a girlfriend?'

'If he does he's done a pretty good job of hiding that fact.'

'A writer with a story of his own,' Janey mocked gently. 'What's his name?'

'Well that's the other thing,' said Laurel, caught up in the fun of it all despite her doubts. 'Athena mentioned he's successful but I've never heard of him. His name is Mark Embry.'

'Wait,' said Janey. Laurel heard her type something into her computer. 'Mark Embry,' she said, reading what had come up on the Internet. 'Prize-winning Irish author, blah blah blah, known for literary fiction.'

'Huh,' said Laurel. 'And you're sure it's him?'

'Yup, if your Mark Embry is thirty-four, born in Dublin, and looks a little like Jake Gyllenhaal.'

'That sounds like Mark,' said Laurel.

'So, now you've found your intellectual dreamboat, how are you going to bag him?'

'Good question,' said Laurel, leaning further back on

her pillows. 'The trouble is I'm really not certain that he's into me.'

'As if!' said Janey, loyal to a fault. 'Tell me what you've done together so far?'

Laurel told Janey about their time at the chapel, their stroll to the harbour, falling overboard, the disaster of karaoke, and their evening walk on the beach.

'Sounds to me like he's into you! It's time you arranged a proper date, just the two of you, find out for sure what's going on in his head.'

'But how, and where?'

'Laurel!' said Janey, despairing at her best friend. 'You're on a beautiful Greek island, I'm certain you can think of something to do on a first date.'

Laurel thought of the beach Athena had suggested and of how she might mention it to Mark.

'You're right,' she said, her mind made up. 'I can.'

'And you will?'

'Yes,' she said, feeling a nervous flutter in her tummy. 'Is everything okay with you?'

'Tickety-boo! Nothing to report.'

'And Tom's okay?'

'He's in his element. Adrian is feeding him too much and fussing him to within an inch of his life, he may not want to come home.'

'Thank you,' smiled Laurel, who'd forgotten how much Janey's fiancé loved cats.

'You're welcome, now go, have fun, send a message to Mark. Let the rest of us get back to the daily drudge of London.'

Having said their goodbyes, Laurel set about the task of writing a message to Mark. She sat for over fifteen minutes writing and rewriting, unable to find the correct words. She was about to give up when a message pinged up on her phone. Her heart skipped a beat when she saw it was from Mark.

Fancy doing something on Saturday morning? Can't do anything until then – deadline, I'm afraid. Mark x

Laurel fixated on the kiss he'd used at the end, her doubts replaced by hope.

Sure. Athena mentioned a beach she loves. Fancy going there? L x

Sounds great. Arrange a time tomorrow? M x

Absolutely. L x

Pleased with the turn of events she sent a message to Janey:

Date planned for Saturday morning! L x

Satisfied, she lay her head down, hoping for sweet dreams of Mark.

16

'I can't believe you got her to agree,' said Emily, the next day in the kitchen. The two of them were sitting with Angie at the large table listening to Chris and Athena discussing the menu for the party.

'She probably realised I wasn't going to take no for an answer.'

Laurel watched Athena as she listened attentively to Chris's suggestions. She reminded her of Marnie – on the odd occasion that she relented to someone else's point of view – in how much joy she found in new things. For all Marnie's stubbornness she wasn't ungenerous, and nor was Athena.

'So,' said Chris, when they'd agreed what they were doing. 'Why don't you show Emily and me how to make your spanakopita, so I don't mess it up on the night?'

'I'll watch from here,' said Emily, rubbing an ache in her side.

'It's simple,' said Athena, reaching for an apron, and taking down a frying pan, which hung above the table. 'Get a chopping board and chop these spring onions, spinach, brown onion and dill.'

Chris did as he was told. 'Now what?'

'Fry off the onions in olive oil until they're soft.'

'Isn't it nice to have an underling?' said Laurel to Athena, with a wry smile. Athena waved her wooden spoon at Laurel in faux-malice.

Once the brown onion was translucent and the spring onions a brighter green Athena instructed Chris to add the spinach, bit by bit, until it was wilted but still vibrant in colour.

'Looking good!' said Athena, seasoning the mix as Chris stirred.

'Do we need to drain it?'

'Absolutely – nobody wants soggy pastry,' said Athena, pleased that Chris got the gist of the recipe. 'Grab that colander, won't you?'

Chris reached to the rack above the table and took down a large colander through which he strained the spinach and onion mix while Athena whisked eggs and spooned in feta.

'Then we need that big dish,' she said, pointing to a large stainless steel tray on the shelves behind where the girls were sitting. Laurel fetched it.

Together Chris and Athena layered and oiled the sheets of filo before combining the spinach mix with the egg.

'Look how fresh and full of goodness that is,' said Athena as she poured it onto the pastry before adding further layers of filo.

'It does look sensational,' said Chris.

'And now, before we put it in the oven, cut it into

portion sizes so that it's easy to serve when cooked.'

'Good tip!' said Emily. 'Filo is always so hard to serve without it crumbling everywhere.'

'I know a thing or two,' smiled Athena, allowing Chris to carry the heavy dish to the oven and slide it in, just as Helena and Yanni arrived.

Helena looked a little shy in the presence of Laurel's friends.

'I'm sorry, Athena,' said Helena. 'My mother can't watch Yanni this morning.'

Athena sighed.

'That's okay,' said Emily, brightly. 'There are plenty of us here. I can play with Yanni outside while you get a bit of work done.'

'I'm not sure he'd—' But before Helena could finish Emily had held out her hand and Yanni had taken it.

'It must be the maternal instinct,' laughed Laurel, reading Helena's surprise at Yanni being happy to play with a stranger.

In the courtyard, Emily set up some football goals made out of two stools, and an obstacle course of flower pots for Yanni to ride around on a bike.

'How are you going to transform this area for the party?' Angie asked, Yanni kicking a ball between her legs, which she failed to get a foot on.

'I thought I'd go for a cosy rustic vibe,' said Laurel, showing Angie the eclectic selection of tables and chairs that's she'd organised in the outhouse. 'It won't take much to give these chairs a lick of paint, a few different cheerful colours, and Athena's got a gorgeous collection of cushions that we could scatter on them.'

Angie stroked the spindles of the old chairs. 'Sounds nice. Have you thought how to dress the tables?'

'Simple seems best. White tablecloths, which Athena has already, and some coloured glassware, pretty crockery, and candles. I like the idea of there being lots of different lights about the place. More strings of lights criss-crossing the courtyard, some fairy lights round the windows and lanterns by the walls.'

'That does sound pretty,' said Angie, dodging a wayward football pass by Emily. 'I remember lots of cosy lighting when . . .' Angie didn't complete her thought.

'When you came with Alex,' Laurel ribbed, gently.

'Yee-ss,' said Angie, quietly enjoying Laurel's teasing.

'He must have been pretty into you to bring you somewhere so special.'

'I didn't think much of it at the time. I probably thought he was trying to impress me so that I would sleep with him but . . .' She paused to reflect. 'Perhaps I didn't give him enough credit.'

'And you still won't consider a date with him?'

Angie rolled her eyes. 'I can see now why Athena caved in!'

'Ha ha,' said Laurel, sensing that Angie wasn't quite as opposed to the idea of a date with Alex as she had been. 'So . . .'

'So I'm not making any promises!' said Angie, which

Laurel took as a step in the right direction. 'What are you doing about the planting?'

Laurel watched Emily help Yanni onto his bike steering him round the pots. 'There are so many planters scattered around the grounds that I thought we could gather them together to really bring in a feel of an Aegean courtyard garden. And I know Athena's got some old blackboards, which we can lean up against the pots with the menus written on them.'

'That's a nice touch – you've really got an eye for all of this.'

'Thanks,' said Laurel, gratified by Angie's comment. 'I like making things homely and welcoming; I wish I could do more of it.'

'You could make a living out of it.'

'Perhaps you're right,' said Laurel to herself, Angie having unintentionally planted a seed in Laurel's mind.

'Oh, this is good,' said Laurel, the crisp sheets of pastry of the spanakopita giving way to soft veggies and crumbling cheese.

'Bliss,' said Emily, as Athena watched them all delighting in her recipe but not tasting it herself.

'Didn't I tell you,' she said. 'Everyone loves the classics.'

'I can't deny it's fantastic,' said Chris. 'But can I show you something that we've discovered – an olive and garlic spread with crushed walnuts?'

As Chris showed Athena how to make the spread in

the food processor, Helena arrived back in the kitchen having finished cleaning the floors.

'Hi,' said Laurel.

'Hello,' she replied, quietly, Yanni running to hug her leg. She set about the washing up, helped by Yanni, while keeping an eye on Chris who was sprinkling sage and cayenne pepper into the spread.

'You're welcome to join us,' said Laurel, assuming Helena might like to.

'Helena has work to be getting on with,' said Athena, in a manner that left no room for discussion.

Infuriated by Athena's attitude towards Helena, Laurel took herself off to the dining room.

'You okay?' Angie asked, joining her.

'Fine,' said Laurel, repositioning a table. 'I'm just exasperated with Athena's lack of respect for Helena.'

'Maybe there's a side to their story you don't know about.'

'Maybe,' said Laurel, slightly ashamed not to have thought of that herself. 'Whatever it is, she's obviously not going to let her help in the kitchen for the party.'

'We could include her in something else,' suggested Angie, helping Laurel with a large table.

'That's true.'

'Maybe she could help us paint the chairs?'

'I like that idea,' said Laurel, who saw it as an opportunity for a proper chat with Helena.

'Are you planning on making this room feel much the same as the courtyard?'

'I think so, painted chairs, cushions, throws, candles

and soft lighting, and we'll take down the curtains, just have the shutters. The plants in here already bring a garden feel and we can open up the doors to bring even more of the outside in. We could set up a little outside dining on the patio.'

'Or maybe do pre-dinner drinks out there?'

'Excellent idea!' said Laurel. 'We haven't thought much about that. Could I ask you to be in charge of which drinks might complement the menu?'

'Sure,' said Angie. 'If anyone knows their drinks, it's me!'

'God, I'd like a drink,' said Emily, from the sitting room.

'Are you suffering, pet?' Angie said.

'I'm okay.' Emily sounded weary. 'Just needing some feet up time.'

Laurel and Angie joined her on the sofas.

'Where's Mark today?' asked Emily.

'Working,' said Laurel. 'He's got a deadline.'

'Shame. How did things go when we left you on the beach?'

'It was nice, he opened up a bit more. I thought there was almost a moment between us but then . . .'

'What?' said Emily, keen to know the gossip.

'Then he told me there was something he couldn't talk about and . . .'

'And?'

'And nothing,' said Laurel. 'That was it. We walked back along the beach, got a cab back to town and said goodnight.'

'How mysterious,' said Emily.

'I know. I told Janey about it and she said I had to set up a proper date.'

'Will you?'

'I already did!'

Emily let out a shriek, which Laurel thought was a squeal of delight but it rapidly became obvious that it wasn't.

'Emily, pet?' said Angie, her voice suddenly professional in tone. 'What's the matter?'

'I'm sure it's nothing . . .' said Emily, concern etched on her brow.

'But?' said Angie.

'I just had a bad twinge.'

She let out a frightened cry – so loud it startled Laurel – as another pain ripped through her. 'Angie!' she said, her voice full of fear. 'What do I do?'

'Come on,' said Angie, helping her up and leading her to the stairs. 'Let's get you to a bed.'

'I'll get Chris,' said Laurel, who'd seen him nip outside earlier with scissors, maybe to cut herbs.

'No!' she said abruptly, bending over to fend off another pain, which took her breath away. 'I don't want him to worry.'

Upstairs, Emily lay on Laurel's bed, the pains still coming but growing less frequent.

'Don't worry, pet,' said Angie, warming her hands. 'I'll give you a quick exam and then we can take things from there. Everything will be fine.'

It occurred to Laurel, thinking about what Athena

had said, that there wasn't a hospital on the island, only a medical centre. If Emily was in labour it might be up to Angie, and Angie alone, to deliver the baby safely. She had a sudden realisation of just how cut off they were on the island, if anyone were to become seriously unwell it would be a long journey to the mainland.

Angie rolled back Emily's top to reveal her bump and began the process of assessing where the baby was lying.

'Do you want me to get Chris now?' Laurel asked, wanting to do something other than nothing.

Emily shook her head. 'He worries at the best of times, he doesn't need to see this.'

'And I don't think there is anything to worry about,' said Angie, continuing her careful examination. 'Baby's lying with feet up but the head isn't engaged. You're not in labour.'

Emily breathed a little easier, so did Laurel. 'What else would cause such a pain?'

'It's probably Braxton Hicks,' said Angie, taking Emily's pulse.

'What causes them?'

'It depends,' said Angie. 'Some people think they come on naturally around this time to soften the cervix, others think it's because of too much activity.'

'You have been doing a lot,' said Laurel, feeling bad that she'd involved Emily in the party when she should have been relaxing.

'Not any more than I'd usually do.'

'Are you usually seven months pregnant?' asked Angie.

Emily laughed and conceded, 'No.'

'So,' said Angie, replacing Emily's top. 'Perhaps time to rest up a bit.'

'If you say so,' said Emily. It was clear to Laurel that she was unimpressed by the idea. 'I guess that's pregnancy for you – some things you just can't control.'

'How about I go fetch you a bit of that orange and almond cake I saw Helena making earlier, when Athena wasn't looking?' asked Laurel.

'Sounds good.' Emily smiled gratefully at her friend. 'And you can send Chris up now.'

In the kitchen Laurel told Chris to go up and see Emily then relayed Emily's news to Athena and Helena, who was mopping the floor.

'She can't be involved in the catering for the party any longer. I don't know how Chris will manage on his own.'

'I can cook with Chris instead,' said Athena. 'We got on well today. I'm sure between us we can cook up a storm.'

'It's really tiring work,' said Laurel, concerned Athena was even less up to the task than Emily.

'I've been cooking for forty years, I'm certain I can manage another day!'

Laurel caught Helena shaking her head doubtfully, and a thought came to her.

'What about Helena?'

A small smile appeared on Helena's face.

'Helena's in charge of washing up.'

The smile faded.

'I'm certain we could employ someone else for the evening to do that,' said Laurel.

'And I'm certain I've made enough concessions around here for one week,' said Athena, taking off her apron and leaving, slamming the door behind her.

17

2016

Laurel and Marnie sat in the bland cubicle of the A & E department waiting for the doctor.

'You gave me such a fright,' said Laurel, whose hands were still shaking. She'd found her grandmother on the bathroom floor less than an hour earlier when she was getting ready to go out for the evening.

'I gave *myself* a fright.'

'I thought I'd lost you.'

Laurel could hardly believe the recovery Marnie had made. When she found her in the bathroom her face was droopy on one side and her speech was slurred, now she was sitting up quite normally drinking a cup of tea.

'I bet it's nothing,' she laughed, but Laurel could tell she wasn't convinced.

'How can it be nothing? Has anything like this happened before?'

Marnie shrugged and changed the subject to Laurel's news. 'You've worked so hard to get another promotion. I'm very proud of you. What's your job title now?'

'Events manager.'

'Janey must never see you.'

'Janey's pretty busy too, plus she has Adrian. You

know they're thinking of living together.'

'Adrian's going to move in with you and Janey?'

Laurel laughed. 'No, Marnie, not with me and Janey. Just the two of them, on their own.'

'But where will *you* live?'

'I've been thinking about a studio or one-bed flat.' Laurel didn't mention that she'd also been toying with the idea of moving back home with Marnie, but her latest promotion was too good to turn down and nothing remotely similar had come up locally.

As they waited a message pinged through on Laurel's phone. It was from Rob, the guy she was meant to be having dinner with – in the chaos of getting Marnie to hospital she'd forgotten to let him know.

Have been waiting for forty minutes – guess you're not coming. I'm out of here.

'Who's the message from?'

'Oh, nobody,' said Laurel, wearily thinking 'another one bites the dust'. It was a shame; this one seemed to have potential.

The curtain of the cubicle was drawn back by a doctor in blue scrubs and white jacket. Laurel figured he was in his thirties and, if his slightly soft middle was anything to go by, he enjoyed a beer and a nice meal.

'Mrs Ferguson, I'm Dr Mather. I've come to have a chat about what happened today.'

'I'm sure I'm wasting your time.'

'You let me be the judge of that. Tell me, has anything like this happened before?'

Marnie was quiet, her eyes cast down to the bedclothes.

'Marnie?' Laurel asked.

'It's happened a couple of times when I've been on my own. But the symptoms resolved quickly and I thought nothing more about them.'

Laurel was incredulous, how could she possibly have missed something so serious?

'Do you smoke?'

'Only occasionally, for fun.' Marnie's eyes twinkled, the doctor didn't respond.

'High blood pressure?'

'Yes.'

'You're not overweight. High cholesterol?'

'A little.'

'Do you drink?'

'A whisky a day.'

'Irregular heartbeat?'

'Sometimes.'

'Diabetes?'

'Pre.'

Laurel sat listening to the long list of Marnie's ailments and thought about all the signs she'd missed. It seemed obvious now, sitting there with the doctor in front of her, that Marnie hadn't been coping in the way that she used to – she realised the house and studio hadn't been tidied to Marnie's usual standard for months.

Having gathered the information the doctor said, 'It sounds as if you've had a series of transient ischaemic attacks.'

'Wh-what does that mean?' stammered Laurel,

terrified it might mean Marnie could die, that she could be left with no family at all.

'It means your grandmother has had several mini-strokes.'

Laurel gave a shake of her head, blinded by shock. 'I don't understand.'

The doctor perched on the bed, his clipboard on his knee. 'It means she's had a temporary disruption in blood supply to her brain.'

Laurel felt as if someone had just struck her hard in the stomach, her worst fear about to be realised.

'But that's *really* bad.'

'It's not as bad as it might sound, but it is a possible pre-cursor to something much worse.'

'A full stroke?'

'Yes.'

Laurel looked to Marnie and held her hand. 'How could this be?'

'It's likely that your grandmother's lifestyle is the cause of the small clot. We'll need to assess her further to prevent more attacks.'

'Is there a treatment?'

'Medication but, more importantly, some lifestyle changes. Don't worry, we'll look after her.'

The doctor left them alone to digest what he'd told them.

'Are you okay?' Laurel asked, wondering if Marnie felt as wounded as she did.

Marnie nodded. 'What about you?'

'I just can't believe you didn't tell me any of this.'

Laurel regretted her choice of words. What she really meant to say was, 'I'm afraid you might die.'

Marnie clasped her hand. 'I didn't want to concern you. I'm fine!'

'You're clearly not fine, or managing,' said Laurel, infuriated that Marnie appeared not to have heard what the doctor said. 'We need to talk – if we sit back and do nothing you're going to die. Do you hear me?'

Marnie said nothing, her silence deafening Laurel, who was afraid the one person she loved the most in the world was going to sit back and allow her life to slip away.

18

2018

The house was quiet for the rest of the day. Chris and Emily went back to their hotel to rest, and Angie had plans to go out on the town. Helena's mother collected Yanni, and Helena remained at the villa; Laurel didn't hear a peep out of her all afternoon despite the fact she was hard at work cleaning the place from top to bottom for the party.

Deciding to make a start on the party preparations, Laurel set about creating a mock-up in the courtyard. With her mother's dungarees on, she dragged a table from the outhouse, and placed a crisp, white tablecloth over it. She positioned some mismatched chairs around the table and imagined them painted in lots of bright colours. She added candles and thought of how it would feel in the evening, with the soft glow of dancing candle-light and the sound of gentle laughter. She could feel it coming together. Content with what she'd achieved so far Laurel hunted for old paint and dug out blackboards, and began the process of moving flower pots from the garden to the courtyard. With the scene beginning to be set, she added rich, textured cushions, and parasols, and she played around with fairy lights, experimenting how to show the house off to best effect. By early evening, her vision of a rustic, Aegean courtyard was taking shape. Laurel leaned back against the whitewashed wall of the villa, hands stuffed in the pockets of her dungarees, and admired her handiwork.

'It's good,' she said, contentedly, breathing in the early evening air. 'It's very good!'

Satisfied but hungry, Laurel went inside to look for Athena. She expected to find her in the kitchen, fussing over some minor details Helena hadn't attended to, so when she didn't find her, she began to worry. She knew Athena well enough to know she was unlikely to be sulking about their earlier tiff; Laurel was confident Athena was more likely to let it all out than to hold anything in. Concerned, she set off in search of her. But having searched the garden, seen the jeep, and looked in the house, Laurel was left with only the option of Athena's private quarters.

'Athena,' she said, knocking quietly on her apartment door. There was no reply.

'Athena,' she called again, feeling uncomfortable about disturbing her in case she was sleeping.

When that yielded no response, Laurel knocked harder and called a little louder. But still there was no reply. Turning the handle of the door Laurel found it unlocked.

'Hello,' she called, creeping in. 'Athena, are you there?'

Laurel heard a light moan.

'Athena?'

'Who is it?' she heard Athena say, groggily.

'It's just Laurel,' she said, following the voice.

'Who?'

Through the small sitting room Laurel found a galley kitchen where she discovered Athena slumped on the floor.

'Athena!' she said, rushing to her. 'What happened?'

Athena looked at Laurel with a dazed expression. 'I must have fallen and bumped my head.'

The memory of Marnie out cold on the bathroom floor flashed into Laurel's mind.

'Wait here,' she said, pushing the thought aside and dashing to find Helena.

'Helena!' she yelled from Athena's door. 'Helena!'

'Yes, Miss Laurel,' said Helena, coming quickly down the stairs.

'Athena's fallen. Can you get a doctor?'

'Of course,' she said, taking the keys for the jeep hanging at the front door.

'Helena's gone to get a doctor,' said Laurel, returning to Athena. 'Let's try and get you comfortable.'

Having learnt how to lift Marnie towards the end of her life, Laurel was able to move Athena easily from the floor to a comfy chair, then she made them both a cup of sweet tea.

'Here you are,' she said, tucking a cushion behind Athena's back. 'Drink this.'

'Is it spiked?'

Laurel laughed, not only out of amusement but also out of relief. Athena showing a sense of humour was a good sign.

'What happened?' Laurel asked, once Athena had drunk her tea.

'I don't know,' she said, feeling the back of her head. 'I remember shouting at you in the kitchen, coming through here to cool off, and the next thing I know you're picking me up off the floor.'

'You don't remember how you got there?'

Athena shook her head.

'Has this happened before?'

She didn't reply.

'Athena?' said Laurel, who knew from Marnie's silences that they usually withheld something significant.

'I've had various episodes over the past twenty years. Nothing worth talking about.'

'Episodes?'

'You know, vascular things.'

'Vascular things,' repeated Laurel, who had a pretty good idea what Athena was talking about.

'They call them mini-strokes,' Athena said.

The mention of the term took Laurel straight back to the A & E cubicle where the doctor had explained about Marnie's attacks.

'How many of these have you had?'

'I forget,' said Athena.

Laurel knew this was either a consequence of the strokes, or Athena's way, like Marnie's, of covering up the true extent of the problem.

Laurel raised an eyebrow in disbelief.

'Several,' she conceded.

'And am I right in thinking they're the reason you're less active than you used to be, why you don't get out as much, or have the same number of guests?'

Athena said nothing, dismissing Laurel's comment with a flick of her hand.

'*Are* they the reason?'

'Maybe,' she said, which Laurel took as a yes.

'And have you spoken to anyone about it?'

'No!' said Athena, defensively. 'And you've not going to either.'

Laurel knew it wasn't easy for Athena to even consider giving up her independence, in exactly the same way it had been almost impossible for Marnie to accept that she must give up hers. After Marnie was released from the hospital they'd come home and managed to talk. Marnie hadn't been ready to accept that it was time for help; she fought the idea zealously, telling Laurel not to mention her condition to anybody. It was only when Laurel said she couldn't return to London for fear of what might happen to Marnie in her absence that her grandmother relented.

Laurel hadn't dared mention a care home; Marnie would rather have 'swallowed a little blue pill' than endure the indignity of that. Equally, Marnie didn't want Laurel to give up London to move back home and care for her, but nor did she feel able to move to London to be cared for there. In the end, they agreed on Laurel coming home each Friday afternoon and leaving on Monday morning – which Jacqui had been entirely supportive about – and Marnie having a carer for the rest of the time. They found Jennifer, the daughter of a friend who was out of work and able to take on the role, leaving Laurel comfortable in the knowledge that Marnie was being cared for by someone she knew in her absence. But all of that seemed a long time ago now, sitting next to Athena in her annexe. Not wanting to provoke any further attack, she agreed not to talk to anyone about it.

'Thank you,' said Athena. 'And what about the party? Perhaps we should postpone.'

'Why don't we continue with preparations for now?' suggested Laurel, remembering how important it had been for Marnie's life to carry on as much as normal, and for there always to be something mentally stimulating for her to be involved in. 'We can always cancel last minute if we need to; it's not as if we're short of people to help. Although,' said Laurel, remembering that Emily had to rest, 'it would be helpful to have one more set of hands.'

'If only Nikos was here.'

'Perhaps you could speak to Nikos about your health,' suggested Laurel. 'I'm sure he'd want to help.'

'Certainly not!' said Athena, sharply. 'He's not to know. Do you understand? You must promise me not to mention anything to Nikos.'

'Fine,' said Laurel, a thought occurring to her; a condition. 'I promise not to tell Nikos if you promise to do something for me.'

'What?' asked Athena, warily.

'Allow Helena to be involved in the party preparations.'

Athena rolled her eyes.

'Or at least,' said Laurel, sensing she might have over-stepped the mark, 'explain why you're so against her helping out a bit more – you could easily find a new cleaner, and Yanni will be in school soon so she'll have more time.'

Athena sighed heavily and shifted in her seat. 'I've known Helena since she was a little girl. Her father was Christos's best friend.'

'That sounds like a good thing,' said Laurel, still none the wiser as to why Athena was so hard on her.

'When Christos and his children came back to visit during the holidays the kids would all play together. They grew up in very different worlds. Nikos in America; Helena here on the island. Nikos became very confident; Helena, well . . . But still the two of them were thick as thieves; we used to joke that they'd marry each other one day.' Laurel saw Athena's eyes return to the time, many years ago.

'And what happened?'

'Five summers ago they had a relationship. Everyone was excited. I thought they'd marry and Nikos would live on the island, I was so proud – I was going to suggest they take over the villa – but then . . .'

'What?'

'Then Helena slept with another man – a tourist,' she said, bitterly. Laurel thought of what Alex had told her about Athena's husband and the 'pretty young tourist' and she felt how awful it must have been for Athena to see it happen twice in her family.

172

'Gosh,' said Laurel, who couldn't quite imagine such behaviour from Helena.

'The result of which . . .' said Athena.

'Is Yanni,' said Laurel, softly, joining the dots.

'Nikos left, his heart broken, and Helena remained.'

'Hence why you resent offering her more responsibility?'

'Not exactly,' said Athena, swallowing hard. 'Whether I like it or not, Helena is like a grandchild to me. Probably more so than most of my biological grandchildren.' Closing her eyes Athena let out a long sigh and spoke slowly. 'Helena has been my constant companion since the boys left.'

A light went on in Laurel's mind. 'And you worry if she had better skills she might leave the island and build a life with her child elsewhere?'

Tears formed in Athena's eyes. 'I know it's wrong, but the idea of life without her, being completely alone, is too difficult.'

'It's okay,' said Laurel, relieved that she'd got to the bottom of the matter, even if she did think it particularly hard of Athena, she understood. She got up and hugged her, resting Athena's head against her own. 'I get it now. I do.'

They sat together until the lights of the jeep shone through the window and Helena returned with the doctor.

'Can you promise you'll at least think about allowing Helena to help out?'

Athena's eyes softened. 'If it makes you happy.'

'It does,' smiled Laurel, going to the kitchen to give Athena some privacy.

'How is she?' Helena asked, reheating spanakopita in the microwave for them both.

'A bit shaken,' said Laurel, thankful that she'd pushed into Athena's apartment when she did.

Helena handed Laurel her supper. 'It happens too much.'

'You've seen it before?'

'The last time was the day you arrived. Just a week ago.'

Laurel thought of Marnie and the growing frequency of her attacks before the final one just two months ago, and of how she had spent all her days worrying, constantly calling to check that she was okay, and asking neighbours to pop by. She still wondered if she might have done something more to have prolonged her life, and she could never shake the regret of her final day. 'You must worry.'

'I do, Miss Laurel. When I arrive each day I don't know if she'll be dead or alive.'

Laurel blinked away a tear and gulped back a surge of grief at the stark reminder of how her own life had been, and thought what she could do in this situation, for both Athena and Helena, which she couldn't for Marnie.

'Helena?' Helena sat down at the large table with her own plate of food. 'If Athena will allow it, would you like to help out more in the kitchen?'

'I'd love to,' said Helena, seasoning her food. 'But Athena will not allow it.'

'What if I could get her to agree? I've asked her to think about it.'

'But who would look after the house? I couldn't do it all.'

'There must be someone else on the island who's able to clean!'

'Yes,' agreed Helena, laughing at her foolishness. 'That's true.'

'So, let's wait to see what Athena says?' said Laurel, excited about her plan, and hoping Athena, after having some time to think about it, would say yes.

19

'How are you feeling this morning?' Laurel asked, surprised to see Athena up and about at breakfast.

'Well enough, thank you. If it wasn't for you I might still be sitting there,' she replied, less brightly than usual, not really pulling off her attempt at levity.

'Helena would have looked in on you before she left.'

'Yes, but still—'

'Have you had a chance to think about my suggestion?' asked Laurel, not wanting Athena to linger in her praise.

'If you're referring to Helena working in the kitchen, then yes, I have, and the answer remains the same.'

Laurel closed her eyes and let out a long breath, in much the same way she'd done with Marnie when she was in her phase of denial. 'The doctor said, categorically, that you're not to work.'

'And I won't.'

Laurel furrowed her brow. 'For what it's worth, I don't really see Helena wanting to leave the island. She has her mum here, and she wouldn't want to take Yanni away from her.'

'You may have a point,' said Athena. 'But still the answer is no.'

Laurel smothered a sigh. 'So what are you going to do if Helena's not in the kitchen?'

'I've put out some feelers,' she said, cryptically.

'Right,' said Laurel, trying not to feel frustrated. 'You do realise the party's in three days, right?'

'I know, I know. Everything will be fine.'

'Things won't be fine unless you start taking things more easily,' pressed Laurel, irritated that Athena's stubbornness was making her sound like a bore.

Laurel caught Athena mimicking her silently as a child might do. Laurel twisted her mouth and flared her eyes, trying to make light of how infuriated she was.

'I promise,' said Athena, seeming to finally recognise Laurel's genuine concern. 'I *am* going to take things more easily.'

'Good,' said Laurel, leaving the details for how she was going to achieve that, without Helena's help, until later. She had enough experience of stubborn old women to know how much you could push them before it came akin to banging your head against a brick wall. Clearly trying to get Helena to help out at the party was a lost cause, but Laurel hadn't given up hope on something longer term. 'Now, can I help with anything before I go out this afternoon?'

'Ooh,' said Athena, her eyes lighting up. 'Are you going on a date?'

'Yes,' said Laurel, who'd woken early with her stomach in knots.

'Where?'

'The beach you suggested.'

Athena's eyes twinkled mischievously. 'Oh goodie! You'll have a blast.'

'I hope so.'

'Trust me, it's the perfect place to relax,' she said, leaving Laurel to her breakfast. 'Just let it all hang loose!'

'This is it,' said Laurel, stopping the jeep, which Athena had lent her for the afternoon. 'We have to walk from here.'

'It looks really secluded,' said Mark, as they left the car behind and set off down a woodland track with a stony path.

'Athena swears it's the best on the island,' said Laurel, following Mark.

'She should know.'

'How did you get on yesterday?'

'I got everything sent off to my editor. Did I miss anything at the villa?'

'You could say that. Emily thought she was having her baby, Athena bumped her head, and now she's searching for a cook, even though she has Helena already.'

'Wait,' said Mark. 'Back up. Is Emily in labour?'

'No, false alarm.'

'And what happened to Athena?'

'Oh, nothing,' Laurel floundered, remembering her promise not to talk. 'Something fell out of a cupboard.'

'But she's okay?'

'Yes.'

'So why is she looking for a new cook?'

'The doctor said she has to rest, and Athena isn't prepared to let Helena have the chance.'

'Why?'

'Your guess is as good as mine,' she said, not wanting to gossip.

The path twisted to reveal the beach below. They stood quietly, taking in the sight of the silvery beach surrounded by cliffs and the crystal clear water.

'I see what Athena meant about it being the best on the island,' said Mark.

'Let's grab some loungers,' said Laurel, spotting two beside the water's edge.

With their towels in place, sunscreen on and books waiting to be read, Mark offered to buy drinks from the small bar and canteen.

'What would you like?'

'Something local,' said Laurel. 'You decide.'

Laurel lay on her lounger, allowing the drama of the last twenty-four hours to melt away. The temperature was high but under the shade of her parasol it felt perfect.

'I could lie here for ever,' said the person on the other side of her.

'Yes,' murmured Laurel, turning to face an older woman on the next lounger, probably in her sixties, with a large semi-circle of sunburn around her collarbones, and toneless white thighs. 'I think I could too.'

'Dorothy loves it here,' said the man with a beer gut beside her – Laurel supposed he was her husband. 'I think it's because of all the young men, starkers, on the other side of those rocks!'

'It is not!' she said, whacking him playfully with a copy of some cheap, women's magazine.

Laurel glanced to where the couple were looking. Several large boulders split the beach in two.

'Nudists,' the woman whispered, for clarity.

'Ah!' said Laurel, finally getting why Athena had been so set on Mark and Laurel coming. She had a quiet laugh to herself as Mark returned with drinks.

'Here we are,' he said. 'Ouzo lemonade.'

'Thank you,' said Laurel, taking the refreshing-looking cocktail that had been garnished with lemon and mint leaves and a sugar rim. 'Let's hope it's not as potent as the last cocktails I consumed!'

'You seem pretty relaxed,' he said, settling into his own lounger.

Laurel took a sip of her drink, which was sharp and ice cold. 'I'm getting there, and this helps,' she said, not quite being able to push the beach beyond the rocks out of her head. If there was one thing on Laurel's bucket list it was skinny-dipping.

'How are you feeling about the party?' asked Mark, drinking a cold beer.

'I'm nervous about the catering, but Chris reassures me he'll be fine on his own. I don't know, there's a lot to do. What about you? Are you feeling more relaxed?'

'More so than usual,' he said. 'Getting that piece of work sent off has helped, until that was done I couldn't think about anything else.'

'Is that what you were referring to on the beach the other night?'

Mark thought for a moment. 'Eh, no. No, that was something else.'

Feeling she'd walked into a conversational brick wall, Laurel changed the subject. 'Athena told me you're a prize-winning novelist, is that true?' she asked, not confessing that her best friend had already googled him.

'*One* prize.'

'Was it a good one?'

'Good enough to help pay the mortgage for a bit.'

'Where do you live?'

'London.'

Laurel whistled. 'That must have been a good prize!'

Mark laughed, which pleased Laurel. 'What about you?'

'What about me?'

'I mean I know you organise events but where do you live, do you live with anyone?'

'I rent a flat in Clapham, with Tom.'

'Tom?' asked Mark, with what might have passed as a hint of jealousy.

'My grandmother's cat,' Laurel reminded him.

He snapped his fingers. 'Of course, Tom, the cat.'

'And that's it really. I was thinking about buying a little studio or one bed with the money I inherited from my grandmother but, I don't know . . .'

'You can't bring yourself to part with half a million quid for two hundred and fifty square feet?'

'Precisely!' said Laurel. 'And then you come somewhere like this and you wonder why you're so hell-bent on clinging on to London in the first place.'

'When it smells, is over-populated, and everyone's rude.'

'And you can never get a seat on the Tube.'

'But we still love it,' said Mark.

Laurel looked out at the perfect water and sky in front of her and couldn't imagine going back to the daily grind of the 'head down' walk to the northern line, her 'face-in-an-armpit' to Stockwell, 'squashed-against-the-glass' to Victoria, and the never-ending queue for the bus to Hyde Park. 'Except, I'm not sure I do love it any longer.'

'No?' asked Mark.

'I'm beginning to see there might be something beyond it – something where I'm my own boss, not a slave to someone else, and in a place where the sun shines and smiles don't cost the earth.'

'Sounds like something you should bottle.'

'Talking of which,' Laurel said, looking at their empty bottle and glass.

'I'm on it,' said Mark, getting up and going to the bar.

After another couple of drinks Mark suggested a stroll.

'Sure,' agreed Laurel, feeling a little tipsy. 'That would be nice.'

'It's nice beyond those rocks,' said Dorothy, with a wink.

'Thanks,' said Mark. 'We'll check it out.'

'Athena was messing with me when she suggested this place,' said Laurel, a little further along the beach, scuffing the sand with her feet.

'How do you mean?'

'You'll see,' she said, teasingly.

At the rocks Mark and Laurel spotted the sign, *Nude Beach*.

'Ah!' said Mark, in a way that made Laurel suspect he was being gentlemanly rather than prudish.

'Have you ever . . .?' asked Laurel, neither one of them so much as peeking beyond the rocks.

'No,' said Mark. 'You?'

Laurel shook her head. 'But . . .'

'But?'

'I quite like the idea.' This was Skopelos Laurel speaking, not London Laurel, she realised.

'You do?'

'Sure,' said Laurel, making it sound more like a question than a statement, not wanting to frighten Mark. 'It wouldn't hurt to look.'

Laurel climbed on to one of the rocks, which sat between the two sections of beach, and glanced between them.

'What do you see?' asked Mark from below.

'Just a bunch of people getting nice even tans.' Laurel jumped down to let Mark up.

From the top of the rock Mark held out his hand. 'I will if you will?'

'Deal!' said Laurel, climbing up beside him, the two of them jumping down together.

'Do you think there are rules?' asked Mark, as they strolled towards the loungers, hand in hand.

Laurel giggled, the excitement, heat and drink, all merging blissfully.

'Excuse me,' said a hairy, pot-bellied man, walking towards them. Laurel noticed his sun hat, perched on top of his head, the only scrap of clothing on him and stifled a laugh. 'This is the nudist section. No clothes allowed.'

'We were just—' Mark pointed to the loungers.

'Go on then!'

'Guess they have rules after all,' said Laurel, bursting into laughter, Mark joining in.

'So,' said Mark, once their laughter had dwindled. 'I guess we have to commit.'

Laurel winced nervously. 'Guess you're right.'

'How about we strip on three and run for the sea!'

'Good plan!'

'Okay, ready?'

'Ready.'

'One, two . . . THREE!'

At once, Laurel and Mark began tearing off their clothes. Flip-flops first, then Mark's shorts, Laurel's tunic, then shorts, bra and finally both of them whipped off their pants and ran – Laurel holding onto her boobs in vain – hell for leather, to the sea.

'Arghhh,' yelled Laurel, wading quickly in, liberated beyond words to be stark naked and up to her chin in warm water.

'Je-sus!' Mark shouted, thrashing his arms in circles,

whipping up the water, which splashed and sprayed Laurel. 'How great is this?!'

'Pretty bloody brilliant,' she said, smiling at him, seeing an uninhibited, carefree Mark she hadn't seen before.

'This is fun,' he said, calming slightly, he too now fully submerged.

Laurel smiled. 'Proper fun,' she said, holding his gaze.

'Proper grown-up fun,' he said, inching towards her, their eyes holding contact.

'I can't remember the last time I had grown-up fun,' she said, feeling his hand reach around her waist.

'No,' he said, their faces almost touching. 'Not this much fun!'

Laurel tilted her head and Mark pressed his lips to hers, kissing her softly at first and then more urgently. As his body pushed closer to hers and she felt him up against her she finally had the answer she was looking for – Mark definitely liked her!

20

Laurel broke the kiss first.

'Was I too forward?' Mark asked, searching her eyes for the answer.

'No!' said Laurel, who felt quite dizzy from it all. 'I just needed some air! The sun, alcohol and, well, you, have left me breathless.'

'We should get out of the water.'

'Yes,' said Laurel. 'A little lie down might be nice.'

'I'll get you a towel.'

Laurel watched as Mark strode up the beach to the towel hut, his white bottom gleaming in the sun.

'Nice,' said Laurel, whose whole body felt like putty. She couldn't remember when she last felt so relaxed.

'Here you are,' he said, paddling in to hand Laurel a towel, one already wrapped around his waist.

Laurel stood up, with newfound body confidence, allowing Mark to see her fully naked.

'Wow!' he said, not diverting his eyes.

As Laurel rubbed her hair dry, for once unbothered by its frizz, Mark moved closer, drawing her in and kissing her again.

'I think there might be rules about *that*,' she whispered, glancing down to what lay beneath his towel.

Mark groaned. 'I'm sure you're right.'

'We should probably . . .' Laurel pointed to the loungers, wrapping her towel around her.

'Yes,' said Mark. 'I suppose we should.'

'Well,' laughed Laurel, once she was settled under a parasol. 'I haven't done that before.'

'Nor me, but I'd do it again!'

'Me too!' she smiled, opening her towel. 'Preferably when there's no one around to impose the rules!'

Mark reached out and took her hand. 'Do you think Athena knew what she was doing when she suggested this beach?'

'Of course she did! I'll bet she's done more than her share of skinny-dipping in her time.'

'I'm glad,' said Mark. 'Though it certainly wasn't what I was expecting at the start of the day!'

'What were you expecting?'

'Just a quiet afternoon with a pretty girl I've been thinking about.'

Laurel suppressed a smile. 'And what have you been thinking?'

'That there's a little bit of mystery about you.'

'Really?' said Laurel, surprised that he should think that of her when she'd been thinking the same about him.

'A piece of the jigsaw is missing.'

'Which piece?'

'I know about London and work, your grandmother

and Janey, even Tom, but you never mention anything about the rest of your family. It's as if they don't exist.'

Laurel stared out to sea. It felt strange to have someone new in her life who saw through the barriers she'd put up over the years.

'It was only ever Marnie and me,' she said, quietly, rubbing her thumb against his.

'How so?'

'My parents died when I was two, I have no siblings. Marnie raised me after that.'

'What happened?'

'They were killed in a motorway collision.'

'Je-sus, I'm sorry.'

'It's fine,' said Laurel, used to people responding as if it was the worst thing in the world. 'It was far harder for my grandmother. The truth is I don't remember them at all, only what Marnie told me.'

'That must be tough.'

'If I could change one thing it would be to have a memory of my own of them, but Marnie told me everything she could, and in many ways I felt I knew them. I guess my only wish is that I'd known something of their essence, their spirit, you know? To understand the chemistry that made me, me. But, now that Marnie's gone . . .'

'So has that hope,' Mark finished for her.

Laurel scrunched up her nose and nodded. 'In the end the only parent I ever knew was Marnie, and I'm happy with that.'

'So really you're grieving for the loss of someone who was your parents, and grandmother?'

'That's about the long and the short of it,' said Laurel, giving his hand a squeeze. 'But moments like this make it easier. God knows Marnie would have loved hearing about this. Me lying naked on a beach with a good-looking Irishman – she would have spat out her tea with joy!'

'My grandmother would have sent me to confession!'

Laurel laughed. 'Talking of which – you've got a mystery of your own you need to confess.'

'I have?'

'Sure! You've travelled alone to a Greek island, you mentioned plans that changed, and there's something you're not ready to talk about. So 'fess up, what's the big mystery?'

Mark let out a small laugh. 'Nothing gets past you.'

'Well?'

'It's nothing very mysterious,' he said. 'Just a nasty break-up.'

'Ah, I'm sorry to hear that.'

'All things happen for a reason,' he said, looking at Laurel's warm body.

'When did it happen?' she asked, moving to show herself to her best advantage.

'A few weeks ago.'

'Was it a long-term relationship?'

'About three years.'

Laurel thought of Phil and the emptiness she'd felt after the years they'd spent together. 'What happened?'

Mark shook his head, indicating he wasn't comfortable offering more.

'Were you meant to be on this trip with her?'

'Yes,' he said, turning towards her and running a finger from her navel to her breasts. 'But suddenly I'm rather glad I'm not!'

They spent the rest of the afternoon luxuriating in the sun and chatting endlessly about anything and everything. It had been years since Laurel had felt the thrill and rush of needing to learn everything about someone in one fell swoop.

'Are you getting cold?' Mark asked.

'A little,' she said, wrapping her towel around her.

'Maybe we should head off. See if we can catch a last bus – neither one of us can drive after all those drinks.'

'I guess,' said Laurel, who didn't want the day to end.

They strolled leisurely back up the path to the main road and caught a bus to town where they lingered outside the entrance to Mark's hotel.

'I'd like to invite you in,' said Mark, another 'but' hanging in the air.

'But?'

'I don't want to rush in and for someone to get hurt,' he said, kissing her tenderly. 'Let's hook up tomorrow, pick up the jeep.'

'Sure,' said Laurel, who, though disappointed, knew Mark's decision was the right one.

'Oh look,' he said, pointing to something behind Laurel.

Laurel turned to discover the little stray cat.

'Hello again,' she said, bending down, but as she did Mark sneezed and the cat bolted.

'Nervous little thing,' he laughed, watching it disappear. 'Do you need me to walk you back?'

Laurel was tempted to say yes, on the off chance he might decide to stay, but, sensibly, she said, 'No, thank you, I'll have Alex take me.'

'Goodnight then,' he said, kissing her once more, neither one wanting the moment to end.

'Goodnight,' she said, walking away, Mark holding on to her hand until she was out of his reach.

'I take you back to the villa?' Alex asked at the harbour.

'Yes, please,' said Laurel. She'd had to fight every bodily urge to peel herself away from Mark, but now she wanted to get to the villa as quickly as possible.

'I've been up already today.'

Laurel wondered if guests had arrived, and if Athena was up to hosting.

'You been with Angie?' he asked.

'No,' Laurel replied, feeling a smidge guilty that she hadn't been in touch with her today. 'But I saw her yesterday.'

'Oh?' Alex looked in the rear-view mirror.

'She told me about your date at Villa Athena years ago.'

'I remember,' said Alex, nodding. 'She was very beautiful. She still is.'

'Yes,' said Laurel, thinking of her first impressions of Angie and how she'd missed so much – her joy, her care, her huge smile. She loved that Alex saw all of that beauty and more.

'She say anything about me?'

'She's thinking about another date,' said Laurel, hoping she wasn't giving Alex too much hope.

'Really?'

'Thinking,' said Laurel.

'I can hope.'

Laurel waved Alex off and walked happily up the track to the villa, recollecting her afternoon's adventure. A smile spread across her face as she thought of Mark, and she felt a spark, a twinkle, she hadn't felt in a very long time.

In the hall Laurel heard Athena's laugh. She found her in the guest sitting room with a man, about Laurel's age, regaling her with a story.

'Ah, Laurel,' said Athena, a hand outreached. 'There you are. I was wondering where you'd got to.'

'The day ran away from us,' she explained, putting down her bag, aware that the strongly built, olive-skinned man, with his short dark hair and inky eyes was watching her keenly.

'A day at Velanio can do that!' she sang, winking at the man.

'Velanio?' he said, standing to greet Laurel. 'There's a place that brings back happy memories!'

'Right,' laughed Laurel, a touch nervously, caught on the hop by the presence of this good-looking man.

'Laurel,' said Athena. 'This is Nikos. Nikos, Laurel.'

'My pleasure,' he said, taking Laurel's hand and kissing it.

'Nikos,' she said, removing her hand. 'Athena's told me all about you. I didn't realise you were coming.'

'Nor did I,' he said, examining her face. 'But when Yaya called last night I thought, hey, it's about time I made my way back to the island. So, here I am.'

'How long are you here for?' she asked, thinking it sweet that he referred to Athena as Yaya.

'A day or two,' he said, sitting back down. 'I'm just passing through.'

Laurel wondered if Nikos was the 'feeler' Athena had put out for help in the kitchen.

'How was the beach?' asked Athena, patting the cushion next to her for Laurel to sit down.

'Unexpected,' said Laurel.

Nikos roared with laughter. 'Yaya, have you been up to your old tricks again?'

'I couldn't help myself,' she laughed. 'Look at this girl, so beautiful. If this girl shouldn't skinny dip, who should?'

'I agree,' said Nikos, his eyes smiling at Laurel. 'And did you?'

'As a matter of fact, I did!' said Laurel, her eyes smiling back, enjoying her new found Shangri-La.

'Yippee!' sang Athena, pleased as punch. Laurel knew

193

Marnie would have been equally as delighted 'That's the Skopelos spirit!'

Yes, thought Laurel – catching Nikos's twinkling eye – and I like the Skopelos spirit, a lot!

21

'Morning!' said Nikos, who was already wielding a screwdriver, tightening the hinges on the dining-room doors. 'Sleep well?'

'Like a log,' said Laurel, who was asleep almost before her head hit the pillow – the sun, sea and skinny-dipping all catching up with her.

'Velanio has that effect!' he winked, testing the door.

Ignoring his comment, Laurel went to the buffet table, selecting some yoghurt and fruit.

'You want some pancakes with that? I make the best pancakes.'

'Sounds good,' smiled Laurel, impressed that Nikos should be both handy about the house *and* a cook.

In the kitchen, Nikos heated a pan and quickly gathered all the ingredients and utensils he needed.

'You know this kitchen well,' said Laurel.

'Like the back of my hand,' he said, cracking some eggs. 'How long have you been here?'

'Just a week, but it feels like for ever – in a good way!'

Nikos whisked the eggs, his biceps flexing strongly beneath his T-shirt. 'My grandmother seems pretty taken with you. You're all she could talk about when I arrived.'

'I'm pretty taken with her,' said Laurel, pleased to learn that her feelings for Athena were shared.

'It's not often that Yaya takes a shine to someone. You must be pretty special.'

There was something about the look Nikos gave Laurel that made Laurel's cheeks flush.

'Athena mentioned you're a vlogger,' she said, trying to divert the attention away from herself.

'Right,' said Nikos, removing the pan from the heat. 'She doesn't get it!'

'No, I got that impression,' she laughed. 'What do you vlog about?'

'Food and travel,' he said, pouring some batter into the pan. 'It doesn't earn me much but it covers my costs, and I've no rent or kids, so . . .'

'You're pretty free.' Laurel's thoughts turned to London and her ridiculously high rent and the job she could do standing on her head.

'I am,' he smiled, flipping a pancake. 'I'm a lucky guy.'

Helena arrived as Nikos was tossing another pancake.

'Nikos!' she said, caught off guard. 'What a surprise.'

'Helena,' said Nikos, going to her. He held her gently at arm's length, scrutinising every inch of her face. 'How are you?'

'I'm fine,' she said, almost defensively. 'When did you arrive?'

'Yesterday,' he said. 'Yaya called. I thought I'd come by.'

'Good,' she said, not quite catching his eye. 'She'll be glad you're home.'

'What about you,' he said, as she put on her apron, preparing for work. 'Aren't you glad I'm home?'

'I'm always glad,' she said quietly, going to the utility closet to get her things.

Laurel remembered something she'd been thinking about for the party. 'Helena, do you know where I can buy some of those little lanterns for candles? I thought they might be pretty as table decorations with some blossom scattered around them.'

Helena gave it some thought, wringing out a cloth at the sink.

'Doesn't Theo make them?' she asked Nikos.

'Yeah, he does,' Nikos replied, snapping his fingers. 'You want me to take you?'

'That would be great,' said Laurel, chuffed that her plan was coming together. 'Thanks, Helena,' she said, though Helena was already heading upstairs with her cleaning basket.

Nikos served Laurel her pancakes with a little less bravado than he'd prepared them, his eyes flickering distractedly to the staircase.

'These are sensational,' said Laurel, her mouth full of light, sweet pancake, creamy yoghurt and sharp fruit.

'Told you so!'

'Do you cook other stuff as well as this?'

'Sure, food is my thing!' he said, sounding a lot like Athena.

'It's just – Athena's having a party on Tuesday and one

of the catering team can't work any more so, could you help in the kitchen?'

'Nah,' he said, scrunching his nose. 'I'll take off again tomorrow, once I've done the jobs Yaya needs doing.'

'It would only be an extra day.'

'Helena can do it – she's great in the kitchen.'

Laurel shook her head. 'Athena won't allow it.'

'Why?'

'I don't know,' she said, thinking it was in Nikos's best interest not to rehash the conversation she'd had with Athena last night.

'So what about Yaya?'

Laurel stalled the conversation by eating some more pancakes, torn between whether to follow her instincts and tell Nikos about his grandmother's health or keep her promise to Athena.

'Athena is the hostess, she can't do both,' she said, her loyalty to Athena winning the toss.

'Hah!' said Nikos. 'You clearly don't know my grandmother! Yaya can do anything!'

And you, thought Laurel, feeling bad for Nikos, don't know your grandmother as well as you think.

Nikos drove a lot like Athena, but with even greater alacrity.

'Who taught you to drive?' asked Laurel, clinging on to the handgrip as Nikos bumped through potholes and tore round corners.

'Yaya!' he grinned.

'It figures,' laughed Laurel, enjoying Nikos's

recklessness and his childlike energy – a mixture of Athena's free spirit and his own unbridled enthusiasm.

'There aren't too many rules on the island when it comes to the road,' he said, whizzing over a blind summit, like something out of *The Dukes of Hazzard*.

'No,' yelled Laurel, holding on to her sun hat. 'I can see that!'

'You English are all about rules,' he chuckled, taking his eyes off the road and turning to Laurel the way Athena had done, with a glint in his eye.

Laurel's mind went straight to London and 'stand on the right', 'mind the gap' and 'don't jump the queue', all the things she found so stifling.

'You think we're stuffy?' she asked, not that she'd blame him if he did.

'Not stuffy exactly.' He thought for a moment before smiling widely. 'More uptight!'

'Oh charming!'

'No offence meant,' he said. 'I like the UK – everything's so proper and in its place. "Cup of tea?"' he mocked.

'Ha ha! I take it you've been?'

'Sure!' he said, turning without indicating. 'First place I travelled to on my own was London.'

Laurel thought of how much she'd missed not travelling after school or uni, too focused on earning money and taking on responsibility.

'You like to travel?' she asked.

'I can't imagine life without it.'

Laurel wondered how he'd feel if she told him about

Athena's health. Would he put his plans on hold? But there was something about his passionate spirit, something she could only imagine he inherited from Athena, that prevented Laurel from asking.

'You?'

'I haven't done that much,' Laurel admitted.

'No?'

'Until recently any time off I had I used to visit my grandmother,' Laurel explained, feeling a little unworldly next to Nikos. 'But I'm loving being here,' she beamed. 'Villa Athena feels a lot like my grandmother's home, and who could not fall in love with Skopelos?'

'Particularly the skinny-dipping part!' he teased.

Laurel blushed.

'I didn't mean to embarrass you – I guess that's the feeling I'm looking for,' said Nikos, his gaze holding Laurel's momentarily. 'A place that measures up to the island, and has that same sense of home.'

'You don't want to settle here?'

'Not yet,' said Nikos. It was easy for Laurel to see that Nikos had too much energy to be confined to one place. 'There's so much out there to discover, and Skopelos isn't going anywhere – I can always come back.'

'Yes,' said Laurel, distantly. Listening to Nikos talking about wanting to leave and exploring other places made her realise how much she felt she belonged on the island, and of how she couldn't imagine leaving it, at all.

'Hey, Buddy,' said Nikos as Theo opened the front door of his small, waterside house.

'Nikos!' he cried, hugging him. 'You're home!'

'Sure am, bud,' said Nikos, slapping his friend's back.

'Come in!'

'You remember Laurel, right?'

'Sure,' said Theo. 'What did you do to deserve being out with this scoundrel!'

'Hey!' shouted Nikos, playfully punching Theo on the arm.

'It's good to see you again,' he said, inviting her in.

'Thanks,' said Laurel, amused by their banter. It was clear that they'd been friends for a long time.

Theo took them out back to a small courtyard with a barbecue, various tools scattered about the place, and a bike.

'Where you been, man?'

'Here and there,' said Nikos. 'You know how it is.'

'Not really,' he laughed. 'I'm up at three every morning making bread and in bed by seven. I barely know anything beyond these four walls and the stall.'

'You've a good life, man.'

'I guess, if work's your thing.'

'You must have something else going on – you seeing anyone?'

Theo laughed. 'You know this place, it's hardly rich pickings!'

Nikos looked to Laurel. 'That's another reason not to settle here—'

'The gene pool!' they said in unison.

'Right,' chuckled Laurel, who saw increasingly why life on the island wasn't the right fit for Nikos. But still, she wondered, if he knew about Athena's health would he see things differently?

'How's business?' Nikos asked.

'The stall's steady enough. The lanterns only sell during the season.'

'Which is why we're here,' said Nikos. 'Laurel's after some to decorate Yaya's courtyard.'

'Oh yeah?' said Theo, opening up the small stone outhouse. 'Take your pick!'

Laurel stepped into an Aladdin's cave of lanterns. On the floor were large lanterns, three foot high, and then shelves of lanterns decreasing in size so that on the very top shelf were the smallest lanterns of all.

'These are so beautiful,' said Laurel, who saw Theo in a different light. There was something about a craftsman that always made her smile – the dedication and care required to create something so intricate spoke a lot about the man.

'Thanks,' he said, modestly.

'I need a selection for the tables,' continued Laurel, 'but I think I'll take some of these big ones too, to sit next to the gates and doors. And we should have a little stall, selling them as mementos of the evening. What do you think?'

'Sure!' said Theo. 'You want me to come along and set things up?'

'That would be so great, thank you – and stay for

the party, it's going to be fun,' she said, grinning about an idea she'd had, and beginning to feel everything was falling into place.

22

'He's handsome, isn't he?' said Athena, sitting on the patio, after lunch, watching Nikos cut the grass.

'Yes,' said Laurel, who could see Nikos was handsome in a macho way – tall, strong and dark – his confidence masking any imperfections he might have.

'He's single,' Athena said, with a twinkle, as if being single was the only prerequisite required to make two people interested in each other. 'But then again, you've got Mark.'

Laurel sat back and watched Nikos effortlessly cutting the grass in the warm morning sun.

'They're very different,' she laughed, thinking how pale and weedy Mark would look next to Nikos.

'My grandson is strong.'

'Yes,' said Laurel, there was no disputing the fact, but she couldn't help think about Mark, reserved and sensitive, and how much more appealing he was to Laurel. 'You know you have to tell him about your health.'

'Why?'

'Because you need someone to help look after you and the villa.'

'I have Helena.'

'Helena isn't family.'

'She's as good as, despite her lack of restraint.'

'But you've said yourself you don't want her taking on extra duties—'

'I don't want Nikos being tied to the island because of me,' said Athena, interrupting Laurel, who immediately heard echoes of Marnie. 'He'd only resent me, and I won't have that.'

'Surely that should be his choice to make?' said Laurel.

Athena shrugged loosely, a sure sign to Laurel that she was on to something.

'How do you think he would feel if he found out you'd passed away and then discovered you might have lived longer if he'd been able to offer help when it mattered?'

Athena harrumphed.

'You know I'm right,' pushed Laurel. 'And it's not fair to put Helena, and me, in a position of withholding information from him.'

Athena turned to Laurel. 'Do you ever get dizzy up there on the moral high ground?'

Laurel laughed. She loved the way Athena broke tension with humour. 'I'm only trying to help.'

Athena put her hand on top of Laurel's. 'I know.'

'Will you at least allow me to coerce Nikos into staying until after the party? We need all the help we can get.'

'I'll certainly allow that,' she said, smiling tenderly at Laurel.

Nikos turned off the lawnmower and came over. 'What are you ladies talking about?'

'Just how nice it is to see a man about the place!' said Athena.

'Doing manly things!' giggled Laurel.

'Oh yeah?' Nikos flexed his muscles in fun, causing Athena and Laurel both to laugh.

'Why don't you have a break?' suggested Athena. 'Take Laurel down to the beach, let me have a nap.'

'How's about it?' asked Nikos, holding out his hand.

'Sure,' said Laurel. 'Sounds good.'

Nikos strode down the steps of the cliff two at a time.

'Don't you worry you'll fall?' called Laurel, from behind, taking her time.

'I've been climbing up and down here since I first started walking,' he said. 'I'm like one of the island goats!'

He waited at the bottom, holding out his hand.

'Thank you,' she said, jumping off the final step.

'You like it down here?'

'How could I not?' said Laurel, seeing the little boat and remembering how she'd fallen in with Mark. She laughed at the memory.

'Nothing beats Villa Athena,' he said, looking up at the house.

'And you definitely wouldn't come back, not even to help Athena?'

'Yaya!' he scoffed. 'Are you kidding me? Yaya doesn't need my help.'

'Right,' said Laurel, frustrated not to be able to share anything about her health. 'But couldn't I twist your arm just to stay until after the party? If not for Athena, then for me?'

'Huh,' said Nikos, stopping and looking at Laurel. 'I didn't realise we had the kind of thing going that would make me want to stay for you.'

'Well . . .' said Laurel, sensing that a dash of flirtation might be her best chance of persuading him.

'Oh really,' he said, smiling back at her, his hands already on her hips pulling her closer. 'You fancy a piece of Skopelos Nikos?'

Before Laurel knew what was happening Nikos's lips were on hers.

'Nikos!' she said, pushing him off, having got more than she'd bargained for.

'You like?'

Laurel was breathless from shock.

As she was about to reply, her lips tingling from his stubble, she saw a figure on the steps, a figure she knew only too well, in a trilby straw hat.

'Bugger,' she said, glaring at Nikos and running towards Mark.

'Mark!' she called, unable to catch him up. 'Mark!'

'What's going on?' asked Helena, in the garden, where she was clearing away Athena's things.

'I just screwed up, that's what's happening,' she said, hearing the gate slam shut behind Mark. She clutched a stitch in her side and decided not to chase after him.

If she'd seen Mark kissing another girl she'd want to be left alone for a while too.

'How?'

'Mark saw me kissing Nikos!'

'Ah,' said Helena, turning a little pale. She put down her tray and took a seat.

Nikos appeared at the top of the steps.

'What happened?' he asked, incredulous that anyone would cut short a kiss from him.

Laurel explained about Mark.

'The guy you went skinny-dipping with?' he asked.

Laurel nodded.

'Oh yeah, baby, you messed up!'

'Nikos!' reprimanded Helena. 'Go make us something to drink.'

'Wait, before you do,' said Laurel. 'You'll still stay for the party, right?'

'Of course!' he said, brushing it off. 'No sweat.'

'He's kind,' said Laurel, after he'd gone up to the house.

Helena inhaled deeply and let out a slow sigh. 'Very.'

'Athena mentioned you and he were close.'

'Once upon a time.'

'Things didn't work out?' Laurel asked not wanting Helena to feel as if she'd been gossiped about.

'It wasn't to be.'

'How so?'

Helena was silent, absorbed in pulling at the flesh on her knuckles.

'Helena?'

She turned to Laurel with a look of resignation.

'What is it?'

'I told a lie.'

Laurel laughed lightly in confusion. 'I don't under-stand. What sort of lie. When?'

'A very big lie that I wish I'd never told.'

'I'm certain whatever it is it can be rectified.'

'I'm not so sure,' said Helena, as Nikos returned.

'Here we are – two home-made watermelon coolers.'

'Thank you,' said Laurel.

'And, if you'll excuse me, I've jobs to do.'

'Thanks,' said Helena, watching Nikos walk away.

'The lie was to Nikos?'

Helena nodded.

'Do you want to tell me?'

Slowly, uncertainly, Helena began. 'We've known each other all our lives, and we've both had crushes on each other over the years, just never at the same time. Nikos was always a bit of a player, and I was always cautious about getting hurt, so there was always a reason for it not to happen.'

Laurel recognised her description as being true of the Nikos she'd spent time with that morning.

'Then five summers ago it did happen – we had a relationship. Everyone was thrilled. Athena didn't say as much but it was obvious she was set on us getting married and taking over the villa, but that wasn't what Nikos wanted, and nor did I; I didn't want to be mar-ried to someone who felt trapped. He'd just found

209

his feet with his vlogging and he was so comfortable with his nomadic existence, I knew being tied to me, the villa, and the island, would suffocate him. I resigned myself to us being the best of friends, instead of lovers.

'And then,' Helena paused, gathering herself. 'Then I found out I was pregnant, and on top of everything else I knew it would be too much for him. So I made a decision.'

Laurel had an idea of what Helena was about to say but she didn't interrupt.

'I decided to make up a story about having slept with a tourist. I said I'd become pregnant with the man's baby, a man I only knew the first name of and had no contact details for.'

'And you told Nikos?'

'It broke his heart,' said Helena, welling up at the memory. 'But I knew a broken heart, which would mend, was better than a lifetime of resentment. I felt certain we'd be good friends again, in time.'

The two women sat together quietly, both with their own reflections.

'And you did become friends again?'

'It took a while but yes, we're friends again. And, of course, I have Yanni now, who takes up all my time anyway.'

'Yanni is Nikos's son?'

'Yes,' said Helena. 'You understand now how difficult it is to undo the lie?'

'Yes, I do,' said Laurel, thinking that Nikos deserved

to know the truth. 'But my grandmother taught me to believe in love, not conflict, and one way or another I'm certain we can sort this out.'

23

'So what happened after Mark left?' asked Angie. The four of them – Laurel, Emily Helena and Angie – were all painting chairs in the courtyard with ABBA playing in the background.

'Alex drove me all round town looking for him. We checked his hotel, the port, the barbecue shack, we couldn't find him anywhere.'

'You must have felt terrible,' said Emily, who was looking much more relaxed after a weekend of doing nothing, though she'd placed her chair on a table to paint to avoid bending. Her painting was perfectly precise.

'Or incredible!' laughed Angie, who was slapping paint here, there and everywhere.

'Don't laugh!' cried Laurel, looking to Helena to check she was comfortable with them discussing the kiss with Nikos. 'Emily's right, I do feel terrible. I had no intention of kissing him – I've no idea how it happened.'

'*I've* an idea how it happened,' said Angie, catching sight of Nikos going into the house, where he was helping out Chris in the kitchen.

'Angie!' Emily said with mock-outrage, waggling her paintbrush at her.

Laurel cast Helena an apologetic look for Angie's behaviour; Helena smiled without malice, knowing Angie didn't know her history with Nikos.

'If Laurel hadn't already been there I'd be making a beeline for him myself,' said Angie. 'Not that I imagine he'd want me after someone as gorgeous as her.'

'First of all – I haven't "been there",' said Laurel, astonished that she, Laurel Dempsey, should find herself in a situation where she had to explain her promiscuity. 'And second of all, you've far more sex appeal than me.'

'Maybe once upon a time.'

'Nobody's judging you, Laurel,' said Emily.

Angie laughed. 'Though some of us are very impressed!'

'Honestly, guys,' Laurel got her brush into the smallest nook of a spindle. 'I'm mortified. Poor Mark. What must he think of me?'

'A little competition never put off a man,' said Angie. 'Particularly when he's just seen you naked!'

Laurel hoped she was right but feared, in this case, that things were a little more complicated. Mark didn't exactly strike her as the alpha-male, boasting about his conquests down at the local rugby club.

'And after all your efforts you still didn't find him?'

Laurel shook her head, pleased that Helena had redirected the conversation. 'Nope. Alex took me up to where we left the jeep yesterday, we checked the beach, but nothing. I haven't seen or heard anything from him since.'

'I hope he hasn't done a runner,' said Angie, ever the drama-queen.

'I doubt it,' said Emily, more supportively.

'I'll tell you who definitely hasn't done a runner,' said Laurel. 'Alex!'

Angie groaned.

'I invited him to the party tomorrow so I hope you're ready!'

'Ready for what?' asked Emily.

'Ready to revisit old times,' said Laurel, winking at Angie affectionately. 'So, you'd better hide your toy-boy – we don't want Alex getting jealous!'

'Hardly,' said Angie.

'God, I tell you,' said Emily, taking a break to stretch her back. 'I'm glad I'm married, I'd forgotten how exhausting all this dating malarkey can be.'

'I wish I had any of your luck with men,' giggled Helena. 'I'd like to be married some day.'

'You can't tell me you don't have someone,' cried Angie. 'You're beautiful! Men must be queuing up for you.'

'No,' she laughed, demurely, tucking a stray hair behind an ear. 'Not now I have a child.'

'There's someone out there looking for you,' said Laurel, repeating what Marnie used to tell her. 'He just hasn't found you yet.'

'Talking of which,' said Angie, giving Laurel another nudge. She looked towards the gate and saw Mark arriving. 'Looks like it's apology time!'

★

Laurel knocked gently on the office door.

'Yup,' said Mark, not looking up from the computer.

'Hi.' Laurel did a funny little wave, which he didn't notice, and she felt suddenly conscious of the paint splattered over her mother's dungarees and hands. 'It's so good of you to come, after yesterday I—'

'I promised Athena I'd help update the website.'

'Of course.' She knew she had no right to expect anything other than curtness.

Laurel glanced round the room at the thousands of photographs of smiling faces covering the walls and ceiling.

'What a great way to have spent your life.'

'How's that?'

'Creating this much happiness,' she said, her hands outstretched.

The thought of leaving all this behind and having to return to London struck her again, she ached at the idea. The prospect of Jacqui's demands, and the basement office with its strip lighting and windows so small you saw nothing but the shoes of passing pedestrians, left her numb.

'I hadn't thought of it that way.'

Laurel adjusted one of the party posters, which Mark had pinned to the wall. 'But it makes you think, doesn't it?'

'About what?'

'About what matters.'

He briefly stopped typing. 'Which is?'

'Love and happiness,' said Laurel, both of which

seemed to be spread across the room and were at the core of Villa Athena.

'I can't argue with that.' He turned a little towards her.

'It makes me feel so ashamed that I might have spoilt your happiness yesterday.'

Mark looked at her with softening eyes.

'I'm so sorry – more than you can know.'

He remained silent, seeming to look more at her nose than her eyes.

'You've no reason to believe me but I really had no intention of Nikos kissing me. I've never kissed two men in two days in my life.' She rubbed her nose self-consciously to discover she had a blob of yellow paint on it. She laughed, hoping he might too, which he did, a little, with his eyes. 'I genuinely don't know what happened.'

'Strange how lightning strikes twice,' he muttered, not unkindly.

'Pardon?' said Laurel, having heard him but not quite understanding.

'It's nothing.' He dismissed the comment with a wave of his hand and returned to his job. 'I like your dungarees.'

Laurel smiled. Nobody ever complimented her dungarees.

'How's it going in here?' asked Laurel, passing through the kitchen.

'Nikos is a great help,' said Chris, who had his hands deep in the meatball mixture.

Laurel looked around the kitchen at all the dishes that were ready for cooking, and the fridge stuffed full of fresh produce waiting to be prepared. 'I can see,' she said, impressed by the order and cleanliness of the place.

'Didn't I tell you everything would work out in the end?' said Athena, entering the kitchen, using a cane.

'You did!' said Laurel, warmly, though still desperate to see Helena more involved. 'Why don't you come outside and see how things are shaping up out there?'

Laurel and Athena walked slowly out to the half-light of the courtyard.

'The old place certainly looks different,' said Athena, taking a seat on the bench by the front door.

Laurel was pleased with how it was coming together – the tables were positioned and their parasols in place with lights strung along their wooden struts like stars.

'You've made it very green,' said Athena, pointing to the planters, which Laurel had gathered in clusters to create the impression of a courtyard garden. It wasn't entirely clear to Laurel whether Athena was impressed or not. 'And the mismatched chairs – all those different colours – are we aiming to give our guests a headache?'

Laurel laughed. 'They're supposed to make it feel homely and welcoming.'

'Well,' said Athena, softening enough for Laurel to know that she was quietly pleased. 'I might be able to see that it works.'

'The final details will bring it all together,' said Laurel, feeling her excitement rising. She thought of the pretty lanterns Theo would bring for the tables, and the blackboards still to be written up with the menu, and all the candles that would flicker in the evening light. 'We're almost there – one more sleep, and it's show time!'

24

Laurel woke to the most glorious day imaginable. The sky seemed to be a brighter blue than on previous mornings and the sea sparkled more brilliantly, even the bougainvillea was bursting with bigger and more glorious blossom. A flurry of excitement pulsed through Laurel's body as she thought of the day ahead – the day of the party! Full of anticipation, she headed downstairs to see how preparations were going.

In the kitchen Chris and Nikos were already hard at work. Chris was manfully whisking egg whites by hand, Nikos prepping meat, and there was a heavenly smell of fresh mint in the air.

'Good morning,' said Laurel.

'Isn't it?' said Nikos, smiling broadly, clearly happy to be back in the kitchen.

Laurel poured herself a cup of tea. 'I can't remember a better one!'

'You guys are way too cheerful,' laughed Chris.

'There's a lot to be cheerful about,' sang Laurel, who couldn't remember looking forward to a day this much in a very long time.

'You've got everything under control, right, no last-minute glitches?'

'All under control,' said Chris, casually, as if he was simply making breakfast for Emily and himself rather than over a hundred guests.

'Great,' said Laurel, brimming with pleasure that the day was off to a good start. 'I'll leave you to it.'

Helena was plumping cushions in the sitting room, making sure everything was perfectly positioned and dust free.

'Wow!' said Laurel. 'It looks gorgeous in here!'

Helena thumped a cushion into shape. 'Like you said, it didn't take much. A new rug, cushions and throws. And you were right to take down the curtains – it's so much brighter without them.'

'Everything's falling into place,' said Laurel, who always liked it when a plan came together. 'The décor, the food . . .'

'They're managing, just the two of them?' asked Helena. Laurel detected a note of disappointment in her voice.

'For now,' she said. 'But don't worry, I still plan on having you working in the kitchen before I leave.'

Laurel felt a pang of remorse whenever she thought about leaving. The number of days was etched on her mind – only four remained – it could never be long enough.

'You know I'm going to miss you, Laurel,' said Helena. 'You've become a good friend to Athena, and to me.'

'I'll miss you more,' said Laurel, looking around the bright room with all its charm, wondering how she could ever return to her beige box in Clapham after this. 'I've got friends back home, but none as colourful as you.'

'As Athena, you mean!'

'I mean both of you,' said Laurel, squeezing her hand, fighting off the rising sensation of sadness. 'We'll have to keep in touch; I'll want to know how things turn out with Nikos.'

'Yes,' said Helena, thoughtfully. 'I've been thinking about that . . .'

'What have you been thinking?'

Helena positioned a cushion on an armchair. 'I've been thinking I should talk to him while you're still here, so I don't lose my courage.'

'Of course. I'm happy to talk to him with you, just let's get today out of the way first, yes?'

'I suppose,' said Helena, not sounding very convinced.

'What are you girls talking about in there?' called Emily, from the dining room.

Laurel went through to find her folding napkins.

'These are incredible,' said Laurel. There were lilies and swans, rabbits and butterflies, fans and bows. 'They're going to add so much personality to each table. Thank you.'

'What else is a pregnant woman going to do with her time?' she said, finishing a turkey.

'Where did you learn to do this?'

'What can I tell you; I learnt for fun,' she laughed. 'I'm just a geek!'

'Lucky for me that you are,' said Laurel, admiring each one.

'Have you spoken to Mark?' Emily asked, folding another napkin.

Laurel felt a twinge of nerves. 'Is he here?'

Emily nodded to the patio, where Laurel saw him crouched down, copying menus onto blackboards.

'I guess there's no time like the present,' she said.

'I guess not.'

'Wish me luck!'

'Good luck!'

Laurel stepped out onto the warmth of the patio.

'These look great – they're so neat and uniform,' she said, with slightly exaggerated enthusiasm. Laurel found Mark's handwriting attractive – it was small and leant to the right with gentle loops. There were few things worse to her than a man with schoolboy penmanship.

'Thanks,' he said, glancing up briefly to acknowledge her.

'How are you?' she asked, sorry that he didn't stop what he was doing to chat.

'Not bad.'

'Good,' said Laurel, nodding, uncertain what to say next.

She watched him for a while, a heavy pause settling between them with only the sound of the chalk on the blackboard to fill it.

'Maybe I'll catch you later,' she said, disappointed in herself not to be able to find anything else to say. There were a thousand things she wanted to say such as:

skinny-dipping with you was the best fun ever; I regret you seeing Nikos kiss me, more than you can know; please believe me, pl-eease! But she didn't say any of those things she just swung her arms, bringing them together in a clap. 'I'll get on then – lots to do.'

Laurel licked her wounds as she walked round the side of the villa, past the drying area where Helena was taking down tea towels, to the courtyard. Suddenly the day didn't seem quite as bright as it had but she was cheered to discover Angie in the courtyard, with Theo, placing tea lights in lanterns on the tables.

'These are the perfect finishing touch,' said Laurel, admiring all the lanterns in different colours, which worked so well with the mismatched brightly coloured chairs.

'And they'll look even better when they're lit up this evening,' said Theo.

'Definitely,' said Laurel, imagining the scene, with everything twinkling, and sweet laughter.

'Shall I take these round to the patio?' Theo asked.

'That would be great,' said Laurel. 'But wait, you need help.'

'I can manage.'

'No,' said Laurel, beckoning over Helena, a ploy in mind. 'Helena won't mind helping.'

'Theo?' said Helena, joining them.

'Helena!' he said, greeting her with friendly kisses on each cheek. 'How long's it been?'

Helena's eyes flickered in delight. 'I don't know,' she said. 'Did I have Yanni last time I saw you?'

'No, but I heard you had a son,' said Theo, picking up a crate of lanterns, the two of them strolling off together, Helena telling him about Yanni.

'He lit her up,' said Angie, when they were out of earshot.

'Yes,' said Laurel, quietly pleased with her match-making, and fetching a stepladder from the outhouse. 'Do you mind helping with the lights?'

'Not at all,' said Angie, picking up a string of white lights.

'Are you bringing anyone tonight?' asked Laurel, up the ladder.

'I don't think so,' said Angie, standing at the bottom feeding the lights to Laurel.

'Why not?' asked Laurel, a tack in her mouth, a hammer in her dungaree side-pocket.

'I don't know.'

'Is it because you know Alex is coming?' Laurel teased, taking out her hammer and bashing in a tack to hook lights over.

'No.'

'Then what?' asked Laurel, who couldn't help notice her friend wasn't in her usual high spirits.

'I don't know, pet. Maybe I've just realised I'm not the person I was any more.'

Laurel stopped what she was doing and came down the ladder for some more tacks.

'What do you mean?'

'I'm older. Guys aren't interested in me the way they used to be.'

'What are you talking about! You've had more men in the past week than I've had in a decade.'

Angie shook her head and twisted her lips.

'Angie?'

Laurel took Angie over to a table where they sat down. Angie fiddled with a piece of blossom and pulled off its petals one by one.

'The truth is, there hasn't been anyone, not for several summers,' she said, only able to meet Laurel's eye briefly.

'I don't understand,' said Laurel, confused. 'All those nights . . .'

Angie breathed deeply. 'I was just out, sitting at bars; I never hooked up with anyone.'

Laurel felt a rush of sadness for her friend, and regret that she hadn't realised.

'I'm so sorry, I—'

'There's nothing for you to feel bad about,' Angie said, quickly. 'This is all my own making.' She threw back her head and ruffled her curls. 'God, I feel such a fool.'

'Don't be crazy,' said Laurel, trying to make sense of the situation. 'I just don't understand why you didn't say something earlier.'

Angie looked at the petals scattered on the table and the stamen she twiddled between her fingers. 'I came hoping for someone to take away that terrible sense of loneliness you get from returning home each day to an empty house. It never occurred to me that the men who frequent bars are getting younger, or at least I'm getting older. It never occurred to me that I don't look the way

I used to, and nor do I have the same spark.'

'I had no idea,' said Laurel, rubbing Angie's arm. 'If it makes you feel any better, I can totally relate to the empty house thing. Since Marnie died I've had nobody, other than Janey, and she has a fiancé and a life of her own.'

'So do all my friends. And that's the problem. Everyone's married with kids. They think it's so much fun being flirty, bubbly, Angie – free to do whatever she likes, whenever she likes. What they don't realise is I really want the thing that they've all got – stability and love.'

'You know, there might be someone who wants to give you those things . . .'

'You mean Alex?'

Laurel nodded.

Angie laughed at Laurel's persistence. 'I'm still thinking about it.'

'Good!' said Laurel, glad to see her friend smiling again. 'Now, let's get this place finished before guests start arriving!'

'Angie,' said Laurel, when the last string of lights was in place. 'Have I forgotten something?'

'I don't know. Have you?'

'I have a feeling,' said Laurel, who knew the heavy feeling only too well from her experience at work when something had been overlooked. 'But what could it be?'

'Promotion's been done.'

'Food's well underway.'

'Menu's prepared. Drinks and glasses attended to.'

'The tables are dressed,' said Laurel. 'And the venue prepared.'

'Helena's been scrubbing the toilets all morning.'

'We've a cloakroom set up and plenty of waiters.'

'You've even got flowers on the table,' said Angie. 'I think everything's taken care of.'

'No,' said Laurel, frustrated that she couldn't pinpoint what it was. 'Something's missing. I can feel it.'

'You're just getting nervous,' laughed Angie, waving Emily over from the house. 'But really, what's there to be nervous about? People are coming for a drink and some food – nobody's performing heart surgery!'

'You're right,' said Laurel, chewing her lip. 'But still . . .'

'What is it?' asked Emily.

'Laurel's concerned that she's forgotten something.'

'Nonsense!' said Athena, who joined them too. 'What could be so important anyway?'

'Would everyone please stop saying that!' said Laurel, with a rising sense of panic. 'It's important to me to get this right. Something has been forgotten and it would really help if everyone could just think!'

'Maybe you're worried about the food,' said Chris, coming out of the house with Nikos.

Laurel was aware that everyone, including Mark, Helena and Theo, was now in the courtyard.

'Forgive me,' she said, looking around. 'Without meaning to sound rude, shouldn't you all be getting on with your jobs?'

227

'We thought we could take a minute,' said Angie, with a glint in her eye.

'What for?' asked Laurel, with a growing sense of awareness that something was afoot.

'To put you out of your misery,' teased Athena, who gave a signal for the boys to open the gates. As they opened the sound of 'Mamma Mia' began to play. It took a moment for Laurel to realise where the sound was coming from but when she did she shrieked in delight.

'Oh. My. God!' she shouted, her hands over her mouth. 'An ABBA tribute band!'

'We thought you deserved a treat,' said Emily, giving her a squeeze.

'For all your hard work,' said Angie, putting her arm around her.

'Yes,' said Athena, joining them. 'You've done more for me than I deserve.'

Laurel swallowed back a surge of emotion but still tears burst from her eyes.

'Thank you,' she cried, hugging everyone – including Mark. 'Music *was* what I'd forgotten. But here it is! We're ready!'

'Yes,' sang Athena, 'we're ready. What could possibly, conceivably go wrong?!'

25

'I can't believe how many people have come,' said Laurel, taking a moment with Angie to survey the courtyard, where almost every table was taken. The air was full of the sound of laughter and chinking glasses, and Athena was in her element, dressed in all her finery – a stunning black and silver silk caftan with countless beads – going round the tables, chatting to people both old and new.

'I don't think it could have turned out any better,' smiled Angie.

'I think you're right,' agreed Laurel, watching Mark circling the tables, a bottle in hand, refilling wine glasses. She dismissed the thought that it might have turned out marginally better if they'd resolved their differences.

'We should get back to work,' said Angie, 'get these starters cleared.'

'Don't rush,' said Laurel, holding her back with an outstretched hand. Her experience told her how to pace events. When a group was merry and light-hearted it was best to keep the wine flowing and take your time between courses, and this party was definitely merry. 'Give the boys time to get the mains fully prepared.'

She noticed Athena head inside and, with the host away, she decided to mingle.

'Odele,' she said, spotting the lady from the market. She crouched down beside her at the table. 'Are you having fun?'

'Very much,' she smiled, widely. 'It feels just like old times.'

'I'm glad,' said Laurel, observing everyone at the table absorbed in conversation. 'How was your starter?'

'Divine!' she said, then whispered, 'The food is even better than I remembered!'

'I'm glad!'

'Everything is perfect: the atmosphere, the food, and such a beautiful spot – so far off the track and overlooking the sea. There isn't another guest house like it on the island.'

'It gets my vote. Enjoy the rest of your evening,' said Laurel, moving on to chat to other guests who were all just as complimentary about the food and the beautiful setting they were dining in.

'Is the feedback good?' asked Angie, as they bumped into each other between the tables.

'The best,' she said, her attention caught by the arrival of another guest – Alex.

Laurel nudged Angie. 'Wow, doesn't Alex scrub up well?'

'I guess he does,' Angie replied, looking at Alex in his crisp white shirt and dark jeans.

Laurel waved him over. 'One might even say there's something of Pierce Brosnan about him tonight!'

'Let's not over-egg the pudding!' laughed Angie, trying to play down her interest, even though she was fixing her hair and rubbing her lips together to tone down her lipstick.

Alex approached them with a handsome smile.

'Good evening.' Laurel kissed him on the cheek.

'Good evening, Miss Laurel,' he replied, but his eyes were on Angie.

'Alex,' said Angie, quite demurely by her standards. If Laurel read the situation correctly, she thought Angie might even be slightly nervous.

'You look beautiful,' he said, holding her gaze and taking her hand.

'Get away!' she giggled, though she didn't divert her eyes from his.

'May I ask you to dine with me?'

'Oh, I'd love to, but I can't,' said Angie, a tinge of disappointment in her voice. 'I'm meant to be helping.'

'I can manage,' said Laurel, directing them immediately to the only remaining table, a small, candle-lit table for two.

'No, I couldn't,' Angie protested, weakly.

'I insist,' said Laurel, winking covertly at Alex.

Chris and Nikos prepared and dished-up the mains perfectly, and between them Laurel, Theo and Mark served them effortlessly. In under five minutes all twelve tables had been served and every guest was tucking in.

'The food looks stunning, guys,' said Laurel, sampling a leftover portion of moussaka, leaving Theo and Mark outside on wine duty. 'And it tastes even better!'

'We aim to please,' said Chris, taking a well-earned five-minute break before starting to plate up the desserts.

'I'm going to grab some fresh air,' said Nikos, his brow covered in beads of sweat.

'I'll join you,' said Helena, abandoning the washing up.

Both Laurel and Chris watched her follow Nikos outside.

'What was that about?' asked Chris, leaning on the table.

'I've no idea,' said Laurel, helping herself to another mouthful of moussaka. But as she ate the sweet, juicy main a snippet of her earlier conversation with Helena about Yanni and Nikos came back to her: 'If I can wait that long'. Laurel chewed slowly. 'She wouldn't, would she?' she mused out loud.

'What?'

'She wouldn't tell Nikos, not now, would she?' Laurel said, more to herself than to Chris.

'Tell Nikos what?'

Laurel swallowed the moussaka with a bad feeling. 'Oh God . . .'

Realising what was about to transpire, she put down the fork and left the kitchen, leaving Chris muttering, 'Nobody tells me anything around here.'

In the garden Laurel found Helena about to catch up with Nikos. She chased after her.

'Helena!' she called, but it was too late. It all seemed to play out in slow motion.

'I've done something unforgivable,' said Helena.

'I doubt that,' Nikos said, stretching his arms up in the air with a groan, ridding himself of the strain of hours of cooking.

'It's true,' she said, moving closer. 'Laurel knows,' she indicated to Laurel who stood at a respectful distance. 'It's time you knew too.'

'Helena—' said Laurel, stepping forward, trying to intervene but Helena's mind was made up.

'I lied to you.'

'About what?' he asked.

She looked down, before saying, 'About the affair.'

Nikos let out a sigh. 'I don't want to drag this up again. It's in the past – water under the bridge.'

Laurel tried again to step in. 'Helena, maybe later would be better . . .'

'No!' she said. 'He needs to hear this.'

'I don't!' he said. 'We had our chance, *you* blew it, we moved on.'

'Except that's not the full story,' said Helena.

Laurel knew there was no going back, for all she wished Helena had chosen a better time, so she stood back and watched, ready to pick up the pieces.

'Then what is?' he asked, exasperated.

'I lied to you about the pregnancy.'

Nikos stood in silence trying to make sense of what Helena had just said. 'You have Yanni. What are you talking about?'

'Yes,' she said, quietly, now with his full attention. 'I have Yanni. I lied about the father.'

Laurel saw the faint look of understanding dawn in Nikos's eyes.

'What do you mean?'

'I mean there was no tourist. Only you.'

Nikos furrowed his brow in thought. 'If there was only me, that means . . .'

'Yes,' said Helena.

Laurel, from where she was standing, saw that the implications of what Helena was saying to Nikos was becoming clear to him.

'Yanni is your son,' Helena confirmed.

For a moment, it felt as if there was no sound anywhere, despite the tinkling of glass and peals of laughter floating down from the house.

'No.' Nikos shook his head, and started to walk away. 'No!'

'Yes!' said Helena, grabbing his hand, trying to stop him.

He shook her free.

'You need to listen to me,' she shouted, causing some of the guests on the patio to turn towards her.

'Helena . . .' Laurel whispered, pulling her back, not wanting to make a scene. 'Let him go.'

'I can't!'

'You can,' said Laurel, holding Helena's wrist, who gave in. 'Let him be.'

'He's done what?!' asked Chris, after Laurel had told him Nikos had taken off and was unlikely to be back for the rest of the evening.

234

'I know,' said Laurel, trying to sound composed, even although inside she was having kittens that they were a chef down with a course still to serve.

'What the hell am I supposed to do?' he yelled, for once losing his cool. 'I've got soufflés to make, brûlées to flame and ice cream moulds to turn out and dress.'

'I can help,' said Helena.

Laurel looked to Chris, who shrugged and threw down his cloth, 'Why not?'

'Are you sure?' Laurel asked Helena, uncertain if she was in the right frame of mind for the pressure of a kitchen.

'I'm sure,' she said, emphatically. 'I'm the reason behind this muddle so I should be the one to sort it out.'

'Fine,' said Laurel. 'Take Chris's lead; I'll ask Theo if he can help with the washing up.'

Laurel found Theo in the courtyard serving wine, where it occurred to her that she hadn't seen Athena for a while.

'Emily,' she asked, handing her Theo's wine bottle to serve. 'Have you seen Athena recently?'

Emily looked around the party. 'Come to think of it, no.'

'Not to worry,' she said, feeling a little concerned but smiling for the guests. 'I'll find her.'

Laurel went round the side of the house, onto the patio, and through the dining room but found no sign of Athena. She hoped she'd find her in the sitting room but when she didn't she began to worry, a rising sense of anxiety, which she'd known before, creeping up inside her.

'Everything okay?' asked Mark, going through to the kitchen. 'You look a bit worried.'

'I'm okay,' she said, his concern not lost on her.

'Everything's going really well, you can relax now.'

'Sure,' she said, knocking on Athena's apartment door as Mark went into the kitchen. 'Athena?'

She pressed her ear against the door. There was no response.

Laurel felt a cold chill run through her heart and thoughts of Marnie raced through her mind. When she called a second time with no reply she went in.

'Athena!' she yelled, finding her lying on the floor, her face and limbs contorted. 'Please, not again!'

She placed her face close to Athena's to check if she was breathing, her hand on her chest. 'Can you hear me?'

Athena let out a garbled moan.

'Oh, thank God,' she said. 'I'm going to get help!'

Laurel placed a blanket over Athena and ran to Angie as fast as she could without the diners noticing anything was wrong.

'I think Athena's had a stroke,' she said, as quietly and as composed as she could manage under the circumstances.

'Where is she?' asked Angie, putting down her napkin and getting up immediately.

'In the bedroom,' she said, leading her friend by the hand, desperate for Athena's fate not to be the same as Marnie's. 'Please help. We need an ambulance!'

'No ambulances on island,' said Alex, as the three of them raced to Athena.

'Then what do we do?'

'I take her to doctor,' said Alex. 'Where's Nikos?'

'He took off,' said Laurel, cursing the timing of it all.

'I lift her myself.' Alex calmly picked her up and carried her to the jeep.

'I'll come,' said Laurel, already climbing in, wanting to be with Athena in the way she hadn't for Marnie.

'No!' said Alex, calmly. 'I take her, then I find Nikos. You stay and look after the guests.'

Laurel had to fight every instinct to stay with her but in the end she knew Alex would take good care of her and that there was nothing more she could do.

'God, Ang,' she said, her body shaking, as they watched the jeep disappear down the track. 'You just never know.'

'You never do,' said Angie, her arm round Laurel to keep her warm. They sat on a low wall outside the villa. 'You okay, pet?'

'I don't know,' said Laurel, who felt rattled beyond all recognition. 'It took me right back to finding Marnie, except . . .' Laurel's voice cracked and all the tears she thought she'd rid herself of over the past two months returned.

'It's okay,' said Angie, holding her tight. 'You've been through the wringer.'

Laurel sobbed and wiped tears from her face, her nose running. 'I thought,' she said, barely able to get the words out for crying. 'I thought Athena was gone too.'

'But she's not,' said Angie, rubbing Laurel's back and handing her a tissue.

Laurel wiped her nose. 'She might be.'

Laurel wished she could fix everything, make Athena well, stop her from dying. Bring Marnie back to her.

'Only time will tell.'

'But what do we do?' said Laurel, beginning to gather herself, the sobbing subsiding, her tears drying. 'What do *I* do?'

'We do what Alex said. We do what Athena would do,' said Angie, stroking a lock of hair back from Laurel's brow. 'We look after her guests and ensure they have the best night possible. And you keep holding it all together. You're doing brilliantly, pet. Athena won't want you to fall to pieces now.'

'I suppose you're right,' said Laurel, who could think of nothing other than Athena and of Marnie, and all that had happened after she'd found her lifeless on her bed. 'But the party just doesn't seem important in the grand scheme of things right now.'

'I know,' said Angie, guiding Laurel back into the courtyard. 'But Athena's reputation is on the line and it's up to us to ensure we hold it up high.'

'Yes,' said Laurel, trying to snap out of the daze she was in, all the fairy lights and candle flames in the courtyard blurring into a haze.

'Are we ready to serve?' Laurel asked in the kitchen, having managed to freshen up and gather herself, even though her only thoughts were for Athena and if she'd survived the ride to the doctor.

'Absolutely! Helena has saved the day, we're back on

track!'' said Chris, who had returned to laid-back mode, unaware of what had just occurred. Laurel decided she would tell them later, not wanting to cause any further disruption.

'Perfect,' said Laurel, who felt guilty for salivating at the sumptuous creations they were beginning to serve. It didn't seem right with Athena's fate unknown.

Adrenalin took over and before Laurel knew it the desserts had been served and cleared, the band was setting up, and tables were being moved aside to make way for dancing. For the guests who enquired after Athena, Laurel simply told them she was resting – it had been a while since she'd partied like this – nobody questioned her further, they simply asked for Laurel to pass on their thanks and praise, which she prayed she'd have the chance to do.

'It's been a huge success,' said Angie, the two of them having a quick rest on the bench. Laurel's adrenalin had worn off, leaving her feeling wrung out.

'Not a sober guest among them.'

'Nope.'

'Helena single-handedly both ruined and rescued the day,' said Laurel, watching her chatting easily with Theo at one of the tables.

'She did,' said Angie. 'And Alex was very calm in a crisis.'

'One might say, vaguely heroic!' said Laurel, wondering if Athena had made it through.

'Yes,' said Angie, her eyes sparkling.

'You agree?'

'Well . . .' said Angie. 'Like I said – you never know.'

At that moment Laurel saw Alex arrive back – she rushed to him, desperate to learn of Athena's fate.

'How is she?'

'She's being looked after,' said Alex. 'I found Nikos at the harbour, he's with her now.'

'Thank you,' said Laurel, dizzy with relief. She reached out to Angie for support.

'Come and sit down, you've gone sheet white.'

'I'm okay,' she said, sitting down, feeling pretty wobbly.

'Put your head between your knees, you'll feel better in a moment.'

When Laurel came back up she couldn't help but notice the way in which Alex was looking at Angie – so full of admiration for the care she was giving her friend. 'I feel a little better now. Maybe I'll take five minutes to myself.'

'Are you sure?'

'Yes,' said Laurel, shooing them away. 'You guys go find something to eat, or dance!'

Angie smiled at Laurel, all too aware of her motive, and was led away by Alex.

Laurel took five minutes to catch her breath. She was about to get on when Mark came up to her.

'Angie told me what happened,' he said, putting his arm around her and pulling her close. She nuzzled in, feeling the stress melt away. 'I'm so sorry.'

'Me too.'

They sat in comfortable silence, listening to the band

playing 'Super Trouper', until Laurel felt steady again. Then she began the process of tidying up and saying goodnight to departing guests.

An hour or so passed before she'd time to check in on Angie and Alex, and when she did she found them on the dance floor, dancing cheek to cheek.

She smiled and picked up a wine glass, noticing that Helena and Theo were still locked in conversation, Theo's hand placed gently on Helena's arm.

'Mission accomplished,' she said to herself with a smile.

26

March 2018

'Marnie, it's me,' said Laurel, standing on the concourse at King's Cross Station looking up at the departures board. 'My train's delayed.'

'Don't worry,' said Marnie, her voice cheerful but frail. 'Tom and I are fine, we're catching up on an episode of *House*.'

Laurel never failed to be amused by Marnie's love of anything with Hugh Laurie in it. 'Has Jennifer left?'

'She had to leave after lunch, off to the dentist for a filling. I've told her a thousand times not to eat those boiled sweets but did she listen . . .'

'I guess not!' laughed Laurel, who was thankful now that Marnie hadn't allowed her too many sweets as a child; it had spared her a lot of time in the dentist's chair.

'Why don't you pick up fish and chips on the way home? By the time your train gets in it'll be supper time.'

Marnie thinking of her stomach reassured Laurel that everything was okay. 'I'll do that. And you're sure you're fine?'

'Yes – now leave me alone, I want to find out what's wrong with the schoolteacher!'

'Okay, see you soon.'

'See you, love. Enjoy the journey!'

Laurel stood on the concourse replying to emails on her phone and boarded the train only a half hour later than scheduled. She spent the journey finalising bits and pieces for the following week's butchery awards ceremony and an Indian wedding celebration.

After her change of train at Leeds, she tucked her phone away and sat back to enjoy the remaining part of her journey, thinking about the weekend and the plans she and Marnie had made. They had a trip to the theatre arranged for Saturday evening and one of Marnie's famous lunches organised with friends on the Sunday. Laurel had been looking forward to it all week – the perfect antidote to the pressure-cooker of London.

She left Harrogate station and walked the short distance to the chip shop, which was on her way home. When she arrived, she found a long queue. Desperate to get back to check on Marnie she thought twice about waiting, but knowing her grandmother would be disappointed if Laurel arrived home without food, she went in and waited, sending a final few work emails as she did so.

Fifteen minutes later Laurel walked home, some forty-five minutes later than planned. She knew there was something wrong the moment she entered the house. Tom didn't greet her as he always did.

'I'm home.'

Marnie didn't reply.

Laurel put the fish and chips on the sideboard, hung her scarf on the newel post, and began searching the house.

'Marnie?' she called, at first thinking she might be out on the patio. When she wasn't outside, Laurel went to the bathroom to see if she was there, when she wasn't she began to panic.

'Marnie, where are you?' Her voice trembled.

It was when she saw Tom, his tail high, meowing at the bedroom door, that she felt the awful dread of what she was about to find.

'Marnie,' she said, quietly, opening the bedroom door.

'Oh God!' she cried, seeing Marnie lifeless on the bed. 'No. No!'

But there was nothing that could be done.

Laurel knelt down beside Marnie, feeling her hand, which was still warm and searched for a pulse. There wasn't one. She listened and watched to see if she was breathing. She wasn't.

Instinctively she pulled her phone out of her coat pocket to call for an ambulance but then she realised if she did the ambulance would take Marnie away. And Laurel couldn't face Marnie being taken away. Not yet.

She climbed onto the bed beside her grandmother, just the two of them, and began to tell Marnie all the things she would have said if she'd got to her in time, if she hadn't stood in the chip shop queue replying to senseless emails.

'I've loved you, more than anyone.' Laurel stroked her grandmother's soft cheek, still able to smell the Olay Marnie loved so much. 'I will never forget the love and support you've given me. And I promise always to live by the wisdom and lessons you taught me.

'Please come back to me, Marnie,' she cried, tears pouring down her face. In that moment, Laurel felt certain she couldn't live without her; her heart was broken, never to mend.

Having cried every tear in her body, Laurel eventually picked up the phone. The ambulance crew arrived in less than ten minutes.

'We'll take care of her from here,' said the middle-aged, male paramedic. Laurel knew that he had meant to sound supportive but the words had sounded clinical and cold. How could a complete stranger possibly take care of the woman she had known and loved every moment of her life?

As they wheeled her body out of the house, shrouded in a body bag, Laurel wanted to scream, 'Stop! Bring her back. Let me keep her forever.'

But quickly the ambulance doors were closed and Marnie was taken away.

The hollowness she felt as she went back into the house was beyond her comprehension. She felt like a shell, as if her soul had left the earth with Marnie's. The only feeling that remained was that of the regret at arriving home too late, a feeling she felt would haunt her forever. The fish and chips lay cold on the sideboard, and the house, for the first time since Laurel could remember, felt still, and quiet, and empty.

27

June 2018

It was long after midnight when the final guest had departed, the villa was quiet again, and Laurel was free to go to the island's medical centre.

She rang the bell, which sounded through the back of the small converted house with its blue shutters, and waited. After a time Laurel heard the shuffle of footsteps and the jangle of keys, which took her back to the night she'd arrived at the villa. She laughed at the memory of how spooked she'd been by Athena in what felt like the dead of night, even though it had been barely past nine o' clock. It was hard for Laurel to believe that only ten days later she was visiting that very same woman who now felt like family to her.

'Yes?' asked the young doctor who opened the door, wearing green scrubs with her curly dark hair tied back.

'I'm here to see Athena.'

'And you are?'

'Laurel.'

'Are you family?'

Laurel was about to say no, when she heard Nikos answer for her. 'Yes.'

The doctor opened the door and allowed Laurel into

the small tiled corridor, where Nikos was standing at the opposite end.

'Thank you,' said Laurel to Nikos, who looked shattered, huge grey circles under his eyes. 'How is she?' Laurel wasn't certain she wanted to know the answer.

Nikos looked to the doctor.

'It's too early to say,' she said, taking Laurel through to the back of the building and a small ward with only two beds, in one of which was Athena, sleeping.

Laurel hesitated, frightened by what she saw – Athena looked so frail and lifeless, almost as Marnie had looked. She had to remind herself of one vital difference: Athena was alive. After a moment or two she went to her, slowly, and held her hand.

'Athena, it's Laurel,' she said, quietly.

Athena lay motionless.

'I've administered medication to dissolve the clot,' said the doctor. 'She arrived in good time so I'm hoping that will be enough. If not we'll have to have her transferred in the morning.'

'Transferred?' asked Laurel, fearful that Athena would be taken far away.

'Only to the mainland,' Nikos explained, 'where there are better facilities.'

'A boat ride?'

'Or helicopter,' replied the doctor. 'But I'm hoping it won't come to that. Let's see what the night brings.'

The doctor left the three of them alone. Laurel pulled up a chair by the bed.

'She owes her life to you,' said Nikos, staring at his

grandmother, who looked unrecognisable with her usual expressive face so motionless and pale. She was so similar to how Marnie had looked when she'd found her that Laurel was taken straight back to that night. 'We can never thank you enough.'

'It was fate,' said Laurel, stroking Athena's hair, feeling guilty that Nikos didn't know the history of his grandmother's illness. 'Nothing to do with me.'

'Still. She'd want me to thank you.'

'She can do that herself when she's able,' said Laurel, who was determined to apply every scrap of positive thinking to the situation that she could muster, refusing to allow another great women to die when she'd got to her in time. She glanced up to see the look of uncertainty in Nikos's eyes. 'She *will* get better.'

'How can you be certain?'

Laurel exhaled, knowing she couldn't conceal the truth any longer. 'She's had other episodes – none as bad as this – but other, smaller ones.'

Nikos squinted. 'What are you talking about?'

'Over the past twenty years, she's had numerous small vascular episodes.' She wondered if Nikos felt as she had when the doctor had told her about Marnie's episodes – winded and disbelieving. 'This isn't unexpected.'

'How do you know?'

Laurel thought back to the day she'd found Athena on her kitchen floor. 'She had an episode a few days ago – I pretty much forced her to tell me then.'

'And you didn't think to tell me?'

Laurel could see in Nikos's eyes the betrayal he felt,

not just from Laurel but from Athena.

'She swore me to secrecy,' Laurel explained, even though the keeping of the promise now felt foolish. 'I should have told you.'

'*She* should have told me,' said Nikos, which Laurel thought generous of him, given the circumstances.

'It's been a tough night,' said Laurel, recalling how exhausted she'd been when Marnie had had smaller episodes, and Nikos had the shock of Helena's news too. 'Why don't you take a break – go see Helena.'

'I suppose you're going to tell me you knew about that as well.'

Laurel said nothing, her eyes confessing for her.

'Jeez,' he said, putting his hands behind his head and pacing the small room like a caged lion.

'Helena's intentions were good,' said Laurel, hoping to soften the events of the night a little for him.

'How do you figure that?'

She paused to try and create an accurate account of what Helena told her had happened when she became pregnant, not wanting to misspeak on her friend's behalf.

'She said she didn't want you to feel obligated to stay on the island; nor did Athena. They both wanted you to have your freedom, to do the things that you love.'

'Unbelievable,' he said, running his hand down his face, devastated by it all. 'Is that what they think of me – that I'm so selfish I'd rather pursue my own dream than face up to my commitments?'

'I think that's just it,' said Laurel, looking to Athena. 'I don't think Athena wants to be seen as a commitment.'

Laurel knew that was the last thing Marnie had wanted either.

'And Helena?'

'She loved you,' said Laurel, softly. 'But she knew you weren't cut out for the island – she didn't want you to live a life of resentment.'

Nikos stood silently, emotionally wrung dry.

'Why don't you go?' she suggested. 'Let me sit with her for a bit.'

'I can't leave her.'

'You're no use to her without sleep.'

'I suppose,' he said, rubbing his jaw.

'Take the jeep, go back to the villa. I'll let you know how she is in the morning.'

'You have to get better,' said Laurel, holding Athena's hand, recalling how she'd held Marnie's after her life had slipped away. Laurel couldn't allow Athena to die too. She wasn't certain she had the strength to survive the loss of two women she loved in the space of three months.

It shocked Laurel to realise that was how she felt about Athena, that she loved her. In such a short space of time she'd become a great friend, someone she cared deeply about, and wasn't prepared to lose.

'You've become like a grandmother to me,' she whispered, rubbing her thumb on Athena's papery skin. 'Don't leave me.'

Athena's eyes flickered.

'Athena?' Laurel cried. 'Athena? Can you hear me?'

Athena returned to her motionless state but Laurel

persevered, believing that Athena had heard her.

'The party was a huge success,' she said, searching for something positive to say. 'You would have been so proud. Everyone loved the food and the atmosphere. I promise, you'll be the talk of the island again!

'And Angie hooked up with Alex, and loads of people were dancing and kissing – it was as if we were serving love potion, not wine! Can you believe Angie and Alex? It's just like Donna and Sam in the movie – back together after all these years.

'Oh Athena,' she continued, the joy of the evening returning to her bones. 'There's so much to live for – the villa, your friends, and . . . and . . . well, you just get better. There's some surprises in store for you, wonderful surprises. I promise you. None more wonderful than—'

Laurel froze, aware that she'd almost divulged Helena's secret. As she sat there she felt the tiniest squeeze of her hand.

'Athena?' she said. 'Did you hear me?'

Again, she felt a minuscule movement.

'That's right,' she said. 'You get better. There's still so much you have to do, I promise.'

28

Laurel sat with Athena through the night, only going back to the villa when Nikos returned to the medical centre.

'How is she?' asked Helena, in the kitchen, from which she had somehow managed to remove every sign of yesterday's party preparations. Laurel figured she'd been up all night cleaning and worrying.

'She's stable,' said Laurel, 'but she's not out of the woods yet.'

Helena stopped wiping the marble. 'What does that mean?'

'It means we could still lose her,' said Laurel, as gently as the words would allow.

Helena, dumbfounded by what she'd just heard, absently wrapped the cloth tightly round her hand. 'What would I do without her?'

'Hopefully it won't come to that,' said Laurel, pulling up a stool, exhausted by the night. She knew exactly what Helena was feeling – Laurel hadn't been able to fathom a life without Marnie either, and now, faced with the loss of Athena, those feelings felt as raw as the night Marnie died. 'We'll find out later this morning if they need to transfer her to the mainland. If they don't then that's good news.'

'So we just have to wait?' Helena asked, who'd begun mindlessly cracking eggs into a bowl.

'That's all we can do.'

As Helena beat the eggs Laurel laid her head on her arms on the smooth wooden surface and drifted into sleep. She dreamt of Marnie and Athena sitting on Marnie's old velvet sofa on the beach below the villa. Laurel served them ouzo and orange, and they laughed merrily at old memories, but whenever Laurel tried to speak to them her words disappeared.

Helena placed an omelette in front of Laurel, which jolted her awake.

'You should eat,' she said. 'Keep up your strength.'

'Yes,' said Laurel, trying to shake off the dream, which had felt as real as Helena standing opposite her. She tried to convince herself that it was only a dream and not as it felt, like a sign that Athena had passed and joined Marnie in heaven. She picked at her omelette, unable to eat for the heavy feeling of grief in her stomach.

'Was Nikos with Athena?' asked Helena.

'He was there when I got there last night,' she said, absently. 'And he arrived to see her early this morning.'

'Did he say anything?'

Laurel chased away the haunting feeling of the dream and did her best to focus on Helena. 'You mean did he say anything about you and Yanni?'

Helena looked over the top of her coffee cup and nodded.

'He was in shock.' Laurel saw Helena's face drop. 'He didn't have much to say about anything,' she added, hoping to soften the disappointment.

'What do I do?'

'You have to let him cool off,' said Laurel. 'You told him something life-changing; he needs time to process it. Plus he's dealing with the shock of Athena.'

'I understand, I am too. I'm just worried I've ruined everything.' She sat down and cupped her mug. 'At least the way things were we had a friendship after years of not having one. What if I've destroyed it again? What if I've chased him away, this time for good?'

'I doubt you have,' said Laurel, reaching out a hand to her across the table. 'It might take a while, but in the long term Yanni's more likely to bring you closer together than drive you apart.'

'Do you think?' Helena searched Laurel's eyes for an answer.

'I do,' she said, nodding. 'The truth will set you free.'

Helena thought about that and relaxed a little. 'I hope so.'

'I know so,' said Laurel, remembering how often Marnie had said it to her in her lifetime – as a young child when she was learning right from wrong; as a teenager when she'd been asked to lie by a friend; and in her twenties when she was having relationship problems – and how Marnie had always been proved right. 'Did you have a nice time chatting with Theo?'

Helena blushed.

'Helena?' she teased, glad to be lightening the moment.

'I've known Theo all my life – we went to school together.'

'And?'

'And I hadn't seen him in years, not since before Yanni, so . . .' Helena's eyes smiled, which made Laurel smile. 'We had a lot of catching up to do.'

'Catching up?'

Helena closed her eyes for a moment, bashfully.

'Maybe I wish for a little more than catching up,' she confessed, her eyes sparkling. 'But for now I must settle with that.'

'Are you going to see him again?'

'I think so.'

'Sounds encouraging,' said Laurel, happy to have some positive news, which Athena would want more than anyone.

Exhausted by the last twelve hours, Laurel flopped down on her bed and allowed herself to close her eyes for just a minute. She woke several hours later to the sound of voices from the courtyard.

She trudged groggily outside to find Chris and Angie moving the tables and chairs back into the outhouse, Mark taking down lights, Helena gathering up table-cloths, and Emily putting candles into crates. Laurel loved the clean-up after an event as much as she enjoyed the preparations. The setting up was so much harder to enjoy with the anxiety about whether everything would turn out all right or not. Clearing up was much more enjoyable – everyone had had fun, the memories of the night were absorbed into the walls, wine stains on tablecloths held stories, even sweeping up broken glass and cigarette butts spoke of happiness and laughter. And while Laurel longed to see the courtyard alive again it was also wonderful to see it full of her friends helping her out, she wished desperately that Athena was there to see it too.

'You shouldn't have started without me,' she said, feeling guilty that they'd been working when she'd been sleeping. She began folding tablecloths.

'You're right, we should have left it all up to you!' laughed Chris, walking backwards, carrying a table with Angie. Chris's hair was a mess – evidence that he'd slept soundly and couldn't be bothered to shower after working so hard yesterday.

'Ignore him,' chuckled Emily, who had neatly gathered up all the candles and was putting them away according to size. 'We're glad to help. How's Athena?'

Laurel explained to all of them as she had to Helena.

'This holiday's thrown more at you than you bargained for,' said Angie, giving Laurel a hug.

'You could say that.'

Laurel thought back to her first day when everything had been so unfamiliar but exciting. Athena had seemed strange and unyielding, she'd known nobody other than Angie, and had no hope of a romance. And now here she was beside herself with worry for the fate of her dear friend but with new friends to help her through, *and* an unresolved romance hanging over her. The holiday couldn't have thrown more at her if it had tried.

'You'll be needing another holiday after this one,' said Emily.

'You'd think that would be the case but . . .' Laurel trailed off, drifting into thoughts of planning another party and feeling the same energy and warm glow she'd felt when it was in full flow with everyone so happy and content. She felt as though she'd been a fairy godmother for a night, sprinkling all the guests with magic dust. And it wasn't the same as it was at work, creating soulless corporate events or extravagant weddings. This had been different – intimate, welcoming. Laurel had let Villa Athena shine, and she had added something more to it, something of herself. And she realised that this was what she wanted to do – not tick off boxes while organising a trade event for some business group or another, but to make people happy, truly happy. 'I wish I could stay forever.'

'So does Angie,' chuckled Chris.

'Oh yeah!' said Laurel, who observed that Angie still had traces of last night's make-up on, though she had changed her clothes, suggesting she'd been back to her hotel rather than Alex's place. Laurel wondered if Alex had joined her. 'Spill the beans, Ang! What happened?'

Angie turned pink.

'She's blushing!' cried Chris. Angie purposefully pushed the table they were moving a little harder to cause him to stumble. 'Oi!'

'Serves you right!'

'Come on, Ang,' said Laurel, enjoying the banter, despite Athena's plight hanging over her. 'Tell us!'

'We had a very nice time,' Angie said. 'He was the perfect gentleman.'

'That means you didn't—' laughed Chris.

'Chris!' shouted Emily.

Chris recoiled playfully.

'And did you agree to spend some more time together?' asked Laurel.

'We did,' she smiled, still blushing. 'He's taking me out to dinner this evening.'

'I'm so pleased,' said Laurel, brimming with delight for her friend. It seemed unthinkable that just over a week ago they'd met on the plane for the first time. If someone had told Laurel then that Angie would become a friend for life, Laurel would have been hard pressed to believe them, but now she couldn't imagine life without her.

'So that only leaves you,' said Helena, turning quietly to Laurel. 'Did you get a chance to speak to Mark?'

Laurel looked to Mark, still up the ladder removing all the lights, and thought of the hug he'd given her last night.

'Sort of,' she said, wondering what he'd meant when he'd said he was sorry. Did he mean that he was sorry about Athena, or sorry for his silence?

'What did he say?'

'Nothing, really.' Laurel thought about their chat in the office. 'He just muttered something about how lightning always strikes twice.'

'Weird!'

'Right,' said Laurel, laughing it off. 'That's what I thought.'

'Men!' scoffed Helena, not very convincingly.

'Maybe Donna had the right idea, living so long without one.'

'Can't live with 'em . . .'

'Can't live without 'em!' they laughed in unison.

Laurel put her arm around Helena. 'Everything will work out in the end for both us, you'll see.'

'And if it doesn't?'

'Then it isn't the end,' said Laurel, with a light shrug.

Helena looked puzzled. 'How do you mean?'

'Even if this door closes, another will open,' she said, quoting another of Marnie's favourite sayings.

'That's what I love about you,' said Helena, smiling at her friend. 'You always see the positive in any situation.'

'I try,' said Laurel, thinking of Mark, but failing to see where they could go from here.

29

The medical centre felt less intimidating in the warm light of day than it had in the dead of night, when the dread of Athena's fate had hung heavily in the air. But still Laurel entered full of trepidation as to what she might be told about Athena.

'Hello,' she called out, when she found no one at reception. She lingered by the desk, listening for signs of where someone might be, for a sign that told her Athena was still there and doing okay.

'Hello,' she called again, wondering if she was allowed to enter the small ward without permission. The truth was Laurel didn't want to go through without first seeing the doctor; she was too afraid of what she might find: Athena in distress, Athena having been transferred to the mainland because her condition had deteriorated since Laurel left her in the early hours or, worst of all, Athena having passed away. All the distraction of her friends and tidying up after the party had failed to quash her sense of fear that she might still lose Athena. The thought was suffocating.

Laurel was about to call out again when a young male doctor came through. He wore a white coat over his scrubs and had dark spectacles, which added gravitas to his youthful eyes.

'Hi,' she said, tensely. 'I'm Laurel, Athena's—'

Fortunately the doctor answered before Laurel had to explain about not being a family member. 'Nikos told me you'd be coming,' he said, reaching for a clipboard on the desk.

'How is she?'

'She's not out of danger yet.'

'How do you mean?' Laurel asked, concerned the doctor may be eluding to bigger, more catastrophic episodes to come.

'For Athena to make any kind of recovery, she's going to have to give up work entirely – if she doesn't, the damage will be irreversible.'

'I understand,' said Laurel, who knew too well the impact stubbornness can have on health. She had wondered many times if Marnie had done less sooner if her life might have been prolonged. 'But for now, she could make some kind of recovery?'

The doctor nodded, Laurel's eyes brimmed with tears.

'Thank you!'

'You're welcome. At this stage there's no need to transfer her but you must ensure she has complete rest.'

On the ward Laurel found Athena, her eyes closed, propped up against the pillows, her dark grey hair spread out over them; she looked small.

'Hi,' said Laurel, gently, sitting beside her.

She sat quietly, tidying Athena's long hair, uncertain if she was able to speak or even hear her. The clock on the wall ticked noisily into the room. Eventually Athena's eyes opened.

'Laurel,' she said, inching her head just a fraction towards Laurel. The strength of her voice was missing but there was something of its playful tone remaining.

'How are you feeling?' Laurel whispered.

Athena didn't respond straight away, causing Laurel to wonder if more significant damage had occurred. When she did reply she spoke slowly, one side of her face weaker than the other, and with a slight slur. 'As if I've been hit by a train!'

Laurel let out the greatest laugh of relief of her life and with it came tears – to know Athena's sense of humour was still intact told Laurel everything she needed to know.

'You're going to be fine,' she said, squeezing Athena's hand, which felt so frail it was almost brittle. Only her eyes had any of their usual vitality and even that was just the faintest glimmer.

'It was a close call,' she said, exhausted by those five words.

'A bit too close,' said Laurel, recalling the events of the previous night, and that awful feeling of panic and fear and complete and utter helplessness that she'd felt too soon after Marnie.

They sat and waited while Athena gathered enough energy to speak.

'Nikos says you got me here,' said Athena, painfully slow in her delivery.

'I'd say Alex was the hero of the day. He's the one

who got you here in time for the medicine to be administered.'

'Hah!' laughed Athena, weakly, stopping again for several seconds 'I'm indebted to him, am I?'

'I'm afraid so,' laughed Laurel. 'Though I don't think he's going to be too concerned – he and Angie got together at the party!'

'Ugh.' Athena attempted a wry smile, which came over more as a grimace. 'I miss all the fun.'

'I wish you hadn't missed it,' said Laurel, watching her recover from the energy she'd expended in simply speaking. 'Everyone had such a good time. The food was amazing and everyone danced into the small hours.'

'Like old times . . .' she said, her voice trailing off.

Laurel poured a glass of water from the tray on the bedside cabinet, and placed the straw between Athena's lips. She took the smallest of sips and lay back, depleted.

'Thank you,' she said, her eyes full of gratitude. 'Without you, I—'

'Best not to talk just now,' said Laurel, not wanting to face up to what might have happened if she hadn't found her, the thought was too dreadful to bear. 'You need every scrap of energy you can muster to beat this.'

'I can't manage the villa,' she said, catching Laurel off-guard – she hadn't expected the doctor to have spoken to Athena in such blatant terms or for Athena to have processed it so soon. It reminded Laurel of the same transition she'd been through with Marnie, from denial to acceptance, and the changes they had to put in place.

'The doctor suggested as much.'

Athena looked at the ceiling, her eyes searching for something she couldn't find the answer to. 'What am I going to do?'

'Worrying about it won't help,' said Laurel, stroking her hand. 'For now there's me, Nikos and Helena. We'll manage.'

Athena swallowed painfully. 'But you'll go home; Helena can't manage, she's got Yanni, and besides . . .'

'You'd have been proud of her last night,' said Laurel, wanting to fight Helena's corner. 'She stepped in for Nikos in the kitchen when he had to leave, everything was done beautifully.' She purposefully neglected to mention that Helena had been the cause of Nikos leaving in the first place.

'But some things can't be overlooked,' said Athena, lacking her usual conviction.

'Well . . .' Laurel wondered if Athena remembered anything of what she had said to her last night, in the dark hours of the medical centre before dawn. 'I'm sure Nikos will want to stay until you've a plan in place.'

'Yes,' said Athena, marginally more brightly. 'I'm sure he will look after the villa now.'

Laurel worried that Athena was clutching at straws. Having spent time with Nikos she felt confident that he wouldn't want to take over the villa, particularly now that things were so up in the air between him and Helena, but she hated to share her doubts with Athena when she was so vulnerable and frail. She was more than aware how any setback could impact on her health.

'Let's see how the next few days go,' she said, buoying Athena's spirits with further tales of the party.

Helena arrived a little while later when Athena was sleeping, with a basket of leftovers from the party.

'How is she?' she asked, visibly shocked to see Athena in a hospital bed.

'She's not great,' said Laurel, not wanting to sugar the pill. 'She knows she won't be able to run the villa again.'

Helena's face fell. 'But what will she do?'

Laurel thought how typically sweet it was of Helena to think of others before herself. After all, if the villa was to close Helena would lose her job.

'I told her not to worry,' said Laurel. 'That you and Nikos and I would help as much as possible.'

'What did she say?'

'She said she doesn't feel comfortable with you taking on so much responsibility.' Laurel left the wording loose to avoid any personal attack on Helena. 'But—' she continued, a thought forming, 'perhaps if she knew Yanni was her great-grandson she might see things in a slightly different light.'

'It's worth a shot, don't you think?'

'I do,' said Laurel, hoping that the timing wasn't completely wrong.

Laurel and Helena sat with Athena for the next few hours. They flicked through magazines and chattered, Laurel told her that Athena had mentioned the idea of Nikos running the villa and how she was worried Nikos wouldn't be interested.

'We'll see,' said Helena as Athena began to stir.

Laurel held her hand and told her they were there.

'Do you feel able to eat?' Helena asked, when Athena had come round fully from her sleep.

'Depends what it is,' said Athena, dryly.

'It's okay,' laughed Helena. 'I brought moussaka, made to your recipe.'

'It was the dish of the night.'

'My moussaka is legendary!'

Helena and Laurel moved her into a sitting position.

'Athena,' said Laurel, as Helena fed her a small mouthful of food. 'How many great-grandchildren do you have?'

She ate slowly and on one side of her mouth. 'None.'

'Right,' said Laurel, offering her a sip of water from the straw. 'Or rather . . . wrong.'

'Laurel,' she said, as if it was Laurel who'd had the blood shortage to her brain. 'What *are* you talking about?'

'I'm talking about the fact you already have a great-grandchild.'

Athena looked confused.

'Helena,' said Laurel. 'Why don't you tell her?'

Helena put down the plate on the bedside cabinet and held Athena's hand.

'Athena,' she took a deep breath, glancing to Laurel to ensure it was still the right time to tell. Laurel gave a nod of approval. 'Yanni is Nikos's son.'

A silence filled the small room. Athena sat motionless. Stunned.

Laurel wasn't sure how to gauge Athena's reaction,

and for a split second she worried that she should call the doctor.

'Yanni is your great-grandson,' said Helena, in case Athena hadn't got it.

Athena closed her eyes, and when she spoke, she spoke even more slowly than she had been doing.

'Ho-ly Mo-ses,' she said.

Laurel and Helena's eyes met across the bed with looks of confusion.

'Athena,' asked Laurel, concerned that the shock might have been too much. 'Do you feel okay?'

'I knew it!' she cried – as emphatically as she was able to – a large, lop-sided smile forming on her face.

'What did you know?' asked Helena, both she and Laurel taken aback by Athena's reaction.

Athena turned fractionally towards Helena and reached out a hand to hers. 'That you weren't capable of an affair!'

Helena brushed a crumb off her cardigan as if to brush away offence. 'You don't mind that I lied?' she said, a little bemused.

Athena thought about it.

'No!' she cried. 'You did it for Nikos, right?'

'Right,' said Helena, incredulous that Athena should understand her motivation without any explanation. 'That's exactly why I did it.'

Athena sank further into her pillows, tiring.

'He must be spitting nails.'

'I think he's probably on emotional overload,' said Laurel. 'And I also think he's more likely to listen to you than to Helena or me.'

267

'Don't worry,' she said, her eyes beginning to close, 'I'll talk him round.' As she fell asleep she laughed lightly and mumbled, 'I knew there was something special about Yanni!'

30

'What a beautiful way to spend a morning,' said Laurel, standing at the bow of Alex's old-fashioned sailboat. Alex had helped Chris moor it next to a small bay with a deserted, crescent beach. It took Laurel's breath away.

'Isn't it heavenly?' replied Angie, who was reclining up front, looking quite at home with her newfound status as lady of the yacht. 'I think we've earned it after the events of the last few days. And it's not long now until we all head off. Best to enjoy it while we can.'

'When we first arrived I thought you were mad to come to the same place every summer,' said Laurel. 'But now *I* wonder how I'll ever leave.'

Laurel tried not to think about the fact that in forty-eight hours she'd be waiting at the airport for her flight back to London, and all this beauty wouldn't be hers to enjoy any more.

She watched Theo and Yanni doing cannonballs off the side into the warm sea, delighting in their joy, and thinking how lucky they were that they didn't have to leave; that they didn't have to think about the Tube, and the noise, and the pollution of London, and returning to an empty flat, with two weeks' worth of junk mail clogging up the entrance.

'What you talk about?' asked Alex, taking round a tray of drinks he'd brought up from the galley.

'About how beautiful Skopelos is.' Angie received her drink with a kiss.

'Nowhere like it in world,' he said, handing Laurel hers then going to offer Emily and Helena who were sunbathing on the cushioned seating at the stern. Chris and Mark were familiarising themselves with the boat's rigging system.

'You might be right,' she whispered, gazing out at the water bobbing gently around them, losing herself in the sway, and thinking of all the fun she'd had these last few weeks, the friends she'd made, and the lessons she'd learned.

Angie drank her champagne. 'It certainly beats London.'

'That's for sure.' Laurel sat down beside her, pushing the thought of leaving out of her mind. She was determined not to let anything spoil what may be her last morning with her new friends. 'Are you still heading back to Newcastle?'

'Of course!' laughed Angie, incredulous that Laurel should ask.

'I just thought, with Alex and you—'

'Steady!'

'You're happy to do the long-distance thing?'

'For now I'm happy to do the "taking-it-slow" thing!'

'Ah, so no plans for another wedding in the chapel at Kastri yet?' she said, tongue-in-cheek.

Angie laughed. 'I'll let you know when to go hat shopping!'

'Make sure you do!'

'I'll make the dress code straw hats and dungarees!'

'Deal!' They laughed together.

'Angie?' said Emily, joining them. 'Can I ask you a question?'

Laurel looked up at Emily, cupping her hand over her eyes to shield the glare of the sun. 'Is it gynaecological?'

Emily nodded with an apologetic look.

'Mind if I duck away? I'm all medicine-ed out for one holiday.'

'Completely understand,' said Emily. 'If I wasn't so totally pregnant I'd be saying the same!'

Laurel left them and joined Helena, who immediately got up, saying, 'I might prepare the picnic. Chris, can you help me?' She pretty much dragged him below deck by the hand.

'Subtle as a Greek wedding,' said Mark, the two of them left alone.

'She knows it's time we talked,' Laurel said.

Mark sat next to Laurel, which felt oddly intimate, despite the fact that only a few days ago they'd been naked together. 'Do you want to go first?'

Laurel looked into his soft, dark eyes. 'Only to say how sorry I am, and that I genuinely didn't encourage Nikos to kiss me – he just—' She made a lurching action.

Mark laughed, wryly. 'The guy certainly doesn't lack self-confidence.'

'Right. The thought crossed my mind that he may be under some kind of Greek god delusion.'

They both laughed, which felt good to Laurel, and she felt herself relax. 'I never meant to hurt you. It's the last thing I ever wanted to do.'

He reached out and gently rubbed the top of her arm. 'I believe you.'

They sat quietly, leisurely in the sun, reminding her of their day on the beach together.

'Is there anything you want to say?'

Mark stretched an arm out along the back of the seat, a little behind Laurel. She felt the desire to snuggle up beside him but didn't. 'I'm sorry I've been so quiet. I tend to go into myself when I've something to work out.'

'Were you trying to work out why I kissed Nikos?'

He shook his head.

Laurel felt a little foolish that she'd been so egotistical as to think his reticence had been all about her.

Mark released a long sigh. 'The break-up I told you about wasn't just a girlfriend – she was my fiancée.'

'Oh, that's awful.'

'And that's not the worst of it,' said Mark. 'This was meant to be our honeymoon.'

'Oh God. What happened?'

He paused, a look of sadness on his face. 'I found her with another guy.'

The thing Mark had said in the office came straight

back to Laurel like the final piece of a puzzle. 'Lightning strikes twice.'

'Right, except they were doing more than just kissing . . .'

Laurel reached out a hand to him. 'No wonder you went into yourself.'

'I should have said something but, I don't know, I just threw myself into work.'

'Of course.' Laurel nodded her head. 'I completely understand.'

'But I shouldn't have allowed anything to happen between us that I knew I wasn't ready for. I just . . .' Mark paused, looking at Laurel as if she was a jar full of sweets he wasn't allowed. 'I couldn't resist you. And it's been great fun getting to know you; it helped me push Imogen to the back of my mind, you know? I had a bit of a breather from the reality of it all.

'But then, seeing you and Nikos together – it brought all my memories crashing down on me like a sledge-hammer and I needed time to sort it out.'

'And have you?'

Mark gave it some thought. 'I guess I have. Imogen sleeping with someone else was a symptom of something being wrong in our relationship, and I suppose I was the thing that was wrong. I was absorbed in my work, I didn't pay her nearly enough attention. If I had, I probably wouldn't be sitting here now.'

'So . . .' said Laurel, wondering where all of this left her.

'And then there's us,' he said, as if reading her mind.

Mark looked at her affectionately and, with a sparkle in his eye, said, 'I had such a great time with you at the beach.'

Laurel felt her cheeks redden at the memory.

'You were exactly the medicine I needed.'

'But . . .' she said for him, hearing it in his voice, preparing herself for what she was about to hear.

'But I don't think it would be fair to get together before I've resolved everything back home.'

Laurel gulped back a wave of disappointment but tried hard not to show it.

'Are you okay?'

It surprised Laurel when she realised that she was okay, that there was no big drama, life would go on. 'You know, I am.'

'You are?' he said, with a smile of relief.

She smiled back. 'The idea of a relationship with you here, cocooned on the island, is a *really* nice one. But the reality beyond these two weeks is very different. You have your life; I have mine. And the truth is that the idea of going back to London kills me, especially with Athena being as unwell as she is.'

'Do you think you might stay on a little longer?'

'I don't know that I can,' said Laurel, who hadn't thought about it up until that point. 'I've a job, and a particularly tricky boss but . . .'

'If there's a will, there's a way.'

Laurel wondered if it was even remotely possible that

she might stay a little longer until she was confident Athena was well enough to be left on her own.

'I'd love to hook up when you're back, as friends – who knows how things might develop,' said Mark.

Laurel thought it sweet that Mark was trying to make things easy on her. 'I'm not sure false hope is the thing I need in my life right now.'

'No, fair point,' he said, seemingly amused by Laurel's pragmatism. 'So what do we do?'

'Recognise we had fun and leave it at that?'

'No regrets?'

'None at all,' she smiled, leaning over to kiss him on the cheek, knowing this would probably be the last time she'd see him.

Laurel closed her eyes and let the warmth of the sun spread over her face. They sat enjoying the movement of the boat and the sound of the boys playing. Helena came back up with a tray of food.

'Watching Theo with Yanni is too cute for words,' said Laurel.

Helena looked over to her son climbing up the ladder on the side of the boat and bombing straight back into the sea, aiming at Theo, who roared in mock-outrage. 'I've never seen him have so much fun.'

'Does Theo know about Nikos?'

Helena nodded, as Mark went below deck to see Chris. 'I thought it best to be honest from the start. And I don't think Nikos would mind him knowing; they're good friends.'

'The start?'

Helena's cheeks flushed. 'If anything *should* happen between us, it's best to be honest right away, isn't it?'

'The truth will set you free!' trilled Laurel, her eyes glinting.

'I just hope Nikos sees it that way.'

'He will.'

'You think he'll stay and run the villa for Athena?'

'I don't know,' said Laurel, not wanting to give Helena too much hope. 'But I'm certain he'll want to be a father to Yanni. Would you want him to take over the villa?'

Helena put down the tray and sat next to Laurel. 'I'm not sure. If he did it would be weird, us working together, but not as a couple as I once imagined we would. But then again, if he didn't, the villa would have to close.' It was clear from the look of sorrow in Helena's eyes what losing the villa would mean to her.

'The only way we'll know is to talk to him,' said Laurel, supportively. 'Why don't we go visit Athena this afternoon when he's there?'

'You think he's ready to hear me out?'

Laurel shrugged. 'We'll never know unless we try.'

As they were talking Yanni, soaking wet and beaming all over, came charging up to Helena. 'Mama, mama!' he called, dragging her up. 'You come!'

'Oh no – no way!' said Helena, sinking her heels into the deck. 'I am not being a human cannonball!'

'Why not?' laughed Laurel.

Helena looked at her as if she were mad. 'You want to do it?'

'Sure – if you do!'

Helena closed her eyes and shook her head, allowing herself to be led by Yanni, who climbed onto the side of the yacht and bombed in with an enormous, SPLOOSH!

'Go, Helena!' chanted Theo from the water, as Yanni bobbed up to the surface, wiping his eyes and nose and shaking his head like a dog.

'Yeah, Helena,' yelled Chris. 'Go on!'

Helena climbed onto the side, held her nose and prepared to jump, then she chickened out.

'Rubbish!' bellowed Chris. Mark, Emily and Angie came up behind him to see what was going on.

Laurel climbed up beside Helena and held her hand. 'Come on. Let's do it on three. Ready?'

Helena nodded.

'One, two – THREE! CANNON-BALLLLL!!!!'

Together they leapt off the side of the boat, raising their knees to their chests and crashing into the water with an almighty SPLASH! For the split second that they were underwater Laurel opened her eyes and saw Helena swimming towards the surface, a huge smile on her face – for a brief moment she looked entirely free of her worries. She looked as Laurel felt.

Laurel emerged gasping for air, and reached for Helena, exhilarated. From the deck Emily and Angie cheered and clapped and whistled before Chris leapt to the side and plunged in beside them.

'You did it!' Laurel beamed, the two of them swimming side by side back to the boat, Laurel reflecting on what a lovely, loyal friend Helena had become, almost like a sister.

31

'You're wasting your time,' said Nikos, as soon as Laurel and Helena entered the ward. Laurel saw immediately that Athena was a little stronger, sitting up with less support from her pillows. She still wasn't anywhere near her old self, but the improvement was noticeable, and dramatic, compared to how she had been when she was first admitted. It gave Laurel hope that there would be many more years in Athena yet.

'We just popped in to see how Athena's getting on,' said Laurel, trying to play down their visit but knowing she was fooling no one. She and Helena drew up chairs beside the bed.

Nikos raised his brow and said testingly, 'So you won't mind if I leave then?'

Athena reached out, putting her hand over his wrist. She wasn't strong enough to physically restrain him but her intention was clear. 'Not so fast, Nikos.'

Nikos released a resigned sigh, unable to disrespect his grandmother's wishes.

'Nikos,' said Athena, in a tone usually reserved for explaining complicated issues to small children. 'You're a father!'

Nikos eyed her moodily.

'Do you hear me,' she said, smiling, placing her hand on his forearm and attempting to give it a squeeze and a shake. 'You're a father!'

'Apparently I've been a father for four years,' he said, looking at Helena, who, rather than lowering her head in shame, cast him a look that said, 'get over yourself'.

'Yes, you have,' said Athena, reading the vibe between Nikos and Helena and taking on the uncharacteristic role of adjudicator. 'You've already lost precious time, so I suggest you don't waste any more sitting here moping!'

Laurel sat back, not certain if Athena's gung-ho tactics were going to work; Helena chewed a fingernail. Nikos fiddled with his charity rubber wristband.

'It's not that simple,' he said.

'Why not?'

'Because most guys get nine months to figure out how to be a father. I get what, two days?'

Athena laughed. 'Nobody's expecting you to know how to be a father straightaway! First you just need to be open to the *idea* of being a father.'

Nikos lowered his head and roughly ruffled his hair as if it might somehow shake all his thoughts into place. 'I don't know.'

'Nikos!' said Athena, as sharply as she was able. 'Were you raised to be defeatist, to turn your back on difficulty?'

'No,' he mumbled.

Laurel couldn't help but chuckle at the way he had regressed into his teenage self.

'Then speak to Helena – the one person in the world,

outside of family, you've loved all your life. Honestly, Nikos – if you're to be a father surely the one person you'd want on that journey is Helena. Now get up and talk to her!'

Nikos, obeying his grandmother, offered his hand to Helena and together they went outside. From the ward window Athena and Laurel could see the two of them pacing the pretty courtyard garden.

'What do you think?' Laurel asked, offering Athena a drink of water. 'You think they'll work it out.'

'Of course,' she said, watching her grandson. 'Nikos may come across as arrogant and self-centred but at his core is a loving, family man.'

'It might be too much to expect them to get back together though,' said Laurel, who saw that both Helena and Nikos were strolling in a more relaxed, unguarded fashion – bodies turning in, arms at their sides.

'I doubt he'll want that after the trust has been broken but he'll want to be involved with Yanni, I can guarantee it.'

Athena and Laurel sat and watched for a half hour or so, Athena drifting in and out of sleep, before Nikos and Helena returned. When they did, Nikos had his hand on Helena's shoulder.

'So?' asked Athena.

'So I'll give the dad thing a go.'

'Oh goodie,' said Athena, a smile of joy spreading across her face. Laurel hoped it was all the medicine she needed to recover.

'That's great news,' said Laurel, hugging them both.

'But I need time to decide on what terms – I still want to travel.'

They sat by Athena's bedside a while longer, chatting excitedly about Yanni until Athena grew too tired.

'Do you want us to go?' asked Laurel.

'In a moment. First I want to share something of my own.'

Laurel and Helena exchanged looks of intrigue and concern.

'What is it, Yaya?'

Athena looked pensive. 'I haven't told you the truth about why I've been reluctant to have Helena help in the kitchen.'

'Oh?' said Laurel, looking to Helena, who was watching Athena keenly if a little nervously.

Athena turned to her. 'I told you it's because you haven't the time and that you have other duties.' She looked down, twiddling the cover on her bed. 'I even told Laurel I didn't want you having new skills in case you left me. And while all of those are true, none are the *real* reason.'

'What is the real reason?' asked Laurel.

'The truth is that the episodes I've been having have, gradually, over the years, caused me to lose my sense of taste and smell, that's why I didn't notice the pan burning, why the food hasn't changed, and why much of the business has dropped off – I've haven't been able to keep up with changing tastes.'

Athena took Helena's hand. 'It was injured pride that stopped me from giving you the chance you deserve.

282

I hope you can forgive me. Of course you must take on more responsibility in the kitchen, if you would like to.'

Laurel let out a long breath, relieved to finally know the whole truth.

'I'd love that,' said Helena, beaming. 'And of course I forgive you. I only hope that you can forgive me. I'm sorry I kept the truth about Yanni from you for such a long time. I wanted to tell you desperately but I couldn't. I had to do what was right for Nikos, and I knew pursuing his dream was the right thing.'

'You've been entirely selfless,' said Athena, brushing Helena's cheek. 'I'm sorry I judged you and treated you harshly, that wasn't fair of me.'

'I understand,' said Helena, her eyes watering with tears of joy and relief. 'I'm just so happy you know now.'

Athena stroked her hair.

'I hate to interrupt all this forgiveness,' said Nikos, 'but jeez, Yaya – why would you keep this from me?'

'Because,' said Athena, 'like Helena, I didn't want you feeling any sense of pressure to return to the island. But now . . .'

'What?' he asked, his defensiveness back with a vengeance. 'Now that I'm a father I should stay?'

'I don't think that's what Athena is saying,' Laurel said, sensing neither Nikos nor Athena needed any more stress in their life right now.

'I'm just asking you to think about it,' said Athena, reaching out and taking his hand. 'Whatever you decide will have my blessing.'

Laurel ate out with Helena and returned to the villa late in the evening to find the lights on in the sitting room.

'Hi,' she said, when she found Nikos in there nursing a Scotch on the rocks.

'Hey.'

'You look as if you've the weight of the world on your shoulders.' She took a seat in the chair opposite him, curling up as if at home.

Nikos let out a wry laugh. 'I've never felt so unsure of what to do.'

'You've some tough choices to make.'

He took a swig of his drink. 'Tell me about it!'

'So, do you stay, or do you go?'

Nikos looked into his tumbler. 'Tell me if I've got this right: if I stay the villa remains open; if I go, it closes?'

Laurel nodded. 'That's about the long and the short of it.'

He looked up at her. 'So I either throw away Yaya's life's work, or I throw away a shot at my own?'

Put like that, Laurel could see the enormity of his dilemma. She tried to think of something to say that might help him.

'If you stay you get to be a father to Yanni.'

'And if I don't?'

284

'Then you'll still be a father to him, you'll just see your son less often.'

'So either way I get Yanni.' He tilted the tumbler from side to side making the ice clink.

'Right. So the only real decision is what to do about the villa.'

Nikos stared into space.

Laurel suddenly remembered a game she and Janey used to play when either one of them had conflicting feelings.

'Nikos, I'm going to ask you some questions and I don't want you to think about the answers, just tell me your immediate, un-censored responses. Got it?'

'Sure,' he shrugged, not seeing how it would help.

When Laurel spoke next she spoke quickly.

'Do you prefer coffee or tea?'

'Coffee.'

'Sex or chocolate?'

'Sex.'

'Would you rather stay or go.'

'Go.'

Nikos froze in surprise at his response then looked to Laurel as if she'd just handed him a winning lottery ticket.

'You see,' she laughed. 'That wasn't so hard.'

'But it's not that straightforward,' he said, his look of amazement fading.

'It is,' said Laurel, encouragingly. 'Athena wouldn't want you to throw away your dream for her. That's not who she is.'

'So I just throw away her dream instead?'

'It won't be her dream when she knows you'd be unhappy fulfilling it. She wants you to go out there and create your own corner of happiness, not live in hers.' Laurel thought of Marnie and of how she would have wanted the same for her: 'live your own life not someone else's' she used to tell her, time and time again.

'But I've so many memories tied into these bricks. I couldn't stand for Yaya to sell it and for me never to return, to not have a reason to come back to the island. I've always depended on Yaya and Skopelos being here for me.'

'But, Nikos,' said Laurel, knowing she had to be cruel to be kind, 'the truth is that Athena won't always be here. She *will* die one day. And what you have to figure out is will Skopelos still feel like home without her?'

Laurel thought of Marnie's beautiful home and the agonising she'd gone through trying to decide whether to keep it or part with it.

'I doubt it will.'

'So why take on the villa if it's only for Athena's lifetime? That doesn't make sense.'

'But it's the only real home I've ever known – I can't just throw that away.'

'It's home because Athena is here,' she said, Marnie foremost in her mind. 'When she's no longer here you'll have made a home for yourself elsewhere, and if you haven't, you will. Home isn't a building, it's where the people are whom you love.'

As she spoke the words to Nikos she realised why she was dreading returning to the UK. It wasn't because London was so terrible, it was because the one person in the world she loved with all her heart, the one person who made it home, was no longer there.

32

'So Nikos has gone, just like that?' asked Angie, the next day. Helena had prepared a beautiful last lunch for Laurel, Angie, Emily and Chris, and they were all greedily tucking in at a table on the patio.

'He'll be back,' said Laurel, helping herself to a salad with feta and pomegranates that looked like little red jewels. 'He said goodbye to Athena; she understands.'

'Does this mean Athena's out of the woods?' asked Emily, rubbing the top of her bump, which now looked uncomfortably large.

'It looks that way.'

Laurel had visited her that morning to check she was okay after Nikos had been to say goodbye. She had found Athena in good spirits and feeling considerably stronger.

'She wasn't upset?'

'Maybe a little disappointed. But she knows she can't manage alone and she doesn't want to quash Nikos's dreams – what choice does she have?'

'And what about you, Helena?' asked Angie. 'How do you feel about this?'

'He came by to explain, and I've managed this far,' she smiled. 'I know he'll help out when he can.'

'I think it's a brave choice that he's made,' said Laurel, thinking about a possible choice of her own. 'It's not an easy option to leave everything that's so familiar in the hope of discovering something of your own.'

'That's true,' said Emily. 'But what will happen if Athena sells the villa?'

Helena shook her head with a shrug. '*Que sera.*'

Laurel rubbed Helena's arm, knowing Helena's real fears about losing her job.

'Nikos has agreed to help financially with Yanni, so if the worst comes to the worst at least I won't have to worry about my boy.'

'That's something at least,' said Angie.

'Yes,' said Helena replenishing everyone's glasses with the sharp cherry juice she'd made that morning. 'Now, tell me about you and Alex.'

Angie flushed then giggled. 'Are you sure you want to know?'

'Go on, Angie!' laughed Chris, polishing off a chicken thigh.

'Well, what can I tell you?' she said, scrunching her hair. 'The older man is quite the revelation!'

'Argh!' squealed Laurel, getting up to hug her friend. '*It* happened?'

'*It* sure did!'

'Well, thank God for that,' said Chris, wiping his mouth with a large napkin.

'Chris!'

'What?! It was like waiting for a baby to be born – it took an eternity.'

'Don't listen to him – we're really happy for you. But, talking of babies being born, we've decided to call our holiday short by a few days.'

'Why?' asked Laurel.

'The Braxton Hicks haven't gone so we'd prefer to be back home; it feels a bit risky to stay much longer.'

Angie smiled sympathetically at Emily. 'It's the right decision, pet.'

Laurel sat back down and thought about how different this stage in her life was to the one Emily was in. She couldn't help wonder if now was the time that she should be taking risks, just as Emily found herself in a time when she shouldn't. And then there was Nikos, following his heart and dreams, searching for something of his own, rather than the safety net of his grandmother.

'I'll miss you,' said Laurel, hugging Emily.

'We can see each other back home. Come and visit us when the baby's born!'

'Deal,' said Laurel, who had a creeping feeling that, in this instance, she may not be true to her word . . .

'Are you really sure you're okay about Nikos leaving?' Laurel asked Helena in the kitchen, once Alex had collected Angie, and Chris and Emily.

'I'm okay,' she said, cleaning the fridge shelves – a job Laurel didn't think she would be doing if she was uncertain about the future of her job. 'It's more the regret of not telling the truth about Yanni years ago. If Athena had known from the start she might have allowed me to work in the kitchen, and I might now have something better on my CV.'

'So you are worried about your future?'

'It's one thing not to have to worry about Yanni, but I still have to carve out something of my own.'

'I understand that,' said Laurel, knowing she must do the same for herself. 'Maybe things will develop between you and Theo – you guys might end up doing something together; your future might be completely different from how things are now.'

'I'm not sure I'd want it to be too different. I like life on the island – my family is here, it's a great home for Yanni – I'm not like Nikos, I don't need anything else.'

Helena's words chimed true with Laurel and a moment of realisation dawned on her.

'In which case,' she said, her mind buzzing with ideas. 'I may just have a plan of my own!'

Laurel sat on the beach below Villa Athena in the fading afternoon sun, feeling entirely at home, and asked herself, 'Should I stay, or should I go?'

She thought about the last two weeks, in which time so much had changed – she'd made new friends, had adventures and created enough memories to last a lifetime, she'd even had a little romance . . . but above all she'd navigated her way through the grief of losing Marnie, and had a new-found sense of direction.

'It's time you lived your own life, not someone else's,' she said, repeating her grandmother's words of wisdom.

'So what's it to be? Risk it all for the dream of Skopelos, or return to the safety of London?'

Never having made such an important life decision before Laurel turned for reassurance from her grandmother.

'Marnie,' she said, looking heavenwards. 'I've an idea you might be interested in. Can I share it with you?'

A warm gust of wind blew over Laurel and instinctively she felt Marnie was listening.

'I'm thinking about leaving London and using the inheritance to buy Villa Athena instead of a flat in Clapham. What do you think?'

Laurel listened to the rustle of the grasses on the cliff and the sea lapping on the sand.

'I know it's a bit out there but I've loved every minute of being here, even the bad ones. Throwing the party at the house made me realise that I don't need Jacqui and the hotel to do that, I can do it for myself – the dream of my own boutique hotel could be right here.'

She hesitated, and moved a stray hair away from her mouth.

'I know it's a risk financially, and I'd feel weird to leave the UK where we were always together but I'd always have my memories of you. I just thought it might bring me happiness in a way that finding a man and settling down in London might not. I'd be a bit like Donna – strong on her own without a man, until the right one comes along, if he ever does.

'But more than that, I have a feeling, a really strong

feeling that this is where I belong, even though I can't say exactly why.'

Gazing out to sea, Laurel began to hum, 'I Have A Dream'. She sat for some time singing to herself and thinking, trying not to focus on the uncertainties she had about investing her inheritance on what could turn out to be a pipe dream, and instead trying to pinpoint what the feeling was that she had about the place.

'Well, it's just a thought,' she said, looking out to the crimson sunset before closing up her deckchair to head inside. 'If you think it's a good one, maybe send me a sign?'

Her mind still in a muddle Laurel went back to the villa and took a tray of food upstairs to watch *Mamma Mia!*. If ever there was a moment that needed Meryl, she thought, this was it. On opening the bedside cabinet drawer Laurel found the letter from Marnie. She put her tray aside and sat down to read it again.

My Dearest Laurel,

I know when you receive the inheritance that you'll want to invest it carefully, probably in a place of your own. If I may be allowed one last request, I ask that you remember that a home is more than bricks and mortar, it is built on hopes and dreams and, most important of all, the love of those who fill it.

If your mother and father had been alive they'd have told you the same – their dream, was to live on the Greek island where they fell in love. They often spoke of their days there in a villa way off the beaten track, perched high on a cliff.

Follow your dreams, Laurel, and you will find where you belong.

Your loving grandmother,
Marnie x

P.S. Never forget the words of Christina Rossetti —
'Better by far you should forget and smile than that you should remember and be sad'.

Laurel read the second sentence of the second paragraph several times.

They often spoke of their days there in a villa way off the beaten track, perched high on a cliff.

'It can't be,' she said, recalling how Odele had spoken of Villa Athena's unique position on the island – 'so far off the track and overlooking the sea. There isn't another guest house like it on the island'. 'Surely they didn't stay on Skopelos, here at Villa Athena?'

Dropping the letter she ran downstairs to the office, telling herself the coincidence of her staying on the same island as her parents was too great, and certainly too big that they would have stayed in the same guest house. But pulled by an overwhelming feeling, she frantically scanned the walls for a picture of her parents. She looked everywhere, all of the faces blurring into one dizzy mass, and she found nothing.

'Of course they didn't stay here,' she said, feeling disappointed and foolish. She took down the photo of herself that Athena had taken at Glossa and looked at the version of herself she hadn't recognised that day – Skopelos Laurel, not London Laurel.

She was just about to head back upstairs to watch her DVD when she noticed that a party poster hadn't been removed. She took out the pin, scrunched it into a ball and had thrown it into the bin when something, where the poster had been, caught her eye – a photo of a couple smiling with the same backdrop of Glossa. She looked a little closer, squinting at them, knowing but not believing what she was seeing.

She pulled the photo off the wall, holding her breath in disbelief.

In one hand she held the picture of herself and in the other a picture of her parents, smiling directly at her, her mother wearing the same dungarees that Laurel had on. Laurel had the same smile and dancing eyes as her mum – Skopelos Laurel was the spitting image of her mother!

Her hands shaking she turned the photo over to find the words, written in her mother's hand, *Wish We Could Stay Forever!*

Laurel's mind was made up.

33

'Janey,' said Laurel, still clutching the photos in a trembling hand, the other holding her phone. 'You will never guess what's just happened to me?'

'Did you get with the writer?'

'No! Well . . .' She remembered she hadn't yet told Janey about skinny-dipping with Mark, Nikos kissing her, the subsequent fall-out, or the amicable 'break-up'. Nor did Janey know about the party, or Athena, or Nikos and Helena. She realised they had a whole lot of catching up to do.

'You did, didn't you?'

Laurel laughed. 'Janey, never mind that; this is so much better!'

'What could be better than getting with the writer?!'

'What if I told you I've just found a picture of my parents in the guest house?'

'What do you mean?'

'I mean, I just read a letter from Marnie, which said Mum and Dad had fallen in love on a Greek island in a villa off the beaten track. I got this feeling that they'd stayed here, so I went downstairs to the office with all the photos on the wall and I found them! They were standing in the exact same location that Athena took my photo.'

'Whoa, that's spooky.'

'But that's not the weird bit,' continued Laurel. 'What's weird is that I was just on the beach chatting to Marnie asking her about something, and I asked her to send me a sign.'

'And she sent you the photograph? That *is* weird!'

'I know. Too weird to ignore, right?'

'Definitely too weird to ignore.'

Laurel heard a scratch at the front door. 'Hello?'

'Who is it?' asked Janey.

'I don't know.'

When Laurel got to the door she found nobody. . .

'That's odd,' she said, looking out into the courtyard.

'What's up?'

She sat down on the bench. 'I must be imagining things.'

'Seems like strange things are happening out there today.'

'Very strange things.' Laurel felt a brushing sensation on her leg and looked down. 'Well, hello!'

'Who are you talking to?'

Laurel laughed, stroking the stray cat from town. 'A cat!'

'Should Tom be feeling jealous?'

The cat circled Laurel's leg. 'How is Tom?'

'A little too comfortable! I'm not wholly convinced he's going to want to come home.'

'Well,' said Laurel, happy to hear that Tom was

content, 'that might turn out to be a good thing.'

'What are you planning, Laurel Dempsey?'

'Janey,' she said, the cat jumping up to sit beside her on the bench. 'What would you say if I told you I was thinking about spending the money I inherited from Marnie on a guest house?'

'Which guest house?'

'Villa Athena, the one I'm staying in here.'

'Is it for sale?'

'Not exactly,' said Laurel, hoping she hadn't got carried away. 'But I think it could be. Athena had a stroke, she can't manage it any more, and she's got no one to take it on.'

Janey thought this through. 'So you'd give up your job and flat?'

'There are lots of jobs and flats in London – I'm pretty sure I could find another if it didn't work out – and besides, it's not as if my flat is a home.'

'But you feel that Villa Athena could be?'

'The only place I've ever felt at home was with Marnie, until I came here.'

'And you genuinely feel that? It's not just because a great holiday is coming to an end?'

Laurel liked the fact that Janey was questioning her, it made her even more convinced it was the right thing to do. 'I've had the feeling since I arrived. At first I thought it was to do with the film and it all being so familiar, but then it became something more – my connection to Athena, and now with Helena. They're like a family to me, but it was something else too.'

'And you're sure that's not just because you're still grieving for Marnie and looking for someone to fill her place?'

Laurel laughed affectionately at how well Janey knew her.

'I wondered that too, because of course I'm still grieving, but always there was this other feeling that I couldn't put my finger on. You know how I've always wanted my own memory of Mum and Dad, not just the ones Marnie gave me?'

'Sure.'

'I've found that here. That's what the feeling was. Mum and Dad fell in love on Skopelos, they stayed here at Villa Athena and wanted to stay for ever. There's something of them in the bricks, I could feel it as soon as I arrived – that same energy I always felt from the film, that feeling Marnie used to have of "coming home" – but I didn't know what it was. Now I've found their picture and put all the pieces of the puzzle together I get it.

'This was where they wanted to live out their dream, it makes sense to me that I should want to do the same. This island feels like home because Mum and Dad were here, not because of it being a great holiday, or Athena and Helena feeling like family, because even without all that I'd still want to stay.'

'Your mind sounds pretty made up.'

'So should I?'

'You're asking me if you should run the guest house that your parents loved on an idyllic Greek island?'

'Do you think it's a crazy idea?'

'No!' yelled Janey, bubbling with excitement. 'I think it's the best idea you've ever had!'

'For real?' Laurel found herself beaming at the cat, who nuzzled into her.

'For real, Laurel! Do it. Don't think. Just do.'

'And you think Marnie would approve? She wouldn't think I was blowing my inheritance on a pipe dream?'

'Are you kidding me? Laurel, Marnie would have been the first to get on a plane to join you! She would have been the first to tell you to follow your dreams.'

'Right, that's exactly what her letter said.'

Laurel let out a huge sigh of relief and with it came a tear of happiness. Having Janey's blessing was almost as good as having Marnie's in person.

'So grab the bull by the horns and do it! Are you confident of doing it alone?'

'I have an idea about that,' said Laurel, not wanting to talk about it until she'd spoken to the person in question. 'For now, are you sure you're happy to look after Tom? Give him big cuddles, and a prawn, from me?'

'Of course.'

After they'd said their goodbyes, Laurel scooped up the cat and went into the house to find it something to eat.

'I think I'll call you Patch,' she said, rubbing its ears and the black marking round its eye. 'We're going to be very happy here. Let's just hope Athena agrees to my plan!'

★

Laurel knocked on Helena's front door and waited, nervous with excitement.

'Laurel!' said Helena on opening the door. 'What brings you here?'

'I was hoping to talk to you about something. May I come in?'

'Of course.'

On entering Laurel found Theo sitting at the table, which was set with candles and a beautiful array of dishes.

'Oh God, I've disturbed you,' she said, horrified to have interrupted their date.

'Don't be silly,' they both said at once, causing them to laugh.

'I'll get some air,' said Theo, kissing Helena's hair before going outside.

'Is it a date?' Laurel whispered.

Helena nodded, her eyes lighting up.

Laurel squeezed Helena's hand in delight.

'Would you like a drink?'

'No, no,' said Laurel, not wanting to keep Helena any longer than necessary. 'I've come to ask you something.'

Helena drew out a chair at the table for Laurel. 'What is it?'

'How would you feel if I said I wanted to buy Villa Athena?'

Helena looked puzzled. 'I don't understand.'

'It's simple. I buy the villa and continue to run it as a guest house and you come on board to run the restaurant.'

'You mean—'

Laurel laughed at her friend's shock. 'You would have complete control of the restaurant.'

Excitement flickered in Helena's eyes then died out. 'I couldn't afford to.'

'It wouldn't cost you anything. I'd purchase the villa and employ you as the chef. It would be a full-time, salaried position. With Yanni starting school this year we could really make it work.'

Helena sat quietly, considering the offer. A few seconds passed before a smile spread across her face.

'I'd love to,' she said.

'You would?'

'Yes!'

'Oh, thank God!' laughed Laurel, getting up to hug her. 'For a moment I thought you were going to say no.'

'And Athena is happy with the plan?'

'Well, that's the next step,' said Laurel, trying to imagine how that conversation would play out. 'But for now, let's just enjoy the excitement of what might be.'

'It's good to be home,' said Athena, the following day, as Laurel and Helena helped her into her chair on the patio.

'No place like it,' said Laurel. She tucked a blanket over Athena's legs and repositioned her cushion.

'But we all know it can't be home for much longer, there's no use pretending.'

Laurel and Helena sat on either side of her. 'What are you thinking?'

'For all it breaks my heart to give it up, I haven't

much choice.' Athena stared out over the garden to the sea beyond. 'Nikos was my only hope, and he's gone. I have to sell.'

Helena and Laurel exchanged a look that expressed their sorrow that a door opening for them should mean one closing for Athena.

'But it's not all bad,' continued Athena. 'I've time left to spend with Yanni, and a smaller house will mean more time doing the things I love rather than cleaning and repairs.'

'And you're not angry that Nikos decided to go?' Helena asked.

'No! I want him to live his own life, find his own happiness, not live in mine.'

'That's almost exactly what Marnie used to say.'

'Marnie sounds like a good woman to me! Have you decided whether to buy a flat with her inheritance?'

'I have.'

Laurel paused nervously. Helena, sensing Laurel was on the cusp of asking, offered her a look of encouragement.

'And I've decided not to. Like you said, Marnie would want me to find my own happiness, and a flat in London isn't going to achieve that.'

'Good for you!'

'But I've been thinking about something else,' she continued, cautiously, wanting to word things sensitively and in a way that Athena would be receptive to them. 'Being here has given me the chance to discover what might fulfil me, and I think that thing is the same thing that gave you fulfilment – spreading happiness to the people who stay here.'

'It's been a great life.'

'And so I was wondering,' Laurel paused again, gathering herself, 'if you might let me buy Villa Athena and allow me to run it, with Helena in charge of the restaurant. You could stay, of course, and we'd look after you.'

Athena didn't speak immediately and Laurel wondered if she'd misread the strength of their relationship, and in doing so overstepped the mark. But then she noticed Athena's eyes welling with tears, and a smile of contentment forming on her lips. She reached out a hand to both Laurel and Helena, the three of them linked together.

'I can think of nothing better.'

'Really?' Laurel laughed, a wave of happiness rushing over her.

'You're both like granddaughters to me – *nothing* would make me happier.'

34

'I can't believe I'm meant to be at the airport and instead I'm sorting the villa for guests to arrive.'

'It's wild!' said Angie, who'd come to say goodbye.

'You promise you'll come back next summer and stay with me?'

'Of course! As soon as I'm home I'm going to book two weeks off.'

'Can you wait that long to see Alex again?'

'He's coming over for Christmas – he's always wanted Christmas in the snow.'

'I'm so happy for you, Angie.' Laurel gave her a huge hug, not wanting to let her go. 'Life won't be the same without you here.'

'You're going to be far too busy to notice I'm gone,' she said, wiping a tear from Laurel's cheek.

'You've been such a great friend – thank you.'

'You've been the same for me. Without you there would be no Alex and Angie.'

Laurel laughed. 'I was persistent.'

'You were like a dog with a bone!'

'It paid off.'

'It sure did. Oh,' she said, digging around in her

handbag. 'I bought you a present.'

Angie handed Laurel a small, rectangular-shaped gift.

'I didn't get anything for you,' said Laurel, feeling a little guilty but touched by Angie's thoughtfulness.

'Never mind that. Open it!'

Laurel unwrapped it carefully.

'Oh, Angie, I love it,' she said, looking at the framed picture of her new group of friends, taken on their boat trip.

'I thought it might be a nice reminder of the summer that changed your life for ever.'

Laurel gave Angie one last squeeze. 'It's perfect, thank you.'

'Well, time I hit the road. Got to get home to all those babies waiting to be born.'

'Come back as soon as you can.'

'I will. Now go, get on, you've beds to make and toilets to clean!'

'You make it sound so romantic!'

With Angie gone Laurel headed inside where Yanni was running down the stairs weaving a toy aeroplane in the air, startling Patch, who ran out of the front door in fright.

Laurel placed the framed photo on the hall sideboard she'd painted. She stood back and admired its position – now whenever she came and went from the house she'd think of the friends who helped her realise her dream of running her own hotel, rather than someone else's.

After agreeing to buy the villa from Athena, Laurel had gone to call Jacqui, to tell her that she was handing in her notice, that, in fact, she wasn't going back at all, but in the end she'd bottled it and emailed her instead. She told her how much she had appreciated working for her, but it wasn't her dream, and now that she had found what she wanted to do with her life, she didn't want to put it off a moment longer. A few minutes after she'd pressed send on the email, her phone had rung.

'I should be mad with you, you know,' Jacqui had said.

'I'm sorry to have let you down,' Laurel had replied.

She heard her boss give a long sigh down the phone. 'To be honest with you, I'm amazed you've stuck it out here as long as you have. You're very good at what you do'

'That's kind of you to say, given that I'm not giving you any notice.'

'You've left everything in order, that's something, though I will miss you round the office.' There was silence for a beat. Then Jacqui said, 'It's good to follow your dreams, Laurel. It's brave. I wish I had been as brave when I was your age.'

Laurel had found a lump forming in her throat. With promises that Jacqui would come to visit when she could – though Laurel doubted that would happen – they had said their goodbyes.

The sound of pans clattering drew Laurel's attention to the kitchen where she found Helena cooking up a storm; the smells were sensational, succulent and rich.

'How's it going in here?'

'Will you try this for me?' asked Helena, whirling around like a dervish.

Laurel sampled the orzo pasta coated in a bright red sauce that Helena had prepared.

'Oooh that's heavenly – what is that?'

'Tomato and lemongrass, it's to go with a slow-cooked lamb shank, which I've had in the oven overnight.'

Laurel had wondered what the succulent smell had been.

'My God, Helena – I'll have doubled in size by the end of the year if you keep cooking like this!'

'More for the men to get hold of,' she winked.

Laurel laughed, relishing seeing Helena so happy. The prospect of eating her food each day was reason enough to buy the villa.

Laurel was about to eat some more when she heard Athena call from the sitting room. She pinched another spoonful of pasta and a fresh plum for later, which she stuffed in her dungaree pocket. 'Gotta go!'

Athena was reclining, her legs up, doing a good job at taking it easy. She had a pile of books by her side.

'Have you placed the drinks order? That needs to be done every couple of months and I know we're low on ouzo.'

'Already done,' said Laurel, replenishing her glass of water.

'And what about the bed linen, has it been aired?'

'It's hanging on the line as we speak.'

'And have we enough toiletries – you know how guests love those little bottles of smelly things.'

'All taken care of,' said Laurel, with just a hint of self-satisfaction in proving herself to Athena. She left Athena and went through to the dining room.

'Because you know there's always something!' Athena called out from behind her.

For all Athena was desperate to have the last word, Laurel could tell from her tone that she was smiling. Laurel knew that Athena was pleased that she was there, relieved she was no longer in charge, and happy in her self-appointed role as general overseer.

In the dining room, Laurel found Rena, a young cousin of Helena's, beavering away with the vacuum cleaner.

'Looks great,' Laurel called over the noise of the Hoover.

Rena smiled, dimples forming on her plump face. 'Thank you, Miss Laurel.'

Laurel adjusted one of Theo's lanterns that she'd decided to use as permanent centrepieces on the tables, always reminding her of the night of the party – the night she found her vocation and realised her love for Athena.

Just then a gust of wind blew open the patio door and Laurel went out. She stood stroking Patch, who'd jumped up on one of the patio tables to join her. She laughed as Yanni ran through the garden, under the archway and disappeared down the steps to the beach, still flying his aeroplane.

'Don't you just love the smell of freshly cut grass?' she said to Patch, tickling his ears. She watched Vasillis, a friend of Theo's, mow the lawn. Seeing him there, busily tidying the garden, made her think of Nikos – she wondered where in the world he was right now and when he might return.

Laurel scooped up Patch. 'Let's go and see Theo in the courtyard.'

Together they walked round the side of the house, under the freshly laundered bedclothes, which billowed in the warm air, and found Theo up a ladder. He was giving the window frames a fresh coat of sky blue paint.

'It looks great,' she called.

'The old place scrubs up well!'

Laurel stood back and admired the villa, so pretty in the sunshine. She thought of Marnie and her parents, and of how very happy they would have been to know that Laurel had at last found the place where she belonged.

'Villa Athena,' she said to herself, having decided to keep its name. 'The place that I call home.'

Acknowledgements

A huge thank you to Juliet Pickering for giving me the chance to bring this story to life, and to Harriet Bourton and Olivia Barber for all their brilliant ideas, hard work and support.

This book wouldn't have been possible without the help of my parents who put in a lot of hours and miles to help look after my son – thank you! And to Lesley next door, thank you for always being at the fence ready to lend a hand.

And to Peter and Rupert, my boys, for their endless love and patience.